chasing butterflies

USA TODAY BESTSELLING AUTHOR

TERRI E. LAINE

CHASING BUTTERFLIES
First Edition

This is a work of fiction. Names, characters, places and incidents are products of the author's imagination or are used factiously and are not to be construed as real. Any resemblance to actual events, locales, organizations, or persons living or dead, is entirely coincidental.

ISBN: 978-1533177742

ISBN- 1533177740

dedication

This book is dedicated to my daughter who got her hopeless romantic streak from me.

acknowledgments

First and foremost a humongous thank you to all my readers for taking a chance on me. There are millions of books to read and you chose mine. That's HUGE to me. And without you, I wouldn't have the opportunity to share all the stories that are in my head. So Thank You again.

Many THANKS go to Nina Grinstead at Social Butterfly PR. She is my IT girl. She listens to me whine and still pulls together a spectacular marketing plan she's worked her ass off. She's opened many doors for me and I can't thank her enough for her support.

There is a group of people, my beta readers, who deserve my upmost appreciation. Their input for project made this book better by leaps and bounds. So Thank You: Nina Grinstead, Jill Patten, Annie Hargrove and Ana Rente. You ladies are the absolute BEST!

A special thanks to Ana for her support and the wonderful teasers she makes without me asking. You rock!

There are not enough special thanks to my awesome writing partner, Annie Hargrove, who is there for me without question or fail. You are an amazing friend and business partner!!!

A huge than you to Sofie at Luminos Graphic House for designing one of the most beautiful covers I've ever published. And to Jeff for the gorgeous photography.

Finally, I want to thank Emily from Lawrence Editing for polishing up my manuscript. And to Max Henry for adding the details to the formatting that make the book even more visually stunning than I thought possible.

part one

prologue

KELLEY

DARKNESS DIDN'T HIDE EVERYTHING AS I WAS JERKED awake by the piercing scream that tore through our silent house. The cry ended as abruptly as it began and was followed by the telltale tinkling sounds of glass breaking. Muffled noises erupted as a struggle continued to play out in the front room. The closed door beckoned me, but the sticky pull of that place between sleep and fear had me stuck to my bed like glue. My gaze, however, was able to cross over the small distance to my brother's bed. His noiseless breathing remained undisturbed as headphones covered his ears.

One thing I read in a book said courage wasn't given, it was earned. Slowly, I forced my limbs to move and stepped into the gap between our beds before frantically shaking my brother awake.

His eyes popped open in alarm, illuminated by the moonlight that streams through our small window.

"What's going on?" he asked gruffly.

I pointed a hesitant finger toward the door that separates us from the madness outside our room.

Ripping his headphones off, he did it in time for a bloodcurdling shriek to pierce the darkness with its lance.

My brother, big for his age, had only grown more in the last year. He was almost as large as the monster who masqueraded as our father, and in that moment was our only hope to save our mother. His arm muscles flexed as he pushed himself up and swung his massive legs over the side of the bed. The weights he'd been lifting and kept hidden under his bed had certainly done their job. I envisioned him as the superhero he was to me.

He unfolded his body as he got to his feet, towering over me by leaps and bounds.

"You stay here, kid."

I straightened my posture, not liking being called a child. I was only five years younger than him. Though at eight years young, I stood no chance against the villain who invaded our walls.

"Even Batman has a sidekick," I protested, hating the squeaky sound that escaped my croaky throat.

He flashed me a smile that warmed my chest in a way I was sure he was proud of me. "Fine, you help Mom and I'll stop Dad."

We traded nods as I watched him stalk to the door with determination in his step. For once, we weren't going to cower in the shadows. We would stop Dad once and for all and save Mom from any more ugly bruises, or worse, a trip to the hospital.

He yanked the door open just as Mom came skidding to a stop flat on her back in front of it. Her wide eyes pleaded with us to stay inside as she made wild gestures with her hands. But not this time. We would save her.

one

KELLEY

HEAT LICKED AT MY SKIN AS SWEAT FORMED AND dripped off my brow. The Texas summer day kicked my ass and messed with my concentration inside the stifling trailer. I didn't let it stop me, though. Determination carved my path with a single purpose. If I didn't get the job done, I knew my friends and brother who waited outside would razz me about it until the day I died.

The useless fan sent a breeze of stale air that smelled like the wharf at the end of the day. The whiff of dead fish was the real reason why I couldn't keep it up.

"Put that big thing of yours inside," the girl beneath me moaned.

"Be quiet," I snapped because her onion breath only made my eyes water.

My sharp words should have pissed her off. Instead, it had the opposite effect. She grinned and fumbled with a few buttons, parting her shirt open down the middle. Her boobs spilled out and caught my attention as she'd meant them to. When she pinched the tips between her small fingers and tugged them taut, everything changed.

Stiff as a board, I was ready for my next try at shoving inside her. Before, with everything so wet and me not so hard, I kept slipping out. My next plunge filled her, and I stayed in place.

Everything in my mind emptied. Home, school, the temperature, and smells, none of it scattered my thoughts anymore. She must have felt it too because her back bowed and her eyes rolled back.

I held there a second, the feeling so intense I didn't want to ever leave the place I would soon dub nirvana. I pulled back and that act made things ten times better. Instinct took over, and I clamped my hands down on her hips and started to pump inside her like the guy in the porn flick I'd seen on someone's phone at school.

It could have been one stroke, five, ten, or twenty. I'd lost count when my brain went offline. I had no idea how long it'd been when I realized she was speaking to me. Nothing mattered as I felt close to exploding.

"Touch me here," she groaned, pointing to a place between her legs.

To know I made her sound so breathy made me feel like Batman, and no longer Robin to my older brother. I glanced down where our bodies joined and then pulled apart in a rhythmic movement. I followed her instructions where she wanted me to touch, having no experience other than what I'd seen and heard. Besides that, I wanted to stay inside her because it was way better than my hand.

Only I couldn't let go of her hips for fear she'd fall off the counter where I held her in place. I extended my thumb and brushed over something small, round, and hard under her curly mound.

Whatever I did caused her to scream, and her insides clamped around me like my fist did when I jerked off. That was all it took to blow my load out of my balls harder than it ever had before. A few more thrusts and I half collapsed with her pinned between me and the wall.

I caught my breath before I could think again. I stood up and pulled out some. The condom started to stay inside her, so I gripped it at the base before finally separating us completely.

"You can toss it in the trash over there."

She pointed to her left. I glanced in that direction, but spun around until I spotted an opening down a narrow hall. I half pulled my jeans up with my free hand and held them in place as I made my way in that direction.

"Where are you going?"

I didn't bother to answer. My brother had drilled into me some things he said I shouldn't ever forget. One was to never trust a girl. Wrap it up and flush it down the toilet when you're done.

The door turned out to be the bathroom like I'd hoped. It was small. I barely stepped inside having to duck my head, and I dropped the used condom in the toilet before flushing it. On instinct, I washed my hands, something Mom had always schooled us about. Her number one thing over the years was to make sure to keep our hands clean.

After zipping my pants up, I made my way back into the kitchen where I'd fucked the tiny girl who now stood before me. Tall for my age, she barely reached the middle of my chest.

She glanced up at me with her half pretty face and the spot between her eyebrows wrinkled. "How old did you say you were?"

"Eighteen." The lie came easily.

Because she and her mom were new to the area, we hadn't gone to school together. And I guessed I'd grown over the summer. So, I looked more the part.

With a wink and a grand smile, she said, "Well, you sure are cute. Your eyes are a little freaky, but you're welcome to come back anytime."

I nodded ignoring her comment about my eyes, having heard it all before, and followed her to the door. When I stepped outside, waiting hands were there to slap my back in congratulations. The door closed behind me and our group moved a small distance away before I was assaulted with questions.

"How was it?", "What the fuck were you doing to her in there?", "She was screaming bloody murder!" were some of them thrown at me all at once.

Sandy, who'd set the whole thing up, intervened. "Guys, give the man some room."

The man comment made my chest puff up as I watched my brother wave his hand. It was like magic, sending everyone to put distance between us.

"Well?" one of my buddies asked as they all stared at me in anticipation.

It was then I realized, friends or not, it wasn't any of their business. The big reveal they hoped for wasn't happening. In grand fashion, I shrugged, sporting what I was sure the biggest smirk ever.

"Aww, man, come on," they pleaded at once, while my brother stood stoic and waiting.

I shrugged again, having nothing to say. I'd never been much of a talker. I was the guy who sat and watched things happen while waiting for my moment.

A torrent of words was hurled at me, trying to convince me not to keep the details to myself.

"Dudes, let the man be."

My brother was the commanding presence that caused all eyes to shoot in his direction. He was well respected by me and my comrades. He didn't treat us like little kids, which earned our admiration. They traded glances with me before I nodded. They looped off in deep conversation, speculating about my first time.

“So?” Sandy asked after they’d rounded a corner of another trailer.

He was one of the two people in the world I trusted. Even though I looked up to him, I didn’t want to give him all the details either.

He didn’t push, so when I remained quiet, he asked, “At least tell me you finished?”

I wasn’t sure why I couldn’t speak. There was so much I had to figure out. The experience had been mind-bending. So, I bobbed my head instead.

He slapped my back hard. If he hadn’t taught me over the years how to take a lick, I might have stumbled forward. But he had and couldn’t kick my ass as easily as he used to.

We walked the long way home, and I half listened to him speak. Mostly, I replayed in my head what it had felt like to be inside a girl for the first time. It was far better than I’d imagined. More importantly, it had drained all my worries away. I’d thought of nothing about how life sucked. Thus I would have to do it again and soon.

What shocked the shit out of me was finding Mom sitting on the porch of our tiny four-room house, if you didn’t count the only bathroom. Sandy was just as surprised to see her as I was.

I found my voice, which was a mix of low and high tones. “Mom, you’re home?”

It was a stupid question and maybe I’d lost several brain cells while having sex. But she worked two jobs, and I rarely saw her. I thought maybe she was there to tell us we had to move again because we were being kicked out.

"I couldn't miss today." She stood and enveloped me in a hug. All I could do was pray I didn't smell like pussy. I had no desire to explain to Mom what I'd been up to. "I had two good reasons to take off this evening."

Her eyes focused on me. "Happy birthday, Kelley."

It wasn't fake. I truly felt the smile that split my face open. Mom had that effect on people, including me. She made everyone feel welcome and happy to be alive.

"Thanks, Mom."

She smelled like fresh flowers, and I closed my eyes a second, fighting the urge to be her baby boy. It felt too good to have her arms around me. I pulled back and glanced at my brother, waiting for the jab.

He ruffled my hair. "How does it feel to be thirteen, little bro?"

He'd stopped calling me kid that long ago night, five years in the wind.

"Don't bother him," Mom chided. "Besides, I'm also here to spend the evening with my oldest son, who's shipping out tomorrow."

That one sentence shifted the mood. The celebration was over that quick as tears threatened to spill from Mom's eyes. Sandy had to report for duty with the marines, and I wasn't sure how I was going to handle things when he was gone.

"It's only four years and I'll be back. They'll pay for school and everything after I'm discharged. Besides, I won't need my paychecks and will be able to send you most of the money I earn. Then you can quit one of your jobs."

We hated that Mom worked so hard for us and always looked tired. It was the reason I hadn't begged my brother to stay because Dad had been manageable since that night. He still drank, but he wasn't as violent.

When Mom's smile melted away, I knew she saw it. My hair half hid it, but Mom's eagle eye noticed most everything. She reached over and pushed the hair from my right eye.

"What happened?"

I sighed. "Got shit from some kid about my name. He got a lucky shot in, but I finished him." Sandy's brows arched. "Why did you give us girl names anyway?"

Mom frowned. "Kelley was a boy's name long before it became a popular girl's name. It's an Irish name."

"What about Sandy?" I asked.

She eyed my brother before answering. "It's your Dad's father's name. Besides, it was originally a Scottish boy's name, not a girl's name."

We'd never known any of our grandparents. Dad never spoke about his parents, and Mom didn't get along with hers. I was about to ask why name my brother after someone he never talked about when through the open screen door, a voice called out that grated on my nerves.

"Jackie, get me a beer, honey."

We all traded glances before Mom looked away, unable to meet our eyes. We'd begged her to leave him, but she wouldn't. She said we didn't understand that he was a good man. No good man would ever hurt his wife the way he did. At least no TV show I'd seen with a happy family showed the father beating his wife.

I reached out to stop her from following that prick's instructions. She gave me a small smile before my hand fell away. The screech of the door opening voiced my silent scream. I hated my father and the shit he put us through.

Sandy placed a hand on my shoulder. "You have to be the man of the house now." I nodded. "You'll be fine. Just keep out of Dad's way." I nodded again. "I'll be back before you know it."

He held out a fist, and I bumped it. I was tall, but I hadn't yet grown as big as my brother. I wouldn't be able to handle our father when he got drunk like Sandy could. The only thing I'd be able to do would be to stand in front of Mom when he felt the need to punch someone. I could take it better than she could.

two

LENORA
months later

WE STOOD IN FRONT OF THE BOARD WHERE THE FINAL list was posted.

"Oh my God, oh my God," Debbie screamed while jumping up and down. She grabbed my hand, and I found myself jumping too. "Lenny, we're in. We're in."

Freshman year of high school was a big deal and to make the cheerleading squad was even bigger. I wasn't sure exactly how I felt about it. It was something Debbie wanted, and I thought I wanted too. Having it didn't give me the flutters in my stomach I thought it would.

When she finally calmed down, she steered me to her locker with subtle glances over her shoulder. A pack of boys clustered nearby, and I thought she was about to comment on them when she leaned in.

She whispered to me while she spun the combination on her locker. "Rumor has it—"

We were interrupted when a shadow covered us. I stood straight and glanced over her shoulder.

It was interesting how my best friend of all my life changed in the presence of a boy. Plus, these days she always did most of the talking. Faster than me, she spun around and greeted our visitor.

"Ox, how are you?"

Odin, better known by his nickname Ox, barely glanced down at her. He gave her a tilt of his head in acknowledgment. Her face soured when his gaze shifted to me.

"Lenny, I was wondering what you were doing Friday night."

Not spending it with you, I wanted to say. Ox had made a reputation for himself over the summer. He'd popped a few cherries and broken a few hearts if rumors were to be believed.

"I'm busy." I was proud of myself for not sounding self-righteous when I said it. No need to be rude.

"Oh. Okay." He nodded and trudged off.

Debbie turned slowly to glare at me. "Why did you do that?"

I didn't cower under her scrutiny as she expected. Most of the time, I gave into her whims, not wanting to fight.

"He's the most popular boy in our class. And he could get us into senior parties," she went on.

"And," I mocked horror. "He's never given me the time of day before. I won't be another check on his list."

She rolled her eyes. "Stop being a baby. He's cute, rich, and on the football team."

"And?"

"You're a lost cause." Her exasperated sigh was her only sign of defeat.

"You date him then," I suggested.

"Well, that's what I was trying to tell you. He's made it known to everyone he's interested in you. No guy is going to talk to you now."

My suffering sigh was more like a groan as I longed for an older brother or someone to defend my honor because what she said was true. Ox was a big, intimidating guy, hence the name. The fact that his family had money would only add to making other guys afraid to ask me out.

"I can't believe it." I groaned.

"Believe it, sister. He wants you, and he won't give up until he has you."

The day took forever to end. My worst fears that Debbie voiced came true. I paid special attention to one guy I crushed on. We'd been trading glances in math class over the past week, but he hadn't looked in my direction at all today.

Mom waited at the curb when I stomped out of school annoyed. I tossed myself in her car, hating how things had turned out. I should have been excited I'd made the cheer squad. Instead, I wished we'd move and go to another school.

"What's with the long face?" Mom asked.

Everyone knew everyone in this small town. So when I told her about how Ox had laid his sights on me, she knew exactly who I was talking about.

"Honey, you should be flattered. Like your father and I have always told you, you are so pretty, and boys are going to beat down our door to ask you out."

"Mom, I'm not that pretty. Besides, I wish he'd find someone else to target," I mumbled.

Debbie, I thought in the back of my head. She would relish the idea of going out with him. I wondered—not for the first time—what we had in common anymore besides being childhood friends. Lately, we had different views on life. I wanted to make something of myself and get out of this sleepy town. Debbie would be happy being the next Teen Mom to the right boy in town, including Ox.

"It can't be that bad," Mom said.

"It is when said boy is only looking for one thing."

That shut her up. I popped my ear buds in and let the music flow for the short ride home.

Around the dinner table that night, it was tense. I wasn't exactly surprised when my father announced there was something he wanted to talk about.

"Lenora, um…"

Dad wasn't ever unsure with his words. The fact that he paused freaked me out. Were they going to tell me they were getting a divorce? Things hadn't been great at home recently. My parents fought constantly behind closed doors. I guess they thought I couldn't hear them through the paper thin walls. But, I'd heard enough.

"Things aren't good at work."

That news felt worse as they pinned me with the weight of it. Suddenly it was apparent my wish for moving might become a reality. We weren't exactly rolling in it. Our small house was barely on the good side of town.

"However, I have an opportunity to make things better. A new potential client might solidify my position in the firm as they continue with cuts."

Suddenly, I wanted to be five again. I didn't want to know we had money problems. My heartbeat thudded in my chest. Was he saying we were almost homeless? What did it mean? And why was he telling me?

"What are you saying, Dad?"

I glanced at Mom, but she quickly looked away.

"It's okay, honey. If the worst happens, we'll survive. We might have to dip into your college fund until we get back on our feet. But we won't be thrown out of our house."

My mouth gaped. It became clear why I was being let in on the news. My college fund was my ticket out of town. And while I understood having a place to sleep was more important, it still stung that I could be stuck going to community college and living at home after I graduated.

"Can't Mom get a job?" I blurted.

It had been too easy to throw Mom under the bus. Still, she had able hands. Why did I have to lose my college fund for her to stay at home? I wasn't a little kid anymore.

"I'm sorry." I quickly backtracked. It was selfish of me and knee jerk reaction to the bomb they dropped on me. "I can quit cheerleading and get a job. I hear they're hiring at the diner."

Dad shook his head. "There's no need. Like I said, I have a solution."

I glanced between them, not getting it. Mom couldn't meet my eye.

"I'm attending a business dinner with the potential client Friday night. You and Mom will attend."

It wasn't unusual for me to go to a business dinner. Especially when I was younger and Dad's clients had kids the same age.

"Okay," I said, not sure why it was a big deal. The way Mom continued to not look at me only made me wonder more what it had to do with me.

"You might know the family. When they talked about dinner they mentioned their son went to school with you."

He hadn't said the words, but I felt his meaning. There weren't many families in town with enough money to be one of Dad's potential clients. Most of his clients were from the city. So it didn't take long for me to put two and two together and why Mom couldn't look at me directly.

"Ox," I shrilled. When Dad nodded, I nearly shouted. "You can't be serious. What are you, pimping me out?"

Mom cringed, and Dad shook his head in a short bust of side to side movement. "Absolutely not," Dad declared. "It's just dinner, and I'm asking you to be nice."

"When am I not nice?"

"Your mom told me about your conversation this afternoon."

Then I remembered how I explained what happened with Ox. Mom had tried to make his intentions okay. I glared at her. Somehow they knew about Ox's interest in me.

"He only wants one thing. What should I do when he makes that clear?"

Twice today, I'd let my feelings known. I hadn't ever been that outspoken. I'd been the good little girl. However, I couldn't let my parents dictate who I dated. They were guilt tripping me into it.

"It's only one night. Let me secure them as a client and you won't have to deal with him again," Dad promised.

Air escaped my lungs and so had the fight in me. Dad needed his job, therefore we needed it. What was one night? Then I remembered Ox asking me out Friday night. I'd told him I was busy. Had he known about the dinner? Would he and his family hold it over our heads?

I couldn't eat another bite. I tossed my napkin over my half eaten dinner and headed to my room. I picked my phone from the charger and dialed my best friend for advice.

three

KELLEY

"OH MY GOD, KELLEY," SHE BEGGED.

"Keep quiet or someone will hear," I whispered fiercely.

It was after school, but her words would carry in the silence. The mostly unused bathroom in the back of the school was a popular spot to make out. Last thing I needed was to get caught. I'd been in enough brawls that the principal had warned me I was on a short leash. And I'd promised Mom I would graduate high school eventually.

Luckily, the girl wrapped around me complied, closing her red stained lips shut. I'd learned over the last two years girls liked to be told what to do during sex, which suited me fine.

I shoved in and out of her until I was close enough. The secret to girls getting off lay between their legs. The magic button would send them into never-never land if I touched it right. I stroked it, not bothering to carry on much longer. She'd already pulled me from the zone with her shouts and who knew if someone was coming.

As soon as my finger made contact, she lifted off. Her back arched and her pussy milked my dick like one would milk a cow. I bit my lower lip, holding in a groan. Everything drifted away in those final seconds. I was lost to the pleasure that coursed through me. The feeling was like a drug, and I'd worked my way through the girls in the school to get my fix.

Everything was silent for a couple of beats as my heart thundered in my chest. Finally, I pulled out and flushed the condom in a stall a few feet away. I turned around to find her straightening her clothes. I tucked myself away and did my pants up.

"So, are you coming to my graduation party Friday night?"

"You don't graduate until May."

She shrugged. "I'm celebrating all year. Are you coming or what?"

I glanced her over as she stood with her hands folded over her chest.

"What's in it for me?"

Her mouth split in a grin, and she moved over to me, swaying her hips. But we'd fucked and it wasn't the first time. Further, I wasn't pussy whipped by girls like a lot of other guys in school.

"Me, of course," she said, sliding her arms up my chest and gazing into my eyes like I should be impressed with that offer.

"And I have you."

Her smile turned into a pout, and she slapped at my chest but without any force.

"You can be so mean sometimes. Is that the green-eyed monster coming out of you? I actually like your blue eye better."

It was my turn to shrug. I ignored her statement about my bi-colored eyes. It was the best way to get people not to talk about it. "What do you want me to say? You want me to come halfway across town to some lame party for what? So you can make him jealous."

I didn't have to say his name. We both knew who I was talking about. The dumbass was the reason we'd hooked up. Mr. Quarterback had left the second game of the season with a shoulder injury. Scouts had been there and he'd lost the opportunity to go to his school of choice because the injury would keep him from completing the season.

Coach had sent me in, and I rallied the team to victory. We'd gone on weeks later to win state with me at the helm.

Her boyfriend took out his frustrations on her by breaking up with her right before the homecoming dance. His reasons had been she wasn't putting out. That's when the future prom queen set her sights on me. Dumbass missed out. Because the prom queen wasn't as frigid as he thought she was. She gave it up to me right after the homecoming dance. And we'd been sort of going out ever since. I refused to call her my girlfriend because who knew if we would move again. This was the longest we'd stayed in any one place. But having a steady girl to bang made things easier.

"Who cares if he's jealous?" she said, bringing me out of my thoughts.

"Who's going to be there?"

"Seniors, of course."

Of course. "I'm only a sophomore."

Her shoulders rose and fell, making her chest bounce a little with the action. Tits were my Kryptonite. I let my eyes find hers again, and she smirked.

"You're the star quarterback. No one cares what grade you're in."

"How am I going to get home?" No doubt the party would run late, and the buses didn't travel out to her neighborhood much after dusk.

"My parents will be out of town. You can sleep over, and I'll take you home in the morning."

The idea of not sleeping at my house won me over. "Fine, I'll be there."

She grinned and moved over to plant a kiss on my lips. I let her but didn't take it further. I got the mechanics of how to kiss. It was a lot like sex, only fucking a girl's mouth with my tongue. But kissing complicated things. Whenever I kissed a girl, they seemed to read a lot more in the relationship than there really was. So I'd stopped doing it.

"See you tomorrow," she chirped before she practically bounced out the door.

I glanced at myself in the mirror, buying time. There was no reason to go home right now and every reason not to. Dad would be home from his current job as one of the crew on a fishing boat. He was gone in the mornings and home in the afternoons. It was better to get home later after he'd had several beers and finally passed out in his favorite chair. Still, I had nothing to do, and I'd been kicked out more than once by teachers who'd caught me in the halls too late after school. I sighed and walked as slowly as I could the few miles home.

When I arrived, Dad's beat-up truck wasn't parked in the drive. My mood suddenly lightened. I wouldn't have to hide in my room. I could get something to eat.

Only when I walked in, Mom was there. Sandy made good on his word and sent her money every month. She quit one of her jobs and only worked at night at the bar because she made more in tips than she had as an administrative assistant at the accountant's office in town. But she was usually gone to work by now.

The sound of the door closing caused her eyes to lift and land on me. She'd been leaning on the counter, and she straightened. She focused red-rimmed eyes on me and my heart sank. Mom wasn't a crier. If she had been crying, then shit was bad. Before I could ask, she moved in my direction with purpose. I'd grown a lot in the past two years, so when she wrapped her arms around my chest, the top of her head was several inches below my shoulder.

"Kelley," she sobbed.

Immediately on red alert, I was unprepared for her tears. I felt helpless under their weight. Did we have to move? Had she lost her job? Had Dad died? If that last were true, I wasn't sure how I felt about it.

"What's wrong?"

When she didn't answer, I created enough distance to glance in her eyes.

"It's Sandy."

The world tilted, or it felt that way.

"Is he hurt? Is he coming home?" I asked, hopeful.

Despite what I saw in her expression, I hoped I was right. Only, her next words would haunt me for the rest of my life.

She shook her head. "No, he's…he's dead."

I stumbled back away from her. I bumped into Dad's recliner and sat, not caring he'd kick my ass if he found me there. A burn started in my eyes, followed by an ache so deep, like an axe was embedded in my chest.

"He can't be," I choked.

Mom came over and hovered over me where I sat. It was her turn to comfort me as she had all my life. She wrapped her tiny arms around me and pressed my face into her chest like I did when I was little. After all, her kisses on all my cuts and scrapes would instantly heal them. Maybe she could somehow heal my broken heart. But it wouldn't heal. That hole could never be filled. My brother, my best friend, was gone.

I'd spoken to him the week before. He was looking forward to coming home in two years. He was tired of death, and it claimed him.

Between sobs and maybe some of my own, muffled words of explanation came out of her. "I got the call. His funeral will be on Saturday."

The next few hours were a blur. I didn't know who clung to who, Mom or me. I couldn't remember the last time I'd seen my brother. We couldn't afford Internet or those fancy phones. So I had only heard his voice over the years he'd been deployed overseas.

I rocked in my chair like a mental case. I wanted nothing more than to break things. But we didn't have much and what we did, Mom had worked hard to afford. So I yelled out my frustrations at God. Why couldn't he have taken our father instead?

When Dad got home, shit got real. "What the fuck, Kelley."

Immediately, my defenses went up, but a moment too late. The first blow came because he thought I'd caused Mom to cry. It was one of the few times he acted like he cared about her, so I took the lick, welcoming the coming numbness. My swing was all air. Dad evaded.

Mom cried out when she stepped between us and caught the punch meant for me. Blood trickled down the corner of the mouth she covered.

"See, boy, what you made me do."

I no longer believed in superheroes, but in that moment, I wished for one. Seeing Mom hurt made me reckless. I barreled into my father only to hit a brick wall. He swung up, catching me in the eye. I managed to stand tall and with my eye swelling, blindly took a swing or two, wanting my life to end knowing nothing good would come from my brother's death.

"James, stop. Sandy's dead."

Dad listened to Mom for once and his hand dropped to his side while I panted. Mom's words echoed in my head, and I dropped to my knees. Water leaked from my eyes as it sank down deep. He wasn't coming home. He wouldn't rescue us. I was Mom's only hope.

"What?" Dad murmured.

"Sandy died last night from IED," Mom answered.

Like me, my father wanted to break something. It turned out I was the only thing he could break that would eventually mend. In my prone position, he gave me no defense. No matter how hard I fought back, the blows rained down as I sought oblivion.

Before it came, I yelled in my head at God and the government. My brother died for his country, making this world a safer place. Only if I lived through the nightmare, his death made me less safe. Dad was sure to continue to show his displeasure that I was his surviving son.

four

LENORA

FROZEN WITH SHOCK, I GAPED AT MY BEST FRIEND.

"Don't judge," Debbie said.

"I'm not judging," I snapped right back.

"Yes, you are."

We were getting nowhere. "I'm not. I'm just surprised."

"We don't all have it easy like you."

The divide between us had been growing ever since we started high school nearly two years ago. We were almost the end of our sophomore year, and I wondered if our friendship would last.

"Easy?" I said, a lot calmer than I felt. "Your house is twice the size of mine. Your parents aren't threatening to use your college fund to pay bills. You don't have to get a job this summer like I do. You're going on vacation while I work."

That shut her up for all of two seconds.

"Maybe not. But you could have any boy you wanted. And you have the hottest guy in school, who happens to be the richest. He's throwing you a sweet sixteen birthday party and you're complaining. All I'm saying is, if he wants to bang you and you don't, throw the guy a bone and give him a blow job instead."

"You say that like you've done it before."

She shrugged, and I was sure my eyes popped out of my head *Looney Tunes* style.

"Why haven't you told me? I thought you were my best friend."

She stepped back and glared at me. Then she folded her arms across her chest like I should know the answer to my own question. Finally, I said nothing and matched her stare.

"You want to know why?" I nodded. "Because of how you're acting now."

"How I'm acting? I feel like I don't know you. And you're keeping secrets. I would never judge you. You are the prettiest girl I know. I think you deserve a great guy. But I wouldn't hold anything you did against you."

A few more seconds passed before she deflated. "Shit, I'm sorry." She hugged me. "I should have told you, and I will. I'll tell you tonight."

Tears stung the back of my eyes as I hugged her back. "We are such idiots."

She agreed. "I'll be at your house tomorrow at eight to pick you up. And I'll call you tonight and give you the details on how to give the best BJ ever."

I tried not to stiffen and managed to maintain a smile on my face. I went to the media center for lunch, wanting to avoid more sex talk with Debbie. What I didn't expect was to see Trina sitting at one of the tables. She smiled at me, and I smiled back. I sat at a different table because it wasn't like we were friends. She actually got up and came over.

"Surprised to see the school slut in the library? Well, newsflash, I can read."

For the second time today I was being called out for judging people. I didn't think I was that kind of person.

"I'm sorry. I guess I was surprised to see you here."

She sat back in her seat and her eyebrow arched. "At least you're honest. Most people in this godforsaken school aren't. But I guess I brought it all on myself. I sleep with one guy who can't keep his mouth shut and I'm labeled a slut. Go figure. But you know what, it's freeing. I don't give a shit what people think. I've slept with less guys than on one hand. But you think anyone cares that there are other more popular girls who have done it with more than they can count?"

"It's not fair."

Her shoulders lifted and fell before she let out a long string of air from her chest. "It's high school. I can't wait to get out of this place."

I smiled, finally feeling like someone agreed with me.

"Me neither."

The light in her eyes danced as the corners of her mouth lifted. "So the girl going out with Ox, the fox, isn't happy."

"Fox, that sounds like something my mom would say."

"Not as in hot, although he's gorg. But he's sly. You have to watch out for him."

I wasn't sure what she meant by that. "Can I ask you something?"

Her eyes narrowed. I plunged forward anyway. "What is it like to have…" I waved a hand around. "You know."

"Sex?"

I nodded.

"It can be really good with the right boy."

She didn't elaborate, and I didn't ask anymore. I didn't know her all that well and didn't think it was my place to pry.

"I have to say, though, Lenora, if you don't want to do it, don't."

She glanced over my shoulder. I followed her line of sight and saw a guy in the grade ahead of us make a beeline in our direction.

"And one more thing."

I frowned by her ominous statement, unsure as to what she was about to say.

"Sometimes you shouldn't trust your so-called friends."

With that, she left. Was she talking about Debbie or Ox? And what did I really know about Trina to trust her? She claimed not to be the slut everyone said she was, but she and that boy who had arrived went hand and hand deep into the stacks. I stared after them until they totally disappeared from sight.

The next night, I stood staring at myself in the mirror. The yellow dress Debbie and I picked up during a shopping trip to Dallas did look really nice on me. It covered almost all of me with the halter style top but left most of my back exposed. The flirty skirt just barely passed mid-thigh. It was the kind of dress I didn't think my parents would approve of. Mom, however, eagerly agreed it was the best choice. Dad hadn't complained when he saw it either.

Half of my hair had been pulled back in an updo with the other half cascading down my back. That and the makeup I'd put on, made me look older even though I didn't feel it.

Despite the rumors, Ox had been really sweet that first night at dinner. When our parents practically dared us to go out, I had. And it had been fun. He hadn't been the boy I'd thought he was. He hadn't tried for more than a quick kiss on my lips when the night was over. And in fact, we had a lot in common too. We liked the same movies. I happened to enjoy superheroes as much as romance. I blamed that on my dad. So it had been really easy to fall into being his girlfriend.

There had been a few times we'd gotten hot and heavy. I'd even let him feel me up a time or two. He'd wanted me to touch him as well. I'd complied, more out of curiosity than anything else. I hadn't let it progress to letting him put his hand under my shirt. Maybe I should let him tonight.

"Lenora, come downstairs for pictures."

I rolled my eyes and trudged downstairs. Not finding my parents in the living room, I glanced around. Mom called from the kitchen, and I found them with a cake and candles.

"You got me a cake?" It wasn't as if they hadn't done so every year, but things had changed. Even though Dad kept his job, he had suffered a pay cut. So I just didn't expect it, not sure why.

Mom smiled and nodded. "Make a wish."

The wish could have been for anything. But I found myself wishing for guidance. I wanted to know if Ox was the right guy for me. So I wished for butterflies. Mom had once explained that you knew if you really liked a guy when your subconscious sent signals that felt like butterflies in your tummy when you were with the right one.

By the time Debbie arrived, I'd already opened my gift, which was an upgrade to my current cell phone. Dad changed my plan to include data. I could go online wherever I was.

"Thanks, Daddy," I said, throwing my arms around him.

"You deserve it," he whispered as Mom captured the moment with her camera.

They waved as we left the house. And I had the feeling it was going to be awesome. Turning sixteen felt sweet.

"This is going to be the best party ever," Debbie announced when we were on our way.

Ox's house was lit up and the two-story dream house was no doubt full of people from school. I felt like a rock star when I walked in. Ox announced me like I was headlining a rock concert.

"My girl's in the house," he yelled over the music, which was great. The best part came when later Ox revealed a huge birthday cake with sixteen candles and everyone sang to me. It felt surreal. When Ox told me to make a wish, I wished that the dream of my night wouldn't ever end.

"Where are we going?" I asked when he dragged me upstairs and away from everyone else.

"Your present is in my room."

My stomach fluttered but not in a good way. Instantly, I was nervous. I wanted to be ready for the next step. It seemed like everyone was having sex, or so it had seemed while wadding through the gyrating people on the makeshift dance floor. As much as I wanted to be, I still wasn't ready. And how could I tell him no after he'd thrown me the amazing party?

The door closed with a click that sounded more like the trigger of a gun. I jumped, wrapping my arms around me, rubbing at the sudden chill. Muffled sounds came from downstairs, which meant no one would hear us. When he turned to face me, he had one arm behind his back. In majestic fashion, he whipped out in front of him a blue box with a white satin ribbon and bent on one knee. My jaw dropped.

"What?"

"Open it."

With shaky hands, I did as he asked. We were only sixteen, I told myself. There was no need to be nervous. Maybe he didn't want to tower over me as I opened the gift.

Inside the box, I found a ring on a bed of felt. It sparkled like nothing I'd seen before.

"I know we're young. And it's crazy. But I love you, Lenny. This isn't an engagement ring, yet. It's a promise that one day we'll be together forever."

I had no words as he took the box from my nervous hand. Then he lifted the ring before slipping it on my finger.

"Do you promise you're mine?"

My stomach was tied in knots. Was this the signal? I had no idea as he waited there, an anxious smile on his face. I found myself agreeing and his grin broadened to show teeth. He leaned forward and kissed me. When his lips met mine, I expected something more. It hadn't happened yet. But surely, the first time a boy tells you he loves you it should be met with fireworks. Only none came.

five

KELLEY

THAT RAINY DAY OF MY BROTHER'S FUNERAL, I LONGED for sunglasses, but I didn't own any. I'd gone to the party the night before and learned what my father found so interesting at the bottom of an empty bottle. *Oblivion.*

I drank until my insides didn't hurt. I drank, becoming the life of the party. I drank, not wanting the numbness to end. I drank until I woke up in a bed just as naked as the two girls on either side of me.

A dried up condom clung to my dick like plaster, and I didn't remember what the fuck I'd done. All I knew was that neither girl was the host of the party. I got up and made a beeline into a ginormous bathroom. I cleaned myself up, pulling off skin cells to free my limp dick from the spent rubber I flushed down the toilet. I dressed in record time, finding my clothes littered in different places on the floor. I didn't bother finding the girl who should have been my ride. I hightailed it out of there and walked my ass home.

By the time I made it home, Mom had carved a path in the worn carpet. Dad had shown his disapproval at me making Mom worry with a fist in my face. That was the main reason I'd wanted sunglasses that day.

After, I was forced to clean my vomit off the floor with a stern warning to Mom by Dad to let me do it. Once I finished, we'd left in Dad's truck for the show the army put on for lost soldiers. I sat next to the window as Mom laid her head on my shoulder. The bruise on my eye forgotten, it would be explained later with a made-up story about my teenage need to fight. I didn't care what lies Dad told. My brother was gone, and I wouldn't get him back.

I hated my life, the one I was forced to live. My father took out his frustrations with life on Mom and me. And she loved him too much to leave him. If that was love, I wanted no part of it. It didn't make sense that love should hurt so much. And losing my brother was proof.

In death, Sandy was treated like a king, including a five-gun salute. I spent my time holding Mom up as she cried like the only person she ever loved had died. And maybe that was true. I hadn't given her anything to be proud of in the last couple of years. I tended to get in trouble at school, using the pent-up anger I had and aimed it at others.

It was business as usual when it was over. It seemed so unfair that the one person in the world I'd looked up to was gone. And why hadn't the world stopped in pause? Why weren't the streets littered with people outraged that one of the good ones had been ripped from this world while protecting them?

Instead, Mom went to work that night, explaining bills still had to get paid. The only spending I saw was when we stopped at the liquor store to get Dad more beer on the way home.

A part of me wanted to steal one from him and find that place where care no longer mattered. But I hadn't liked losing part of my memory to the drunken haze. So I sat outside, away from my father's line of sight.

I sat on the back porch alone and dreamed of a life like those on TV, with a father who cared and wanted me to succeed. With a mother who didn't work her ass off, but stayed at home to make warm meals. And a brother who wasn't six feet under. I wanted just one day to live a normal life without fear, without going to bed hungry because it was better not to be seen. And going to the kitchen meant I might be fed a knuckle sandwich instead.

In the days to come, Mom picked up a day shift as a waitress to make up for the loss of Sandy's income. On a rare occasion I saw her, I pleaded my case.

"Mom, I can get a job."

She cupped the side of my face. "No. Promise me you'll finish high school no matter what."

There weren't many things Mom asked of me, so I easily said, "Okay."

Then she forced my hand open. "What?"

I felt the cool metal in my palm and realized she'd given me Sandy's dog tags. "You should have these." When I started to protest, she put a finger to my lips. "He would want you to have them." I slipped the chain over my neck, and would wear them every day that would come after.

Knowing he wore them made me feel close to him. And maybe somehow all the strength he possessed would leak into me. I missed him like crazy and didn't want to spend the summer in my head. So, I found relief working construction.

My coach hooked me up with it, and I'd been working my ass off with many side benefits. I was growing out of my scrawniness, picking up lean muscle with all the manual tasks, like lifting, I was given. Also, I was able to give Mom whatever she would take from my paycheck. More importantly, the time spent working meant less time thinking about my dead brother. Because he hadn't been home in a while, I could pretend in my head he was still overseas, not buried in some cemetery.

One afternoon, I'd gone to the deli down from my worksite to get lunch and met a cute redhead. I was sure she'd make a comment about my eyes, which was the norm for someone meeting me for the first time, but she asked about the dog tags around my neck.

"Are you in the military or something?"

"Or something."

There was no way I'd admit I would be in eleventh grade the coming year when she looked like she was in college. I wasn't hard on the eyes, or so I'd been told, so my age might not have been a factor. In the short moments she'd talked, I learned she was visiting family in town, which explained why I'd never seen her before. We made plans, or rather I had plans to be inside her later on that day. My head was so far up the memories of her short skirt, I didn't pay attention when I walked in the front door.

"Where the hell have you been?"

My head shot up, and I realized my mistake. I knew better than to enter the house at that time of day if Dad was home. I could already tell he was in that mean place, drunk but not quite enough for him to be passed out.

"At work," I said, knowing that nothing that came out of my mouth would be a good enough answer. However, experience had shown it would be better than no answer at all.

"Working? You little shit. You probably had your head in pussy."

The best way to survive that encounter was to say nothing more unless he asked me another direct question. It was like a replay of a bad dream. I knew the script all too well.

"You think you're some Romeo. You better remember it's my face you wear. Now go get me some beer money. I'm out."

I never forgot I was the spitting image of him. Sandy had taken after Mom, and God hated me. That's why I looked like my father.

"No."

The word came out softer than I meant it, but I'd said it. I'd earned that money for Mom, not for Dad to waste on getting drunk.

"What did you say, you little fuck?"

Dad jumped to his feet from his chair. By that point, we were about the same height and his eyes narrowed as he stalked closer. He staggered some, causing me to stand a little straighter with the knowledge that I might have a shot.

He jabbed a finger in my face. "I said give me some goddamn money for beer, you little shit."

"No."

The air left my lungs after I dodged a right cross to the jaw and my punch caught him in the side. Only I missed his gut punch. I bent forward and had my light snuffed with an uppercut to the face. I went down before I could take a swing. Only, he wasn't done. A solid kick to my stomach and parting words to *Get the fuck up*, was how he finalized my humiliation. In that moment, I thought of a hundred different ways to kill my father. Slowly, I rolled to my side, not wanting to be kicked again. It took several tries before I found my feet and braced myself against the wall. Jail was the only thing that stopped me from acting on the many ways he could die that played out in my head.

Sandy. I missed my brother with a soul aching pain that mirrored the physical one Dad left me with. I wiped at the tears that burned to unleash from my eyes. I wasn't a pussy even though I felt like one. Why couldn't I be bigger, strong, more intimidating so Dad wouldn't use me for a punching bag. One day, I would make it out of the hell hole and take Mom with me.

Somehow, I managed not to slam my bedroom door as I tossed myself on my bed. I lay there a few seconds before I could totally reclaim my breath. Then I stayed longer, adding up all the things I needed to make a break for it.

There was only one thing on the list—*money*.

According to the bills Dad often left around for Mom to find and pay, I needed much more than I had to make it on my own.

A short time later, I heard Dad banging around in the kitchen in search for alcohol Mom might have hidden. It wouldn't be long before he came looking for me again. I managed to roll off the bed without hurting too much. Then I lifted the mattress and found my duck-tapped baggy filled with my earnings still there. I let the bed back down and straightened the sheets so Dad wouldn't think to check under there.

Having experience with bruised ribs and pain in general, I didn't have a lot of trouble moving around without grimacing in pain. I made my way over to the window and opened it. The humid wall of night air hit me as darkness rolled in while I'd been curled up in a ball on our living room floor. Somehow, I managed to climb out the window without causing myself more injury. I stumbled around to the back of the house, trying to figure out my next move. No way could I take my dad. I tried and failed before, which only resulted in a worse pummeling.

My face hurt enough to know it had swelled, which meant meeting the redhead was off. Because I couldn't afford the expense of a cell phone there was no way I could call her and cancel. That was unless I risked walking into the kitchen near where Dad was to use the house phone. That was a no go. I wasn't giving him beer money no matter how many times he caused me pain. The redhead was a total loss. And if I saw her again she'd probably never forgive me for standing her up.

"Hey, you."

The sweet voice drifted from next door. I turned to see a shape cloaked in shadows on the porch. She stepped down the stairs into the moonlight, and I watched in fascination as the dress she wore fluttered by the movement.

I stood, hoping night would keep my injuries hidden.

"Hey," I called back.

We met at the fence that separated our yards. Fast moving clouds hid the moon, shrouding our view of each other. But she'd starred in my dreams plenty of times for me to know exactly what she looked like. At about two years older than me, she'd graduated from school the past year. I also knew she had a boyfriend and hadn't given me more than a brotherly glance for as long as we'd lived next door to her.

"Why are you out here? I'd figured you'd be out on a date or something."

She'd noticed? "Or something. What about you? Boyfriend taking you out?"

As if the lucky bastard knew what I was thinking about his girl, her phone chirped. She pulled it out from a hidden pocket and glanced at the screen. The light coming off the phone highlighted her smile, which soon dipped into a frown.

A gasp escaped her as she moved to put the phone away. As she did, the light passed over me and gave her a view of my battered face.

She was quick to step forward with a scowl marring her features. "That bastard. He hit you, didn't he?"

I shrugged, which turned out to be a mistake. The movement caused the pain in my chest to grow sharp claws.

"Come in and let's get you cleaned up. I can't believe that asshole messed with you, let alone your gorgeous eyes."

"You don't think my eyes are weird?"

"Of course not. They're both beautiful and uniquely you."

She tugged my hand so I would jump the short fence that separated us. I didn't want her pity, but going into her house was a better option than entering my own. Stifling a wince, I got over and found her house was almost a mirror of ours the little that I saw. We'd entered the bathroom, and I sat on her counter as she played nurse with cotton balls, water, and antiseptic like what Mom used on me. I'd cursed a few times, but mostly I stared at her mouth.

"All done," she announced.

Call me crazy, but I figured I had nothing to lose. If she hit me, it couldn't cause any more pain than I already suffered from. I lifted my hands to her face and drew her close. I pressed my lips to hers and kissed her. When she didn't fight me, I did everything I'd wanted to since the day we moved in.

I couldn't be sure it was me or whatever her boyfriend had texted her, but we ended up in her bed. My movements were slow, but soon enough, my aches were forgotten. She'd given me a condom, and I'd made good use of it, losing myself inside of her. Later on our backs, we panted before laughing.

"You were—"

"Incredible," I offered.

"Cocky bastard, but yes."

"Better than your boyfriend?" It was probably a bad idea to remind her of what she'd done.

"I swear I didn't know you had an ego. But yes. Two for two."

I smirked because my skills were legend, which kept a steady stream of girls giving it up. My ego was my own. I never boasted, but getting the one girl whom I thought unattainable was too much for even me to ignore.

That night, I spent it at her house, in her bed. Her parents were out of town and it just kicked off, us spending the entire last half of the summer exploring each other. She had a book about sex positions she'd wanted to try out. And several times a week we did just that.

Her boyfriend had stupidly enlisted in the army, which he'd shared with her via text that first night and had shortly gone to basic training. So I had no competition for her time. Her mom and dad worked nights like my mom. After I got off work, I'd go straight to her house, avoiding my dad. She cooked me dinner and shit. And the rest of the time we fucked like rabbits. It was the best summer ever.

That was until one night, a week before school started, I left through her back door and hopped the fence. Mom waited for me on our back porch.

"So that's where you go every day?"

The disappointment in her tone cut me.

"You're not at work," I said, unable to answer her.

She patted the spot next to her. "Sit."

Mom could have asked me to jump over the moon, and I would have found a way to do just that. So I sat next to her.

"You know how I wanted you to have a normal high school experience with the same friends and give you a chance to play on the same team."

"We're moving again," I said flatly. It had been a good couple of years in the same place. I thought for sure we'd make it a few more.

She nodded. "I'm sorry about this. I didn't want to."

I believed her, but I did want to know why. "What happened now?"

Did Dad drink the rent money? Were we kicked out because their fighting was too loud for the neighbors? Had Dad gotten in trouble with the law?

"I'm sick," she began, shocking the shit out of me.

Her words coalesced in my head like a tornado. She went on to explain that she had some disease, but it wasn't cancer. MS, she called it. It attacked her nerves or some shit like that. The air thinned, and I was sure I would pass out. Thoughts I tried hard to suppress about my brother's death came roiling back. The idea of losing Mom clogged my throat.

"I've known for a while." She sighed. "But without good insurance I couldn't afford to go to the doctor that often or pay for the medicine."

Cash… Wasn't that what it always came down to?

"So why didn't you accept the money I offered you? You took Sandy's."

She jerked, and what kind of shit son was I to bring up my dead brother?

Swallowing, she said, "It wouldn't have been enough. But things have gotten worse." That's when I noticed the tremor in her hands. "We're moving in with your aunt Joy. She's letting us stay at her house and offered to help pay for the doctors and medicine I need."

We'd lived almost two years in Galveston. It was the longest we'd lived in one place that I could remember. I wanted Mom healthy, but I also didn't want to move…again. Would I ever be able to visit my brother's grave?

"Why can't we stay here?"

She blinked back the shine of tears in her eyes. "Things have gotten too bad. I can't hide it at work anymore, and I've been asked to leave."

I had no idea what she couldn't hide and couldn't bear to ask. Wrapping my arms around her, I cursed my father for being a no good drunk and not being able to keep a job. I cursed because I would go. I would do what was best for Mom. I cursed because I knew it wouldn't be the two of us. Dad would undoubtedly come with us.

"She has a big house north of Dallas. You'll see it will be great," she added.

Mom's sister's house was big, but when we arrived, everything was far from great.

six

LENORA

IT WAS HARD TO EXPLAIN. I WASN'T SURE WHETHER IT was because the hall got a little quieter or I felt something different in the air. All I knew was when Debbie spoke. I wasn't at all surprised to hear her words.

"O.M.G.," she clucked.

I pulled out the book I needed for first period and turned around. My stomach dropped like the floor fell away beneath my feet. Near the school office stood a guy as tall as Ox, but not as wide. That wasn't the jaw-dropping thing about him. He was gorgeous, like movie star beautiful. His dark brown hair was streaked with strands of gold most likely from the sun and fell in his face. His skin bore the hue of someone who spent a lot of time outside. But it was his lips that had my insides turning out. They were perfectly bow-shaped and made for kissing.

"Holy hottie."

I glanced to Debbie's other side to see Trina standing there, gawking with the rest of us spectators. She'd been the one to speak. Debbie was in a state of stupefaction because she didn't cry foul at her frenemy standing near her.

The vice principal held a paper he and the hottie stared at, which was most likely his schedule. And my eyes were transfixed to him. Seconds later, the vice principal looped off, and the boy lifted his gaze to find us in the peanut gallery gaping at him. And it wasn't because he was gorg. It was his eyes that made us pause while sucking in air. One was the color of a typical ocean and the other was bright green, freaky but so incredibly cool.

His smirk drew my attention back to his lips after I watched his eyes trace to Trina. No surprise there. Her blond hair was almost pale enough to be white and caught most boys' attention. Though her curves were more likely the cause. Her outfit left little to the imagination. After obviously looking her up and down, he trained those amazing eyes on Debbie.

She preened under his scrutiny, kicking out her hip for good measure. I glanced back at him in time for his eyes to lock on me. I felt the heat rise in my checks as butterflies the size of bats beat wings into high gear in my stomach. He pushed back a mop of hair, which only spilled back into his face. And what a face. After his eyes skimmed down my body, they traveled back to Debbie.

Good for her, I thought. She didn't miss a beat. She marched forward and held her hands out to him. No doubt names were exchanged.

"Well, that was interesting," Trina muttered before stalking off.

I shut my locker and didn't stay for the show. I wasn't jealous, or I didn't want to be. I had Ox and it was time my best friend got her due. She was really pretty and lacked confidence in herself, which led her to make questionable decisions.

The day passed, and I managed not to run into the boy who made my insides go gooey. I stepped out of the teacher's lounge and headed to the table where we were setting up. My balancing act with the tray in my hands had me paying close attention to what I was holding and not who was in front of me. It was a setup for disaster I should have predicted.

Somehow I managed to keep the tray of cupcakes from all spilling to the ground when I ran cliché style straight into *him*.

"Sorry, I didn't mean to," I said, glancing up into those unfathomable bi-colored eyes.

"You should watch where you're going."

I almost missed the cocky grin he gave me because his voice sounded as good as he looked. Then I caught the smirk. I glanced down where metal hung from his neck. They gleamed against his white shirt. I almost asked about the dog tags but stopped myself.

"You could help me, you know," I said, glancing down at the few cupcakes that took a nose dive to the ground.

"I could."

Though he made no move to do it. I huffed and set the tray on the table before turning around to pick up the mess.

"You are an ass," I sniped, wishing the feeling like I'd just ridden down the biggest drop on a roller coaster would go away.

"And your ass is fine."

I glared over my shoulder after realizing my mistake. As the bake sale was a cheerleading fundraising, I'd changed into my uniform. When I'd bent down, I'd given him a perfect view of my backside. I jumped to my feet with messy hands and stalked back into the teacher's lounge. When I came back out, he was gone.

Ox showed up just as I finished with the table setup.

"Babe."

His pale blue eyes held onto mine. "I want us to go somewhere after I'm finished with practice."

I bit my lip, knowing damn well where he wanted to go and why. "I'm not sure. I have to see if my parents will be okay with me missing dinner."

He grinned. "I've already talked to your mom and they're cool with it."

That was something I didn't like about him. He made decisions for me without talking to me first. And part of me hated my parents for agreeing without seeing if I was okay with it. Then I pictured my father jobless and forced the words from my mouth.

"Yeah, sure."

He hadn't yet pushed the sex issue. But his attentions weren't pure either. We would end up at the park where I would endure his groping and wet kisses, which weren't that horrible if I were honest. I should be strong enough to back out of the relationship. Then I thought of all those women in history who had endured before me. Why couldn't I date a decent guy to ensure my family had a roof over their heads? Debbie kept telling me there were worse hardships.

After he left, it wasn't long before my wayward friend showed up looking extremely pleased with herself.

"What's up?"

Her face split with a grin. "Oh, that's right. You didn't come to lunch. Hung out in the library, or should I say you hid in the library?"

"I wasn't hiding. I had to get some research done."

"Yeah, sure."

"Whatever." I waved a hand and laughed when she playfully slapped at it.

"So I'm meeting Kelley at the game."

I frowned. "Kelley?"

She nodded. "The new guy. His name is Kelley."

"Oh."

So that was his name. I opened my mouth to tell her what a jerk he'd been to me when she babbled on.

"I was so afraid he'd be into you, but he picked me."

That shut me up for a second. "Why wouldn't he pick you? You're beautiful."

She beamed, and I had to be happy for her. I just hoped his doucheness was only for me. I was grateful we got our first customers and I didn't have to lie about my true feelings for the ass.

Our conversation steered to gossip after the sugar rush wave of customers. Debbie was a wealth of information. People talked to her, not knowing she kept no one's secrets except mine. We didn't have much to clean up by the time Ox arrived. As we left, Debbie teased us mercilessly.

He treated us to burgers and shakes before he drove out to the field surrounded by trees where makeshift parties happened, or where people went to make out.

"What's wrong?" Ox said when I didn't respond to his touch.

I decided to be honest. "I really don't want to."

"When do you ever?" he snapped.

His anger forced me to act. I wrenched his truck door open and stumbled out.

"Wait! Fuck. Lenny, I'm sorry."

I kept stomping toward the road. Taller than me, with his long strides, he was able to catch me quickly. I swung around when his hand circled my arm.

"What?"

"Fuck, Lenny." He'd already said that. "I love you. I gave you that ring to prove it. You'd think you'd trust me by now. I just want us to be closer."

Closer? "You want to have sex. Just say it."

Maybe his honesty would get us somewhere.

He shrugged. "Maybe. And not because I'm a guy. Hell, there are plenty of girls willing to give it up."

I lifted my hands up. "I'm not stopping you." I didn't wait for an answer. Instead, I headed toward the road again.

"Come on, Len. We don't have to do it. But I can make you feel good. I've done it before and you could do the same for me."

We had fooled around, rounding some bases. But he'd never created bat signals in my stomach. One boy had and it was stupid of me to think about it because Mom had been totally wrong. My subconscious was way off base. Kelley was a douche of epic proportions. I should be gaga over the guy I called boyfriend.

Not wanting to walk a couple of miles home, I stopped because I couldn't be mad at his honesty. But it didn't mean I was giving in either. "Just take me home, please."

seven

KELLEY

MOM HADN'T LIED ABOUT THE SIZE OF MY AUNT'S house. We could easily fit four of our former house inside theirs. I hadn't made up my mind yet if things would be better or worse.

It took a week for Mom to get me enrolled in my new school. A week without losing myself inside a girl had nearly driven me to sneak a beer from Dad's stash. Stuck in my head hadn't been a good place to be. Mom knew it too. On day two of my new surroundings, she'd given me a battered copy of a classic book, she'd called it. The title was *Of Mice and Men.* Considering the alternatives in my stark confines, I didn't balk. The book was pretty thin, and lacking any other options for entertainment, I finished it, which left me to think more. The story was full of irony I could relate to.

Grief was hell, and I had no one to talk to. I couldn't tell Mom how much Sandy's death broke me because it broke her too. So I hadn't complained. Not after seeing how much Mom needed help from Dad to walk, which came out of nowhere.

During one stop on the long drive to Dallas, Dad pumped gas. Mom must have caught my distress.

With a hand on my cheek, she said, "The disease is progressing quicker, which isn't unheard of, only rare. This is why we are moving so I can see a better doctor."

Her eyes were soft with love, and the idea that she may leave this world filled me with my lungs with cement. I couldn't imagine life without her with my father in charge of my existence.

We arrived without fanfare and kindness really. My aunt treated our arrival as if we were putting her out. A week with nothing to do had been too much.

Never had I looked forward so much to school. Getting enrolled meant I could get out of my head and use the school library's computer to search for a job so I could help pay for whatever Mom needed to get better.

By the time the vice principal's scripted talk about what a great school I was attending and how I would make a lifetime of experiences, I felt eyes on me. I'd grown used to it and semi-enjoyed it if the right girl was watching.

Girls. They stared and giggled and when they saw my eyes, they'd gawk. At first I didn't get it. In fact, I still didn't totally understand it. I just went with it because the ones who did it so obviously were normally open to my brand of conversation, which didn't include a lot of talking. And damn if I didn't need that kind of distraction.

So when I glanced up and saw a trio of them, I almost smiled but stopped myself. I had to admit the school wouldn't be all that bad if the three were a sample of the rest of the girl population.

First up was a blonde with serious curves who wore a *been there done that* smile. I moved on to the brunette next to her. The girl was clearly a virgin, but she stared me down like she wanted me to be her first. I'd done several virgins, so I wasn't scared off.

Then the last. I sucked in a quiet breath. She was fucking gorgeous, the full package, from her perfect face framed by dark hair, to her body that created an instant reaction in my own to the way her cheeks colored in a blush when our eyes met. That was her virgin calling card. And damn if that didn't mean she wasn't ready for the likes of me. As much as I craved her, I settled for option number two.

I couldn't have been more right. When I challenged the first brunette with my stare, she skipped her way over to me with her hand extended.

"Hi, I'm Debbie. Welcome to our school."

I lifted my chin and ignored her hand. She dropped it to her hip, trying to play it off.

"So, do you talk?"

I said nothing, still considering whether banging this girl was worth the virgin blues that came after. Because no matter how many times I'd made my intentions clear, there were always some who thought they'd be the one to change my mind.

"Are you going to tell me your name?"

I needed to say something if I planned to get any. Admittedly, I'd been watching the other brunette over her shoulder. She'd turned around when Debbie came bouncing over. Still, I tracked the other girl's movements as she strode away before I said, "Yeah, sorry. I'm Kelley."

Coolly, I watched her reaction. If she snickered over my name, we were done. Lucky for her, she grew a smile worthy of the size of Texas. Bingo, I was in.

"Why don't you let me give you a tour of the school?"

I snickered. "Sure thing."

During said tour, she linked her arm in mine. She prattled on about stuff I didn't remember. I kept envisioning the other girl on my arm. So when eventually asked if I wanted to hang out during halftime at the football game that Friday, she had to repeat her question. Hearing her the second time, I gave her a non-committal response, which she'd taken as a yes. Time would tell. I'd have to see how clingy she was before I made up my mind.

After school, I met with the football coach only to find out I was a summer late and dollars short. Playing on the team required money for certain equipment the school didn't provide. And it cost more than I had, which was nothing. I'd given all the money I'd earned over the summer to Mom. I didn't want us to be a total charity case to my aunt and uncle.

Coach said, "Sorry, son, I would offer you help, but I've already given out all the donated money to returning students who needed it as well. And even if you could come up with the funds needed, I most likely couldn't start you."

Spots on the team had been earned over summer practice and according to him it wouldn't be fair to start me even if my reputation preceded me. So I'd be riding the bench with money paid for equipment I wouldn't use. And money didn't grow on trees. I wouldn't dare ask Mom for the cash I'd given her because she needed it more.

Football was my ticket away from my life and making a better one for my mom. If I couldn't play this year, I would still have one more year to make my mark and get into a college, anywhere far from my dad. Meantime, I'd used my brain. Most people thought I was dumb, but I'd cruised through many exams, passing easily without studying. It was one of the reasons my former principal would give me a pass when I got into trouble.

I have to say when I saw her, I was pissed about something that had nothing to do with her. It was the fact that my dad was a jobless useless drunk who couldn't take care of his family, forcing us to move, and me being unable to play ball, I narrowed my eyes and spit venom from my tongue.

So when she'd called me an ass, I hadn't been expecting it. She seemed sweet like apple pie. Taken off guard, I'd said the first thing that came to my mind while doing nothing to help her pick up the cupcakes that tumbled to the floor. When she'd bent down, it sent my dick rising up like a football during the kickoff. Fuck, but I wanted her way more than that Debbie or the blonde.

And it was fucking cute when she stomped off after I told her I liked her ass. Her mouth had been perfect, and I was ready to give up my no kissing policy, which wasn't as strict as it sounded. I was selective in who I kissed.

"Dude, don't bother. She belongs to a guy named Ox, and he didn't get the name for no reason."

The guy materialized out of nowhere. He was a few inches shorter than me and had the look of the perfect wingman.

"Yeah, belongs to, huh?"

"Exactly. Lenny is like Ox's future wife. He put a ring on it, dude. You didn't see it? You don't stand a chance."

I eyed him. His words didn't sound like he was jealous. "Lenny?" I questioned because I'd yet to find out her name.

"Lenora, but everyone calls her Lenny. And Ox claimed her freshman year to make sure no one else could talk to her. So forget it. Trust me. Not only is the guy built like a Mack truck, he's richer than anyone here. I'm Joel, by the way."

He gave me more than enough reasons to leave the girl alone. I slapped him on his back and turned us toward the door. “So, Joel, what can you tell me about Debbie?”

“Her best friend?”

I nodded, even though I hadn’t been sure of that until he said it. He grinned. “Do you need a ride home?”

“I sure do.”

“I’ll tell you all about Debbie on the ride there.”

And he did. The girl had quite the reputation for a virgin. From what he heard, even though she didn’t put out, she had other talents. *Interesting.*

“Holy shit, you live here,” he said when he pulled up into my aunt’s driveway. Joel’s shit car had coughed and sputtered all the way to my place, and was ancient and far older than my dad’s truck.

Figuring by his car and his stunned eyes at my aunt’s house, I assumed he wasn’t well-off, like me.

“I stay here. I don’t live here.” I pointed for him to pull next to the garage. “This is my aunt’s house. We’re staying here for a while because my mom’s sick.”

“Shit, man, sorry.”

I shrugged, not knowing him well enough to say more. “It beats back home. Besides, I get the apartment over the garage.”

My uncle didn’t like kids. And though I was taller and bigger than he was, he didn’t want future guests to have to deal with teenage bullshit, whatever that meant.

Even though I’d made my room over the garage sound sweeter than it was, there had been more words I’d said to him than most people since Sandy died. Joel didn’t judge. He only nodded.

“I’d kill for my own place. My sisters drive me insane.”

“Sisters?” I waggled my eyebrows.

"No fucking way. They're too young anyway."

We laughed, which was another thing I hadn't done in a long time. After he left, I walked toward the house. And not to the front door, since we were forbidden to enter that way. Mom's room was the first door on the left after entering the designated side entrance. It was private at least.

"Kelley," Mom said, reaching an arm in my direction from where she sat propped up on pillows. "How was your day?"

I sat next to her on her bed. "It was all right. How about you?"

Since moving here, Mom's condition changed rapidly. It was as if she'd given up to the disease. She tired easily and couldn't stay on her feet long. Which was the excuse my aunt used as to why Mom had been given the maid's quarters. Aunt Joy had claimed it was for the best. She wouldn't have to walk upstairs and would be close to an exit in case of an emergency like for an ambulance, not because of a fire, or so she said.

"I'm fine," Mom answered.

Aunt Joy, who'd been sitting in a chair in the corner, said, "You need to tell the boy the truth, Jackie."

I glanced up and managed to hold back the glare I wanted to level at her. Aunt Joy may have kept a pleasant smile on her face when she discussed our family like we were a charity case, but she'd given enough clues that she really didn't want us there. Her rich husband was reminded of her humble beginnings with the likes of us in their house, which was the real reason we'd been tucked out of sight.

Family or not, I didn't like her, and disliked my uncle even more. He barely said two words to us and it was clear he was counting the days for us to be gone. As far as my aunt, I'd only seen her once before and briefly when they'd been in Galveston. They'd managed to slum it long enough to come say hi to our dinky home. She hadn't even sat down when she'd stepped inside, making excuses about not being able to stay for the dinner Mom had agonized over.

"Joy, stop," Mom said with more defiance than I'd heard from her in a while. She turned to me. "Now tell me, how was school? Were there any cute girls? I know there were."

I never intentionally lied to my mother. She asked a question, I'd answer it truthfully or say nothing about it at all.

"There might have been a few. Anyway," I said, changing the topic. "I can't play ball. The season has already started. Coach said I'd be riding the bench and not to waste my time."

Her hand pushed my hair back. "I'm so sorry."

I shrugged. "It's cool. Gives me more time to study."

She laughed. "When was the last time you've had to study for anything?"

"Well, we know where he gets his brains from and it sure isn't his daddy."

"Joy, please," Mom begged.

"If he isn't stupid, he sure knows what I'm saying is true. He was cursed with his father's looks, though. Just remember, Kelley, no girls allowed in my house."

I nodded, wanting to argue. But Mom got a word in before I did.

"Can you please stop talking about my husband?"

"Why? Mom and Dad warned you not to marry that good for nothing boy. He wasn't any good then and he's not any good now. And maybe if you hadn't gotten knocked up, you wouldn't be living in my house with a man who can't take care of you."

Part of me wanted to fist bump my aunt, but I still didn't like her. The other part wanted to defend my dad because even if he was a shit, he was my shit. And I didn't like her looking down her nose at him. Because, really, she thought we were all worthless and just wouldn't say it.

"I love him, Joy. And I never say anything bad about your stuck in the mud husband."

That got my aunt to her feet and pointed her nose high in the air. "If it weren't for my husband, you wouldn't have a roof over your head. Don't ever forget that."

Before my aunt made it out the door, Mom asked in a small voice, "How are Mom and Dad?"

My aunt stopped and cradled the doorframe with her hand.

"Mom's starting to show signs of dementia. No surprise there, considering her age. And Dad's got a cold. But otherwise they are good."

"Have they asked about me?" Mom asked.

"Mom barely remembers me half the time, and Dad pretends not to remember you. Nothing's changed, Jackie, since the day you left choosing to marry that boy."

She left the room, and I saw the disappointment on Mom's face. She'd never hidden that she had a strained relationship with her folks. They'd never come to see us. They were a great deal older, as was her sister. Mom was their *oops baby,* and they'd been too old to pay attention to her growing up, but too religious to give her up when they found themselves in their mid-forties about to have another kid.

I wrapped Mom in a hug, feeling my heart break for her as my strong and proud mother tried to look tough for me.

"They don't deserve you, Mom. Anyone who can forget their kid so easily should lose their memory and their mind."

"Kelley, they aren't bad people."

But that was exactly what Mom would say. She wanted to see the best in people, even when they didn't deserve it. Her body shook, and I didn't know if was the disease or silent tears that caused it. I didn't ask either. She'd felt bad enough. No reason to remind her how fucked up the world was.

For the longest time, I just held on. I glanced around the room that had no personality. We hadn't had much, but our walls in Galveston hadn't been white like these were, along with the only small dresser and chair in the room. It felt more like a hospital than a guest room. Mom glanced up and caught me looking at what we'd been reduced to. Our house hadn't been much, but it felt like home even when Dad was there. The only thing good here was she had a private bath attached. I had to use the bathroom in the pool house, which was across the other side of the backyard from the garage. Still, I didn't complain because I had my own space and didn't have to share with Dad.

Speaking of, "Where's Dad?" I finally asked, not wanting to bump into him.

Her smile looked brittle. "Out finding a job. He's been better to you, right?"

It was true he hadn't hit either one of us since Mom's news to me, but he hadn't been around much either. What she hadn't said was my aunt probably required Dad to find a job if he wanted to stay there. Good thing my room wasn't near. No doubt he would take his frustrations out on me if he didn't find anything soon. So far, he hadn't visited my room. Too many stairs, I guessed, for his drunk ass to handle.

Mom patted my hand. "Don't be late for dinner."

That statement was a gentle reminder that meals were served at six am, noon, and six pm. If I missed them, I wasn't allowed to scour for food in the kitchen. I would be out of luck. Good thing I qualified for free breakfast and lunch at school. When Mom finally fell asleep, I left for my room.

Friday, I found myself in a shed behind the bleacher during the football game. I'd walked straight into the gate while a line waited to buy a ticket. No one was watching, and I didn't have any cash anyway.

Debbie panted as my hand worked the short distance under her cheerleading skirt. Before I could snake a finger under the material between me and getting off, she jumped back.

"Wait, I can't. I'm a virgin."

The news wasn't a surprise. I guessed right, and Joel had warned me too. But the chick had practically been begging for it. Her hand had stroked my dick through my jeans. If I were another guy, I might have taken what I wanted. No one liked teases, but I wasn't down with taking it. There were always other girls.

"Yeah, okay," I said, backing off.

"Wait," she called out when I headed for the door.

Turning, unsure why I did, I left a good distance between us. And I made no move to touch her again.

"I can give you a blow job."

Joel's information had been good, and who would say no to that? I stood there with my hands lifted, palms up. She got on her knees, and I braced my hands against the walls. It might have been an unspoken dare. It might have been I hadn't gotten any in so long. What it was, was all on her. I hadn't asked, and I didn't expect anything.

Only when she got down to it, she was all teeth. So much for her reputed skills. My half hard dick went completely limp, so I carefully guided her off me.

"Sorry, this isn't working." I wasn't one to lie.

While I began to put my dick into my pants, she pleaded with me for reasons I halfway understood.

"Please, I can do better."

Can't say I'm a total asshole. She didn't want to be a failure. I got that. Girls were complicated, and I'd been around enough to know when they did it, they wanted to please. So I took control and let her mouth cover the head. Then I basically jacked off using her wet tongue as motivation. Only it took more than that to get me off. Somehow my mind drifted to Lenny. Imagining her on her knees in front of me sent me coming unexpectedly into Debbie's mouth. She jerked back and ribbons of it covered her face.

"What the hell? You're supposed to warn me, you jerk!"

I sighed. "Sorry, I guess I forgot." I didn't think telling her the truth that I'd been thinking of her best friend would win me any prizes.

She found a questionable towel lying on a table and wiped her face clean. I'd tucked myself away, and we stood there staring at each other.

"So what now?"

Shit. We hadn't actually talked before she dragged me out there. Once we were alone, she'd placed my hand on her tits and it was a moaning fest until my release, except that bit in the middle.

"You're a virgin, and I'm not. It's never going to work between us."

"So what you're saying is, because I won't have sex with you, you're dumping me?"

The whole dumping thing stumped me because I barely knew the girl. But there was no reason to throw eggs on her ego.

"I like sex, you don't have sex."

"What?" she snarled and things were going nowhere good fast.

Her eyes narrowed on me. Before she could fuss me out, I added, "A little advice. If you don't want the wrong guy to get pissed, maybe you should be more like your friend Lenny."

Her next words came out of nowhere when all I'd tried to do was warn her there were assholes in the world who wouldn't take kindly to her *I want it, but I'm not giving it up* game.

"You want her. Of course you do. Just like everyone else. You're a total asshole."

She stomped out of the shed, and I groaned loudly, watching her march away. I hadn't meant that I wanted Lenny even though most of me did. I'd meant it because Lenny didn't pretend to not want to be a virgin the way Debbie did. Debbie should keep her legs closed and mouth shut before she ran into trouble. Instead, a girl like her had a mouth with a lot to say. I could imagine the uphill battle I would have with the female population by the time Monday rolled around.

eight

LENORA

HALFTIME HAD JUST ENDED WHEN DEBBIE CAME barreling onto the field. Her hair was slightly out of place and her legs had a layer of dust on them.

Quickly, I scrambled over, while the other girls got into position.

"What happened?"

Her mouth formed a sneer and then it flattened. "Nothing. I'll tell you later."

She pushed past me and dusted off her legs before she grabbed her pom-poms off the ground. I studied her for a second. She'd left to meet Kelley. Apparently nothing good happened, but what did? My glance around netted me nothing. He hadn't come after her. My concern made it hard to get through the rest of the game as Debbie refused to talk during the breaks.

When I piled in her car after the game because my parents hadn't come, she had no choice but to speak.

"What?" she snapped. "Can't you give it a rest already?"

I breathed through her anger, trying to hold back my own. "Look, I know something happened between you and Kelley. Spill!"

The long breath she exhaled could have gone on for days. "Okay." She shifted the car back in park because we hadn't moved from the spot yet. "You need to stay away from that guy. He's bad news."

My forehead wrinkled in confusion. "What guy? Kelley?" She nodded, but so slowly my heartbeats slowed. "Just tell me what he did to you."

It had to be bad considering she didn't blurt it out. Debbie wasn't one for keeping secrets, or so I'd thought.

"He tried to rape me."

I gasped and covered my mouth with my hand. "Are you okay? How could you not say anything? We need to go to the police."

Vehemently she shook her head. "No way I'm going to the cops. What do you think they're going to do? It will be his word against mine."

There was panic in her eyes as she glanced out the window, as if the people walking through the parking lot could hear us. I reached out a hand and clasped her arm.

"I'll be there with you."

Her eyes snapped back to mine. "No! I'm not. Do you know how they treat rape victims?"

I couldn't say that I did. You heard stuff on the news occasionally, but nobody I knew had ever been hurt that way.

After I shook my head, she sniped, "They make them out to be whores. They'll ask me all kinds of questions about my sex life."

"You haven't had sex." It hadn't been a question. She would have told me, right?

"No, but I've done everything. And you know how guys are." I didn't, but I let her continue. "They'll say I'm easy or that I've done this or that."

I stared at my best friend, wondering what I really knew about her. What was this and that? And what guys?

"My parents will know I'm not their precious little daughter. I can't do it. I won't do it," she practically yelled.

My shoulders slumped a little. But I tried one more time. "What if he does it to some other girl?"

She shrugged. "Not my problem. So promise me you won't say a word."

"Debbie—"

"Promise me."

I closed my eyes in defeat. "I promise."

"And stay away from him. He mentioned your name."

That caught my attention. "What?"

"It was nothing. It just sounded like he may try to talk to you next."

My jaw couldn't have been opened any wider. "Why would he do that? That's crazy. He knows you're my best friend." Okay, I wasn't sure of that. "He has to know you'd tell me."

"Just stay away from him," she said again.

Then she shifted the car in drive and took me home. Music filled the silence between us as I didn't pepper her with any more questions. She obviously didn't want to talk about it. I wasn't stupid enough to think it wouldn't be hard telling the cops. But I didn't understand why she didn't care that he could do it to someone else. And why would he target me? Something seemed off. But how could I possibly doubt my best friend over a guy I barely knew? One who hadn't been nice enough to help me when I dropped the cupcakes. One who'd made crude comments about my body. Maybe he was a creeper, even if he hardly seemed the type to have to force a girl to do anything.

After school on Monday, I stared at the cursed ring on my finger. Debbie was right. I hid in the library so I wouldn't have to sit with my boyfriend at lunch. I wasn't in love with Ox. But what was love? I headed to the room where I tutored along with some other students with good grades who needed an extracurricular activity on their college applications. Though I had to admit I liked helping people and had toyed with the idea of becoming a teacher.

When the classroom door opened twenty minutes later, I didn't bother looking up. Students came and went during the session as needed. Only the mood in the room shifted. Slowly, I glanced up to find my worst nightmare. His eyes searched the room before landing on me. My heart sped up and my stomach took a nosedive. I don't know what he saw in my expression, but he headed in my direction anyway.

"I need you."

Any other time, those words might have been powerful, even romantic. But after what he did to Debbie, I suddenly believed she'd been right that he'd targeted me.

"I'm sorry, but I'm helping someone right now. You have to wait your turn. Anyone who frees up first can help you."

A freshman with a face suffering from a bout of acne sat next to me as I helped him with algebra.

"I don't want someone. I want you. Dude, beat it."

Carl, with his mop of ginger curls, grabbed his stuff and took off out of the room. Kelley's *I'm going to kick your ass* expression had been enough to do the trick.

He sat without my permission. With my eyes narrowed, I attempted to get up from my seat and find someone else who needed assistance. He gripped my arm, stopping me.

"You're a bully," I spat.

"Maybe, but that kid didn't need your help either. Did you see how he was looking at you?"

"No." I hadn't. Carl wasn't dumb and seemed to get the concepts, although he claimed he didn't. "It doesn't matter anyway. I'm here to help people."

"And I need help. Mr. Wilks sent me here to find you. I need to get caught up and fast. He said you're the best person to get me there. Although I can think of better ways we can spend our time together."

I was flattered that my trig teacher placed me in high regards. But his last statement made me roll my eyes, and I chose to ignore it, ignore him the best I could. Only, it was hard to ignore his kissable lips. And why was I thinking like that? Time to bring the conversation around. "Why didn't he help you himself?"

Seemingly having an answer for everything, he said, "I need to get caught up with all my subjects, not just math." Then he leaned forward, and my breath caught thinking he might kiss me. "I passed Biology and Chemistry, but maybe we could work on some practical application of Physics."

Was he flirting with me? Suddenly hot, I reached for my next words and blurt them out. "Let me see your schedule."

The paper slid through the pages of one of the books he carried as he pulled it out. When he held it out, I made sure I didn't touch him. Only my eyes locked on his lips a second too long, and I watched them curl into a smirk before I jerked my gaze to the paper in my hand.

He was in AP Algebra 2, which surprised me. We didn't share classes, but his schedule didn't include one remedial class. Talk about not judging a book by its cover. He'd been too pretty to be smart too, and boy I was wrong.

"Based on your schedule, I don't see why you can't help yourself. I'm sure there are other more willing victims for you to prey on."

Crap, I hadn't meant to say that. He rubbed me the right way, not the wrong like he should have. He smelled faintly of soap and his hair flopped over his left eye. A part of me wanted to reach out and push it back.

"Victim?"

I swallowed, because the way he said it, I felt like I was on the witness stand. His whole flirty smile had darkened into a scowl.

"Is that how she played it? She didn't like I wasn't into her and she tells you she's a victim. *Maybe* she didn't like that I told her she should be more like *you*."

He stood, and I felt small because I'd judged him based on hearsay.

"You know what? I can figure this out myself. I don't have time for this shit. Lying about shit like that ain't cool. And of course you believe her because I don't wear the right clothes or I'm not from the right part of town."

He plucked the schedule from my hand and stalked out of the room with his stuff. I sat dumbfounded as the classroom was way too quiet, and I realized that everyone had been watching us. The thing about it was, I didn't know him. But his actions and words had me questioning the truth of my friend's story, and I hated myself for that.

nine

KELLEY

AFTER CHECKING ON MOM, I'D SPEND THE REST OF THE night between worrying about her and worrying about what one girl thought of me. I shouldn't give a rat's ass about the latter. Yet, I couldn't get the gorgeous girl out of my head. Smart, confident enough to speak her mind, and beautiful was a deadly combination. Most girls I messed around with were more into clothes and reality shows.

I'd chosen poorly with Debbie and decided I should have gone with the sure thing when my mind wanted option number three, Lenny. Over the next week in school, I decided to move on and cut my losses and try and forget about the unforgettable girl.

A tap on my shoulder pulled me away from the blonde who was so ready for my kind of fun. Debbie's stories hadn't reached everyone, or maybe some just didn't believe her. I glanced over my shoulder to see the tiny girl who'd invaded my every waking thought over the past week.

"Hey, give me a minute. Then I'll find you, and you can give me the tour you were talking about," I said to the blonde in front of me.

I squeezed her waist, sending her into a giggling fit.

"Don't be too long," she replied with better things to come.

She sauntered away. Her short skirt swayed with promise that I'd end my drought that night. Over a week of not getting any made me stupid like what I was about to do. I crossed my arms over my chest and turned around to glare at the brunette.

Her eyes were laser tag focused on my *sure thing*'s back as she walked away.

"What is it you want?" I asked, gaining her attention.

Whip fast, she turned to face me again. Only she met my eyes a second before turning her gaze to the floor.

"I'm, uh…Debbie cleared some things up."

I wasn't going to make this easy for her. She'd summed me up without giving me a chance to defend myself. Plus, she was cute as hell when she blushed. "You're what?"

Her gray eyes rose, chin up, and she said, "I'm sorry, okay? I was given bad information, and I treated you horribly because of it. I want to help you get caught up."

"There are things you can help me with." I let my gaze fall over her, watching her pout change as I made myself clear. We didn't have classes together, so I hadn't seen her all day. She wore jeans and a tee that fit her. And even though she was all but covered, my imagination filled in the blanks. "But today's no good." I glanced behind me, but the blonde was gone. "And I can't risk missing dinner."

I had just enough time to make good with the blonde and walk the few miles home.

"If you think being crude will scare me off, you're wrong. Let me buy you dinner?"

She didn't have to buy me anything. I could feast on her all day.

"I'm not some charity case."

She frowned, not getting it. "It's not charity. I totally owe you for how I treated you. I'll buy you dinner at the diner just down the street, and I can help get you caught up."

The fact that I was wavering was a bad sign. I knew better.

"What will your boyfriend have to say about it?"

Joel had pointed the guy out as if in warning. Although he was one of a kind and stood out like a Cyclopes, I would have pieced it together myself. He was about my height, but stockier. He probably packed a serious punch, but he would be slow to my quick moves and have to catch me first.

"What can he say? It's not like this is a date. Besides, he doesn't own me."

Her defiance was cute. But then everything she did I found cute. I reached out and touched her hand. Her skin was as soft as I imagined. Then I held it up, ring finger sparkled in the light from the windows.

"This ring seems to say otherwise."

She snatched her hand from mine. You would think she'd been burned the way her eyes flared.

"It's a promise ring. Not an engagement ring."

Interesting choice of words. "Could have fooled me and not what's being said around school. Guy doesn't put a ring like that on a girl for a promise. He's stating his claim loud and clear that you are his forever."

"It's a promise ring," she said, and I scoffed. "Now do you want to go get burgers or not?"

Blonde forgotten, I shrugged. "Will I get in trouble for being out with the town's princess?"

“I am not…” She snapped her lips closed and didn’t bother saying anything else. She stalked down the hall, and I moved to follow.

The view from behind was just as good as the front. My dick leaped for joy thinking he was getting some action. I groaned a bit, remembering the sure thing I left behind for the sure no, yet I followed like a dog wanted a bone.

She hadn’t lied. The diner was only a few blocks away. Seeing that it was just after four, the place was deserted. School was over and it wasn’t a Friday night. Everyone who didn’t have to be at school had gone home somewhere, to study or to bang. And I wasn’t doing either. The pretense that we were going to study was lost on her, because I hadn’t brought a book with me. Not that she’d given me time. She had a backpack, but we didn’t share any classes, to my utter disappointment. Needling her in class could have been the highlight of my day.

“Burger,” she said to the waitress who appeared.

Then they both turned their eyes on me. I’d been watching Lenny, studying her face like the answers to a pop quiz were there. She was more than pretty. Yet, she didn’t paint her face or even wear that gloss shit on her lips. I wanted to kiss her and that was a first. I did it mostly because I had to on occasion. Wanting it was an entirely different thing.

“Yeah, what she’s having,” I said to end the scrutiny the two were giving me. “And fries.”

“Fries come with it, hon,” the older woman said. She stared at me. Finally, I turned my attention to her and stared back. Turned out she wasn’t exactly that much older than me. Maybe two or three years at most, and she had a decent smile. I was used to older girls. They liked me, and I liked them back. They didn’t play the games girls my age did.

"I'll have a Sprite," Lenny said, gaining the woman's attention.

The cute waitress shifted her focus back to me. "Shake, vanilla."

"Coming right up."

She sauntered off with swaying hips. I watched in appreciation.

Lenny's finger snapped in front of my face. "Are we going to study or what?"

"I didn't bring any books." When she started to frown, I added, "It's not like you gave me any time to get to my locker."

"I thought that was your locker."

"No, that was *her* locker. You know, how you interrupted us."

"Interrupted. You should be thanking me. She's been passed around the entire football team."

With an arched brow, I said, "I thought you knew better than to believe rumors."

She sagged in her seat. "You're right. That was mean. I shouldn't have said that. I don't know why I said that."

"I know why," I tossed out.

Straightening, her eyes challenged me, and I liked it. "Why's that?"

"Because you like me. Jealousy was written all over your face."

"I…I…" she sputtered. "I'm not jealous."

"Snapping your finger in my face so I wouldn't check out our waitress."

"That's not true."

"Lie to yourself. It's okay."

"I have a boyfriend." Though she was grasping at reasons.

"Yeah, where is he?"

She closed her mouth and good thing. I imagined all kinds of things as our waitress materialized with piping hot food in record time. Then again, we were the only customers. The smells made my stomach stretch. It totally beat the school lunches I forced down unless I wanted to starve.

After the waitress set down our food, she placed the bill face down with her number face up near me. Lenny snagged it like a snake strike.

"I've got this," she declared.

I smirked because she was so jealous. Bad thing was, her declaration that had nothing to do with me couldn't have been truer. She had my complete attention like no other girl had ever before. I couldn't resist needling her.

"Sure you do. But I'm pretty sure that phone number is for me."

Her mouth dropped open. "She's like too old for you. You're like sixteen, right?"

"Soon to be seventeen."

"Then I'm doing you a favor. She could go to jail."

The paper crumpled in her hands. And I decided not to point out that the waitress not going to jail was a favor to her and not to me.

"Are you going to catch me up with school or what?" I asked, shoving a fry in my mouth.

"You said you didn't have your books."

"So, tell me all I need to know about my teachers. What they expect and shit. Who's the hardest...yeah, that kind of stuff."

And she did while we ate. She made me laugh as she gave me the lowdown, giving me rumors and pointing them out as unsubstantiated. Her use of a word like that made me wonder more about her. She was smart and beautiful, which only made me more interested when I shouldn't have been.

"And don't ever mention Mr. Wilk's cowlick in his presence if you want to pass the class. I swear the guy could use plaster and it still wouldn't stay down. And that's so mean to say because he's a great teacher."

I chuckled, enjoying whatever she had to say.

"Your turn. I've done all the talking."

"What do you want to know?" I asked, curious about what she would say next.

"Where did you move from? What brings you to our sleepy little town?"

There were a hundred things she could have asked, yet she'd given me an easy one.

"Galveston and my mom. She's sick."

"You don't talk much."

"Nope."

By the time I made it home, it was well past dinner. Dad wasn't home, or at least his truck was missing. Mom lay in the bed looking frail. I hated how fast things had changed.

"Kelley?"

I sat. "Yes, Mom. How are you feeling?"

She reached out and took my hand. "Better. Tell me about your day. Your aunt informed me you missed dinner."

"It's cool. I ate dinner with a girl from school."

Her eyes perked up before they softened. She squeezed my hand. "Kelley, I know girls flock to you like pigeons.

But you need to be smart. Don't be like your father. A pretty face and he forgets himself."

I didn't respond. We both knew Dad cheated on Mom. Why she stayed, I didn't understand. Plus, her statement was a departure from the day before when she acted as though me finding a girl was a good thing. Maybe that'd been for my aunt's benefit.

"It's not like that with this girl. She's got a boyfriend. She's just helping me get caught up with classes."

"Oh, that's nice."

It had been. But seeing Mom put everything in perspective. She hadn't said it, but I assumed that's what my aunt wanted her to tell me. I'd used the library computer when I left lunch early to do some research. I'd found out that although MS wasn't deadly, there were the rare few who did die from complications related to the disease. Mom followed that pattern. She was going to die. I could see it in her eyes and the way she held my hand.

I lay in bed that night, tossing my football up in the air. I needed a plan, and I needed a job. If Mom did die, I wanted to be able to be on my own. And wasn't that a sucky way to think about things, which only made me think of my dead brother and how very alone I was.

ten

LENORA

SILENCE RANG OUT LIKE A SCHOOL BELL ON THE OTHER end of the phone. I'd called Debbie once I got home.

"Well?" I demanded.

Debbie said nothing at first, which made me want to reach through the phone and smack her. "I can't believe you called him out on it in the middle of a classroom."

"I didn't mean to." I hadn't. "But you know I'm not the type to smile in someone's face and talk behind their back. I just blurted it out. So were you telling the truth or not?"

There was a pause, and I was about to demand an answer when she finally spoke.

"It's complicated."

A huff escaped my lips. "Complicated. I think it's an easy yes or no. Did he or didn't he—"

"No," she blurted. "No, he didn't try to rape me."

I fell back on my bed with the phone pressed to one ear, and I covered my eyes with the other. There was no way to understand.

"Why?" I asked softly.

"Why?" she repeated, only grating on my nerves.

"Why did you lie?" I didn't get it. I didn't get her.

"Because I was embarrassed. He rejected me and told me to be more like you."

He'd told me he'd said that. But I still didn't quite comprehend why she would make up a lie that big just because he compared her to me in some way. It seemed stupid. Was she lying about that too? Could I even trust her? My thoughts circled to the offhand comment Trina made about not trusting people close to me. Had she meant Debbie? What did she know?

"When I told him I didn't want to because I was a virgin, he basically wrote me off. So I tried."

"Tried what?" I asked tiredly. I knew I should be more sympathetic, but I couldn't muster the energy to do so.

"To give him a blow job. But I failed at that too. That's why my legs were dirty. He had to jack himself off because I couldn't even get that right."

She'd seen him naked? Why did that bother me? And not for her sake, but a jealousy that she'd seen him bubbled up in my chest.

"Why do you allow yourself to get in these situations?"

"Because I'm not pretty enough, okay? You're like my parents. You see something no guy sees. The only thing I have to offer to keep their attention is sex. And I'm a virgin."

Her sobs broke through the hard feelings I had toward her.

"Debbie, you have to believe in yourself and not let some guy place value over you."

These were some of the things my parents had told me until Dad's job had become more important than my self-worth. So why was I even repeating their words when they didn't truly believe it themselves?

The next day I swallowed my pride and approached Kelley after school. He was saying something to the girl flattened against the locker as he leaned in. She giggled, and I saw red. I had to breathe through the insane thoughts I had. I was with Ox, not Kelley, I repeated in my head.

He hadn't seemed excited to see me, but somehow I convinced him of my sincerity. After an awkward start, we actually laughed during dinner. When I mentioned Mr. Dunnon's unibrow, he nearly spat out his drink.

"I didn't think you had it in you to go there, princess."

I shrugged and ignored the princess comment. "It's not like it's a fact. It all moves as one."

He laughed so hard. And boy when he smiled, he was even more gorgeous. When the check came, I saw the number the waitress had left for him. She'd graduated from school a few years ago when I'd been a freshman. The fact that she worked there and gave her number to him was sad, but pissed me off. Did she assume there was no way I was his girlfriend? Had to be. Otherwise, why had she blatantly done it?

I'd snatched the check, which he'd thought was hilarious. I'd said half-truths to hide my jealousy, but bought him dinner as I promised. I'd seen the pride in his eyes and was sure he would pay, so I hurried to do it first.

He'd walked me back to school where Mom was waiting. I had an urge to hug him then lift on my toes and kiss him. Only he waved and was gone, moving fast down the sidewalk.

"Who was that?" Mom asked once we were off. "I've been waiting fifteen minutes."

"Just a guy I'm tutoring."

Her next words shocked me. “What does Ox think about you tutoring a boy? And you didn’t come from school.”

I glared at her. “We went and had burgers. He’s new, and Ox doesn’t own me. I can have friends, even ones that are boys.”

She clammed up, and I felt more like the parent. I popped ear buds in my ears to drown out any further conversation.

The next day Kelley showed up to tutoring with books in his hand. Carl got up without being asked to. When Kelley plopped down in the chair next to me, I wanted to roll my eyes but managed not to.

“You should really put the guy out of his misery and kiss him,” he said.

“What?”

He shrugged. “He’s what you girls call hopelessly in love with you.”

“He is not.”

“Believe what you want. But if your fiancé finds out, he and the rest of the football team will fold him in a locker and leave him to starve to death.”

“Boyfriend, not fiancé.”

“Interesting you didn’t say your boyfriend wasn’t a bully.”

I couldn’t. He was and he was right. If Ox thought Carl liked me one bit, he’d shove him in a locker just like Kelley said.

“You’re too good for him.”

His statement was flat and said without any emotion.

“And you?” I breathed, because I held my breath after.

“You couldn’t handle me, princess.” We stared at each other for a while and my heart raced. I wanted to challenge his statement, but who was I fooling. He was beautiful in a way no boy should be. On top of that, I liked our conversation, which turned into sparing matches. I liked him. Before I could put voice to any of it, he opened his math book. "Show me."

His words were simple, but I wasn't sure what he was asking. His bi-colored eyes held mine in challenge. I licked my lips before I took the easy way out. I started tutoring him. Well, that was a stretch. He was smart and caught on quick. The ease at which he grasped everything I showed him made me lose myself in time.

"You've got this. You don't really need my help," I said. "You'll get in whatever college you apply to."

"Maybe." His response was nonchalant.

I wanted to know more about him. He was a contradiction and that fascinated me.

"Are you going to college? What do you want to be?"

He pushed his dark hair back. "I hope to play ball. You?"

It was as if he hated talking about himself. There had to be more to it. He was too smart and didn't want to show it. But I answered him anyway.

"I want to go to Layton University in Oklahoma. Far enough from my parents, but not too far."

"Babe." The word was said like a dog pissing on a tree. I glared up to see Ox. "It's late. I'm sure your parents want you home for dinner."

I didn't like the way he told me what to do. "We're not finished. I can find my way home."

Ox opened his mouth, but Kelley beat him to it. "It's cool. I got plans with a hot girl anyway."

My ass of a boyfriend couldn't leave it be. "Yeah, you should leave."

Kelley stood, making Ox raise his eyes to meet Kelley's head-on. "You think your intimidation tactics scare me. Think again. Or maybe that word is too big for you, like my dick."

Ox got red in the face. "Then why are you leaving, freak? I'll shove your little pacifier down your throat."

"Sorry, I'm not into dudes. And my pacifier would choke you anyway." Kelley's eyes assessed Ox like he wasn't a threat. "And you should stop treating her like property. That ring doesn't mean you own her. As far as history goes, slavery ended a long time ago."

Ox wisely said nothing else as Kelley walked away.

"Are you into that guy?"

"What? This is after school tutoring, Ox. I help whoever needs it."

I slammed the book shut, only then realizing Kelley had left it. I tucked it in my backpack, saying nothing about the fact that it wasn't mine. If Ox had known anything about me, he would have realized I wasn't taking AP Algebra 2.

"You should stay away from that guy. His eyes are freaky as shit."

"His eyes are cool, and he has a name."

"Yeah, what is it? I'll be sure to mark that on my to-do list."

"His name is Kelley."

Ox barked out a laugh. "He's got a bitch name."

"The name is universal. Besides, he doesn't look anything like a girl. And that's all that really matters."

That shut Ox up as I sauntered from the room.

eleven

KELLEY

THE HOT GIRL I HAD TO GO SEE WAS MY MOM. I PROMISED her I would have dinner with her that night. Dad had been MIA, which was a good thing for me and, well, it bothered Mom.

"Have you seen your father?"

"No. He hasn't been home?"

She moved her head side to side, so sad I wanted to kill the fuck even more. I was pretty sure it was Aunt Joy's rules that had scared him off. Still, it was pretty shitty of him to leave Mom the way he did. I had to wonder if her worry over what he was up to was causing her to suddenly look far older.

"What did you do after school?"

I shrugged. "I went and got help to catch me up in my classes."

Mom's knowing smile broke up some of the tension I felt for watching her waste away in a bed. I wished we'd never come here.

"Does this have anything to do with a certain girl?"

"She has a boyfriend."

"Un huh." She dug into her food, but I knew the subject wasn't over.

I took a bite, resenting our situation. Aunt Joy was grateful we took our meals in Mom's room and not in the dining room.

"It's not like she's married. Maybe she likes you too."

The conversation differed far greatly than the one we had yesterday.

"Maybe she's not, but the guy she's dating doesn't see it that way. He gave her a ring, and she wears it like she's married."

Could this be any more unreal? Then again, with Sandy gone, who did I have to talk about girls with?

She patted my hand. "Regardless, she'd be lucky to date you. You should bring her by so I can meet her."

My denial of that request was evident. I shook my head.

"Why not? It may be the—"

She stopped herself, but we both knew how that sentence ended.

"You're getting out of here. I'm going to break you out. Maybe we can go sit by the pool this weekend."

"Maybe."

I decided to ask another question. Normally I didn't pry, but I didn't want to talk about Lenny anymore.

"Why doesn't Aunt Joy have kids?"

"She can't have them, and she found a husband who didn't want them."

Our conversation died after that. I lay in my bed last night, the only piece of furniture we'd brought from Galveston. I needed to get a job so I could help Mom pay for a place of our own. Being where we were wasn't helping her at all. I wanted to move back to Galveston. I'd talk to Mom about it. I could take care of her and go to school at night.

The door to my room banged open, and I stared at the darkened figure in the doorway. Rain fell hard, and he dripped water on the floor as he came forward. Bile rushed to my throat because it was bad.

"Where is it, boy? Where's the money? Your mom says she gave it back to you."

The money I'd saved and had given to Mom, she had in fact returned it to me that night. But there was no way in hell I would give it to him as he swayed forward, slurring his words.

I'd grown, but not enough. He took a fistful of my shirt and hauled me to my feet. His beer stained breath blew in my face with each of his words.

"Give me the fucking money, Kelley."

Trying to push him off me didn't work. He only laughed when I swung wildly with little distance between us. He let go of me next, sending me stumbling a few steps back. With everything I had, I connected a right with his jaw.

He shook his head and said, "Bad for you."

The warning was apt. He took one step forward, closing me in with nowhere to go. I raised my arm to protect myself and braced for the blow to come. It was better than taking a punch and leaving myself open. He wasn't that drunk as his fist came straight at me like a sledgehammer. The crunch only confirmed he'd broken something in my face. But the lights went out, and I had a vague sense of falling.

I woke up face down and rolled, realizing my mistake too late. My ribs ached. Dad must have kicked me while I was down. Light poured into the room, and I shifted my head to see shit everywhere. He must have torn up my room searching for money. I groaned and rolled back to my stomach. Lifting my head up, I saw the nightstand still had the lamp on it. It glowed and remained untouched. I scooted across the floor and reached out a hand underneath and found the sealed bag still taped there. I sighed and lay there a few moments longer.

When I was able to prop myself up, I carefully removed my shirt and wiped my face and floor. Then I slowly got to my feet and staggered to the door to toss the smelly shirt on the landing just outside. I turned to face the damage. The mattress was tossed, along with everything else. I went to the mini fridge, the only good thing my aunt had provided. I righted it, suppressing a groan when sharp pain darted across my chest. I put the few bottles of water and napkins full of leftovers back inside. I cracked out one bottle of water and drank.

Then I forced myself to straighten the bed where I flopped back down, deciding school was out. I didn't have a mirror, but I knew my face was shit. I forced my eyes closed and willed myself to sleep. I had no clock and no idea what the time was.

Sometime later, a hand patted my shoulder. I blinked, praying it wasn't my dad for a second round.

"Kelley, what happened?"

Mom came into focus. "What are you doing out of bed?" I asked, scrambling to sit up.

"I'm not dead, and I was worried about you. Your aunt said the school called and you hadn't shown up." I closed my eyes. Cool fingers pushed at my hair. "He did this, didn't he? Damn him."

I didn't answer. Mom was in no position to fix it. "I'm okay."

"No, you're not. He won't be allowed back here. We aren't alone anymore."

She was dreaming. My aunt wouldn't do anything, and my uncle was more like a scared rabbit. Dad would eat him alive.

"I'm going to get some ice. I'll be back."

"Mom, it's okay." I tried to get up and my ribs made me go back down. I pressed a hand to the sharp pain.

Mom was back. "Are they broken?"

I shook my head. "I'm okay."

"We need to get you to a hospital."

"No, we don't have the money."

"You let me worry about that."

She hobbled out the door, and I saw how she struggled to walk. The disease that brought us there was taking hold. I felt so fucking useless because I couldn't help her.

Some time later, Mom came in with a stranger.

"Kelley, I've brought a doctor to see you."

Next thing I knew, the man sat on the side of the bed, ignoring the destruction in the room. He poked and prodded me before declaring I would be fine with rest.

"Nothing appears to be broken," he said wearily.

"What about my chest? It hurts," I mumbled.

He turned his attention back to me. "Does it hurt to breathe?"

I took in a breath and winced. "A little."

"Most likely they are bruised. If the pain worsens over the day or you have a harder time breathing, then I suggest you go to the emergency room."

"My nose?" I touched the bridge of it and closed my eyes. I ached all over.

"Again, it looks fine, although swollen. You can ice it, but if it is broken, there is nothing we can do but let it heal on its own. It's not out of alignment, so it's just a matter of time."

"Can you give us a minute?" Mom asked.

"Sure," the doctor said, surveying the damage of the room. "You took quite the fall."

So that was the story they were spinning. He stepped outside and headed downstairs.

"Who is he?" I asked.

"He's the doctor Joy hired to come check on me."

I nodded. She pulled a cooler I hadn't noticed over toward the bed. The doctor must have carried it. "There are some ice packs in here. Your meals will be brought to you by Carla. You should rest." She took a pill bottle from her pocket. "And take these for the pain. I'll come check on you later."

"Don't," I said. "You don't need to keep walking up and down the stairs, Mom. You need rest so we can get out of here and get our own place."

Her eyes didn't carry the smile her mouth did. "You're my baby. And there is nothing I wouldn't do for you."

I wanted to say except leaving Dad, but I didn't.

She opened the bottle and handed me two pills. She shuffled over to the fridge and handed me a bottle of water. I had no choice but to take the medicine as it didn't look like she would leave until I did.

I closed my eyes and listened to her unhurried steps as she navigated walking when her muscles didn't want to cooperate. It was hard for me not to jump up and try to carry her back to her room. I would have if merely sitting up didn't cause massive pain. So I sank into my sleep as a dark-haired girl filled my thoughts.

twelve

LENORA

CLEARLY, I WAS BECOMING BORDERLINE OBSESSIVE. Every day I'd been searching for Kelley. I had to return his book, I told myself. There wasn't another reason I wanted to see him.

Finally after school, I turned to Debbie. "Have you seen Kelley?"

Her eyes narrowed. "Why?"

"He left his book in tutoring, and I want to return it." I tried for innocence, but I could tell she wasn't buying it.

"Does Ox know you're spending time with him?"

I took a step back. "What does it matter? There is nothing going on between us. I tutor a lot of people, and I don't need Ox's permission to do so."

"I haven't seen Kelley," she said. "Are you still going out with Ox tonight?"

The divide between us never felt greater. I wasn't sure I could trust the girl I'd grown up with. She acted as though aliens had taken over her body.

"Yes," I said.

She lopped off, and I was left to wonder if our friendship would survive the year. She always came over, and we got ready together. That wasn't her plan tonight.

I didn't bother to go to my locker. I kept Kelley's book in my backpack and headed outside where Mom waited to take me home.

Later that night, I stood in front of the mirror, not really wanting to go out with Ox. Mom called upstairs when he arrived. I smoothed the front of my dress down, wishing for jeans. Ox said we were going to a fancy dinner. I didn't think sneakers would be seen as fashionable in those types of places.

Downstairs, Ox stood smiling at me. "You look beautiful, Lenny."

"Thanks." I felt a blush creep on my face. The way he stared, I believe him.

"You kids have fun tonight," Mom said. Dad gave a grunt in the living room. He was watching something on TV that was far more important. He'd seen Ox and me go out plenty of times.

We didn't end up at a restaurant. Instead, he parked in front of someone's house.

"I thought we were going to dinner."

He grinned as if he had the best kept secret. "I told your parents that so they wouldn't get suspicious."

"Suspicious of what?"

Instead of answering me, he got out of the car and came to my other side where I stayed. I wasn't waiting for him to open my door. I was trying to decide if I wanted to go along with his harebrained scheme. There were several cars lined on the street.

He opened my door, and I glared at him. "I thought the party wasn't until tomorrow."

"It isn't."

"So what's this?"

He took the arm I'd used to wave around to prove that all of the cars surely looked like a party to me. He yanked me to my feet, and I collided with his chest.

"It's just a few guys and their girls. Nothing big."

Somehow, I let him guide me in the house where burly football players and several cheerleaders sat around with plastic cups.

"Don't you have a game tomorrow?" I whispered.

He shrugged, keeping a hold of my hand. "Let's get you a drink."

The cup cradled in my hand cooled my palm as I pretended to be interested in drinking. Guys were trading stories about the nasty things they did to unsuspecting freshmen. The girls laughed, and I wore a hesitant smile, trying to figure a way out of this.

I sat cradled between Ox's legs and held in place by his big arms. I pretended to drink but took nothing more than a sip over the last hour if I could guess.

More people started to show up, including Debbie. She barely glanced in my direction as she sat with the rest of the cheerleaders. I took the opportunity to get away while Ox was otherwise occupied with his friends. I walked outside and sat on the porch after the last round of people came in. Music started and things were getting rowdy.

My phone screen remained dark as I considered calling my parents to pick me up. Ox wouldn't be in any condition to drive me home. And I didn't plan on becoming a statistic.

Far down the street, I saw a figure dragging a trash can to the curb. I squinted to see, mainly because there was no other movement. Things were pretty quiet outside despite the music. Ox's house held most of the sound in.

Then the figure stepped under the glow of a street lamp. I wasn't sure, but he looked a lot like Kelley. Without thinking, I jumped to my feet and hesitantly moved quickly down the lawn, holding back from a full out run. He disappeared into the shadows, but I knew which house he'd come from.

The mini mansions had sprawling yards, so he had fully disappeared before I got halfway there. By the time I came to a stuttering stop, he stepped out with another trash can. I froze, unable to form words. He hadn't been in school the rest of the week, and I could see why.

"What happened?" I breathed.

He stopped short and glanced in my direction as if he hadn't noticed me until that moment. His eyes narrowed and glanced over my shoulder.

"What are you doing here?"

"I—I'm here for a party," I stuttered.

"Ain't no party here."

"Ain't isn't a word. And I know you know that. I've seen your class schedule, remember?"

He shrugged. "You still haven't answered the question."

"Ox is having a party at his house."

I felt totally off balance. He didn't seem angry, but he also didn't seem happy about me being there.

"You should get back there."

There were many reasons for me to heed his advice. Instead, I stepped into his space and lifted my hand. "Who did this to you?"

He stepped back, and I let my hand fall.

"None of your concern. Go back to the ball, princess. You won't find any castles or princes here."

"Princess," I snapped. "You should talk. I don't live in a house anywhere as big as this."

His words were sharp and took me by surprise. “I don’t either. I’m barely tolerated as a guest. Don’t make judgments on what you don’t know. I’m two steps away from living on the street if my aunt kicks us out. And you want to know the truth? I’d feel more at home on the streets than I do here.”

He turned away and started off. But I couldn’t let it go. I followed him, because damn it, that was more information than he’d ever shared about himself.

“You still haven’t answered my question.”

He spun to face me. “You want to know who did this to me? Dear old Dad wanted cash I’d earned to buy beer and whatever else he’s into. When I didn’t give it to him, he commenced teaching me a lesson about who was in charge.”

With his arms folded across his chest, he held my gaze in defiance to anything I might have to say.

“That’s fucked up.” Normally, I didn’t curse. But his words hit me much like his father had beaten him. Surprisingly, he laughed. “What’s funny?” I didn’t understand why what I said would cause a burst of real laughter from him.

“That word sounds funny coming from you,” he said.

“What, fuck?” There, I’d said it again. Probably more times than I ever had in one day.

His head fell back and the belly ache of chuckles made me smile.

“I curse.”

“Sure you do. I bet you don’t even know what that word means. Or do you let Ox touch you down there until you scream?”

My jaw hit the pavement.

"That's what I thought. Go back to your boyfriend, Lenora."

"How do you know my name?" He'd called me Lenny like everyone else. He wasn't in any of my classes.

"You'd be surprised what I know about you."

thirteen

LENORA

IT WAS PROBABLY CRAZY OF ME, BUT I FOLLOWED HIM UP a set of stairs, needing to know what he meant by what he said.

He opened a door, and I followed him inside. There were boxes everywhere and clothes on the floor. But what surprised me most was the bed in the corner to the right of a small window with a nightstand underneath.

"This is—"

"This is where I sleep, Lenora. Impressed? I'm like garbage and this is where forgotten things are kept."

I turned in a circle, taking it all in. The ceiling peaked with exposed beams. Most of the left side of the room was filled with boxes of stuff. The right side was where he lived.

"I think it's cool."

"Cool?" he repeated, shocked.

"Yes." I glanced back at the door he'd closed. The top half had a window that let in moonlight opposite the window. “It’s like having your own place. No one knows when you come and go. Talk about freedom.”

When he said nothing, I spun around and found him standing right there. My breath caught in my throat.

“What’s wrong? In a strange place with a guy you barely know? I bet no one even knows where you are.”

His face was dark with shadows.

“Why are you trying to scare me?” I tried to sound confident, but his words chilled me. Had I made a calculated mistake?

“You should be scared. You should run off back to your boyfriend. You’re safer with him than with me.”

He pointed at the door and took a step back.

I lifted my chin. I didn’t believe him. I saw clothes on his bed and a trash bag next to the door. “Maybe I want to stay.” I turned and started to lift boxes back in place. They had spilled like dominos.

“If you were in my headspace watching you bend over like that, you’d run far from me.”

Nearly tipping and stumbling head first, I stood straight and faced him. “Stop being a jerk. I’m trying to help you.”

I gave him a little shove to put some distance between us. My stomach was a riot of butterflies but in a good way.

He winced and took several steps back before plopping on his bed with his hand on his chest.

“Oh, you’re hurt,” I pronounced like a dummy. I stepped closer, nearly between his legs, and lifted his chin. “Are you okay?”

His hands landed on the back of my bare thighs, and my heart skipped a beat.

"Better now."

I wanted to swat him away, but I had no idea the extent of his injuries. And if I could admit it, I liked him touching me. It was nothing like I felt when Ox put his hands on me.

"You should go, Len."

He swallowed, but didn't let go. In fact, he gripped my legs tighter while his thumbs stroked up and down the sides of my legs.

"Why?" I choked the word out.

There was silence for more seconds than I could count.

"Because I can't give you what he can. I can't take you to homecoming in a limo or even buy you flowers and shit."

My throat was dry, but I managed to croak out, "Maybe I don't want those things."

"Trust me, you do. And even if you don't, I'm no one's boyfriend. I can't be yours. I told you before, we move a lot. And as soon as I can manage it, I'm out of here for good. Besides, I like to fuck, Len. And you're nowhere near ready for that."

It had to be dumb that I couldn't keep my mouth shut.

"How do you know what I want?"

He still hadn't let go. Instead, his hands started to glide slowly upward.

"Has he touched you, Len?"

There was no good answer. But there was truth between us. He'd told me about his family. So I should be honest with him too.

"Yes."

"Hell," he growled.

"What?" A slice of fear rolled through me at the way he'd said the word.

He didn't answer my question, though. "Did you like it? When he touched you there?" he asked through gritted teeth.

"Truth?"

"Yes." But he didn't sound like he wanted the truth.

"Yes, a little."

His hands were nearly touching my underwear. A thrill skipped through me.

"I bet I can make you feel a thousand times better."

Despite his words, his hands were gone. Then they landed on my waist as he turned me to face the door while he stood up behind me.

His next words fanned across my neck like electric shocks. I shivered.

"Leave, Len. Because if you stay, I'm going to show you exactly how good I can make you feel."

I hesitated, knowing he stood towering behind me. There was no stopping me apparently. I turned to face him.

"Dammit, Len. Today's my birthday and I didn't get any fucking candles to blow out. You know what I got?"

He sounded on the edge, and danger emitted from every coiled muscle in his body. I shook my head.

"I got to heal from the bruised ribs and a nearly broken nose my dad gave me. And what I see in front of me is a very pretty present I want to unwrap. And ask Debbie, I'm not a toy to play with, Len. The only kind of play I want to do with you is all hands on, kind of like naked twister. So, I suggest you go before I won't let you leave."

Everything he said should have frightened me. But it didn't. There were strange sensations going on between my legs. Finally reason won as I remembered I had a curfew. And I had a feeling I would lose time if I stayed there with him. Plus, I needed my parents to pick me up because no way would I let Ox drive me.

Kelley waited, and I lifted up on my toes. I had to brace my hands on his shoulders and move in quickly to press my lips to his. They were incredibly soft, and I wanted to taste him. Heat flared on my cheeks as I sank back down to my real height. Then I met his eyes as they burned a hole through me.

"Happy birthday," I said softly before spinning around and heading out the door.

I took the stairs two at a time with a stupid grin on my face. I didn't look back, afraid he would be standing outside watching me. I wanted to believe he was. So I jogged back down the street on a high that was all Kelley. Nervous and giddy at the same time, I was ready to admit to myself I really liked him. He wanted to act tough, but I saw something softer inside him.

All I had to do was break things off with Ox. Maybe Kelley wouldn't be my boyfriend. And maybe that was okay. I had a boyfriend for two years. I was ready to have fun and with someone I chose, not because my parents chose the boy for me.

"Where have you been?" Ox slurred when I came in the house.

I dodged his handhold and went to find my purse. I closed myself in a bathroom with Ox beating softly on the door, begging me to come out. The call netted my mother, who promised to be there in fifteen minutes. I waited there until Ox finally gave up. When I opened the door, Debbie was there.

"Ox is worried about you."

She had the same glassy eyes, and I shook my head. "I hope you are enjoying the party."

"I am. Don't be such a party pooper." The last word was more spit than voice as she giggled. I shoved by her and out the door. Mom was at the curb, waiting for me.

"What's going on?" she asked.

"Ox didn't take me to dinner. He brought me here where he and his friends decided to drink. This is the guy you want me to date?"

I shouldn't have been surprised by her next words. "Kids. I remember when I was that age. Everyone makes a mistake. But I am glad you called me to pick you up."

"You're not mad. What if I drank? Don't you want me to break up with him?"

"It's one mistake, honey. Besides, your father will get his bonus in a few weeks. If you can just hang on until then."

My mouth gaped. I loved my parents, but I didn't like this side of them. I shut my mouth because it was for a good cause, wasn't it? Dad's job, I chanted in my head. As long as Ox didn't force the sex issue, I could hang on another few weeks, couldn't I? Then a plan started to form. I may have to wait to break it off with Ox. But that didn't mean I couldn't make a new friend in the meantime.

fourteen

KELLEY

HER KISS LEFT ITS MARK ON ME. I TOUCHED MY LIPS, sure I still felt hers on me. But she was gone, and I was left to lie on my bed and remember as if a punishment. It was worse than any blow my dad could lay on me.

Sleep was a daydream that played over my mind. Forced to remain conscious, I started putting the room to rights. My jaw still ached but not as much as my lips. When the boxes were stacked back and my clothes in garbage bags, one clean and one dirty, I wondered not for the first time what it would have been like to live differently.

With nothing else to do, I got out the book Mom had given me, *Of Mice and Men.* The thin book was fat with ideas, hopes, and dreams much like my own. George and Lennie, like me, had only dreamed of a better life. Yet fate had other plans, thwarting them from reaching their goals because they were misunderstood or treated differently because they were poor. I could so relate. Even though I'd read the book before, I began again as morning sunlight rolled into my window like it would be a good fucking day. Only I knew better.

As I read about the Lennie in the story, the overgrown simpleton, despite the similarity in names, Lenny was nothing like him. She was more like the beautiful woman Lennie accidently killed. The parallel lines there was Lenny being with me would be like me killing her dreams. I had nothing to offer her other than a good fuck. And I'd just gotten to the part where Lennie was patting the girl's dress when a rap came at the door. No one knocked. Fear was my first thought until I realized Dad would never knock. So I achingly got to my feet.

"Hi." She stood the picture of innocence on the other side of my door with a tray of cupcakes in her hand.

"What are you doing here?"

I made no move to let her in. Something about that act would seal my doom, especially as she stood there in a dress that made me imagine what was underneath. More times than not, when a girl wore clothes that truly hid her, those were the times my mind really wandered.

"You left your book at tutoring. Plus, I brought you birthday cupcakes."

"It's not my birthday," I said gruffly.

Her big, beautiful eyes blinked in rapid succession. "I know. But it was only yesterday and you deserve a celebration."

She was fucking sweet, like one of those kids on a sitcom. I bet she lived the life I longed for. But the last thing I wanted from her was pity.

"You can't fix me, Len."

Her face fell, but it was better this way. I couldn't allow her in and hope for something that could never be. If I let myself feel, I would be torn away from this place in a blink of an eye. Moving to the next town, the next place where our lives would be *better*. And I couldn't take much more heartache. I had a dead brother, an ailing mother, and a father who cared nothing for me to fill those holes.

"I'm not—"

I cut her off. "Look, go home before your parents find out you're trying to make friends with trash instead of taking it to the curb to be picked up."

Those pretty features of hers scrunched up in a mask of anger. I thought she would stalk off and I'd be done with her as much as she would be with me. Only she shoved past me and into my room. She set the tray down on my bed and turned to face me.

She pointed a small finger in my direction. "You don't get to talk about yourself like that."

One perfect brow arched up under her bangs. I had an urge to reach out and push her hair back so I could admire her stubbornness.

"You try to pretend you're this tough guy that words just bounce off of. But I know better. You're sweet and your heart is pure."

I glanced away, unable to face her when I said the next words. "You wouldn't call me pure if you knew I was picturing you naked on my bed."

Then I met her glare as she shook her head slightly side to side.

"You're trying to piss me off and it won't work this time. You will blow out a candle if it kills me."

A chuckle burst from me as the line of her jaw mirrored her wide stance with her arms crossed over her chest. She was fucking adorable, if ever that word fit something in my life.

"Fine, I blow out your candle. Then you're leaving."

Her lips curled in a smile I felt all the way to my toes. She moved, pulling out a candle and a matchbook from a hidden pocket from her dress. Then she was just there in front of me, making my mouth water.

"Make a wish, Kelley," she breathed, stealing my unhappiness and wrapping it with her joy.

She was so close I could smell the fruity scent of her shampoo or perfume. I didn't have to think about what I wished for. The idea, the fantasy was right there in front of me as I blew a slow stream of air past my lips. The flame flickered as her hair fluttered around her head. She was the most beautiful girl I'd ever seen.

With quick fingers, she plucked the cupcake from my hand and placed it back on the tray.

"What did you wish for?"

There was no way in hell I would reveal that. "If I told you, it wouldn't come true."

"I know what I wish for."

Then she seemed to grow before I realized what she was about to do. She stood on her toes and her face inched toward mine. How much I hungered to taste her again. It was evident in the weight of my balls as they drew up with anticipation.

I placed my hands on her thin shoulders, holding her back, and watched humiliation grow on her face.

"Sorry, Len, but you and I can't."

I wondered if she realized she poked her lip out like a five-year-old and it would be so easy to kiss her.

"Why not?"

I could tell her how shitty my life was, but that hadn't stopped her last night. I could tell her I wanted to know for myself the color of her underwear, but my sexual innuendos were also lost on her. So I went with the truth.

"Because the next time I kiss you, you'll be mine not his."

Her eyes filled, but not with tears. She got it that I wasn't joking.

"You don't understand—" Her head shifted side to side.

"I do."

"There are reasons, and I wish things could be different…"

But things weren't different. They were the same as always and maybe worse. In Galveston, I had football. Here I didn't have that. I had nothing to look forward to except that maybe Mom would get better.

As she eyed me with admirable defiance and a little remorse, I offered a bargain and half hoped she would accept.

"Then stop being a tease and call him to break up with him so we can finish what we started."

She glared at me. And I saw when she made up her mind and hated myself for it.

"Happy belated birthday, Kelley." And she left. The cupcakes and the tray remained on my bed as she made her hasty exit. Why did I feel like such a shit? She had a fucking boyfriend.

The six cupcakes were devoured hours before heavy footsteps made their way to my door. I scrambled to sit up in bed with only lamp light to scare away the dark that streamed through my windows.

"What the fuck, Kelley?" Dad bellowed as he banged through my door. "What did you say to your mother?"

Words would only fuel his anger, so I remained mute with one hand on the empty metal tray Lenora had left. Her forgetfulness may save my life, because there was murder in my father's eyes.

He bent over me, grabbing the collar of my T-shirt. Fabric gave way, which only made him grab more as he hauled me to my feet. I brought the tray with me. I was just about to slam it in the back of his head when Mom's voice rang out in the night like a broken bird.

She called my father's name, but not in an angry way. It was more of a plea that stopped my dad in his tracks. His choking grip on my shirt released. And then he was out the door. From his profile on the ledge, I saw his eyes widen. Fear spiked through me as the tray clattered from my hands to the floor. I moved like chilly breeze to the door. Dad was already making his way to where Mom was crumpled at the bottom of the stairs.

"Mom." It didn't matter that my voice sounded like the boy I'd once been. Mom looked so helpless and lost as Dad scooped her up.

"You shouldn't be out here. I can't lose you, honey."

Those words and how he reverently said them stole the fight out of me. That was the first time I realized Dad loved Mom. Maybe he hated her and us too. But he'd once loved her and she had him. Somewhere they'd lost their way. In that moment, though, I knew I could trust him with her.

I watched him carry her into the house and debated on whether I should follow. I sat on the stairs, knowing that Mom needed this time with that side of Dad. I planted myself and listened. If she cried out, I would go and kill the bastard if I had to. But until then I would wait it out until he left as he would.

Good Dad may have shown up, but I didn't expect it to last forever. Everyone eventually let me down. Sandy, my brother, died, leaving me alone without his protection. Mom had grown ill and would probably die by the looks of things. Dad had never once masqueraded like a real dad. And Lenny had walked out when I told her she would have to choose between me and her asshole of a boyfriend. No one ever chose me in the end.

fifteen

LENORA

We stood in our kitchen as Mom gave me a speech and then a list of the rules.

"It's one night," I said, slightly annoyed she thought I couldn't take care of myself.

"And a school night," Mom added. "We trust you, honey. We really do. It's just..." I tried really hard not to roll my eyes, but I failed. She sighed. "Here are the keys to my car so you can drive yourself to and from school. I've texted you the hotel information, and you can call us if you need anything. We should be home by dinner tomorrow. If not, I've left some money in the cookie jar for you to order pizza or something for both nights."

I nodded.

"Come on, let's get going. I want to beat traffic," Dad called from the front room.

"All right," she said, angling her neck as if she could see Dad. Then she turned back to me. "Be good." She kissed my forehead before walking out of the room.

I waved for good measure. Once the front door closed, I raced to the window and watched them drive off before I danced around the living room.

"Freedom," I called out.

I gripped Mom's keys tightly in my hand as I continued to dance through the house. It wasn't often I was given such a gift. I was actually quite happy it was a school night. If it had been the weekend, Ox or Debbie would have found a way to ruin my solitude with a last minute party. Instead, I grabbed my backpack and headed for school.

After school, Ox hovered over me like a mother hen. "You don't need a ride?"

"No, I told you I have Mom's car."

"You don't want me to come over?"

My glare did nothing. "They trust me. For all I know they'll come back home tonight to test me. And if you're there I'll be grounded for life."

He sighed. "Fine. But I'll call you later to see if you changed your mind."

The nod I gave him didn't match the unspoken words in my head. *Don't worry, I won't change my mind.*

As I got in my car, I thought about how Debbie didn't even know my parents weren't home. She and I had barely spoken in days. She'd spent more time with the other cheerleaders on the squad, and I felt like the odd man out. Cheerleading had been her dream, which was why I considered quitting. She'd barely talked to me at practice and neither of us made the effort to call the other in over a week. I considered ending our stalemate by inviting her over for dinner. We could watch movies or do something like we'd done before boys came between us.

I slowed the car as I watched Kelley walk achingly slow down the street.

"Need a ride?" I called from the open window.

He jerked in my direction with a wince on his face.

"No, I'm good."

"Don't be like that. Your place is like two miles away. Let me drop you off."

I pulled to a stop on the side of the road. He came over to the car and peered in. "Won't your mom be waiting for you to arrive home on time?"

"My parents are out of town. No one's waiting on me."

He opened the door without giving me a response and slid into the seat. He had to crank it back to comfortably fit his long legs. Mom's Subaru Forrester masqueraded like a family car but it was a compact version of one.

Before I could strike up a conversation, he turned on the radio and found a station he liked. Sitting back, he closed his eyes and effectively ended any possibility of conversation. I sighed, knowing it was for the best. He'd warned me off so many times, why was I pushing the possibility of a friendship with him?

Parking the car near the garage, he got out without a word. He set his backpack on the stairs then headed over to my side of the car. I rolled down the window.

He leaned down and got so close. His lips were there, and I'd bet money they'd be as soft as they had been the last time I'd kissed him.

"You should go, princess, before your ride turns into a pumpkin. Your parents probably have GPS installed and are tracking your movements. Or maybe your boyfriend does. Wouldn't want him to find out you're here with me."

He tapped the top of the car and strode toward a side door. I turned off the car, not wanting to be so goddamn predictable.

"Wait," I called out. He had the door open as he turned back to me. "I'm not the perfect princess you think I am." I marched over to him with confidence I couldn't quite pull off. "Yes, my parents trust me. But that's not a bad thing. I'm free to do what I want even if it means spending time with your grumpy self."

Those lips of his bent in a smile. "I know how we can spend that time." He winked at me. My jaw dropped as if I should be surprised. "But I have something I have to do first."

Okay, he hadn't exactly told me to follow him, but I did anyway. At the first opening on the left, he turned in. I was already there before I realized I shouldn't have been.

"Who's this?" a beautiful woman asked from the confines of a bed.

His floppy hair covered one eye as he tilted his head back in my direction. "Mom, this is Lenny, or Lenora. Lenny, this is my mom."

As awkward as it was, I walked forward to take her hand. Only she tugged me closer. Taken off guard, the little pressure she exerted pulled me closer to the bed, so I was practically dropped on it.

"Nice to finally meet you."

I couldn't hide my shock. Had Kelley talked to his mother about me? A scattering of wings beat in my belly.

"Mom," Kelley admonished.

She let go of my hand, and I took a step back. "She is the girl you were telling me about?" He gave her a curt nod but avoided looking at me. "It's not often, how about ever, that my son talks about a girl."

"I told you she has a boyfriend. So don't start, okay?" he gritted out.

"So she's a friend. You need more of those," she said to him. Then her bright green eyes met mine. "He's a very private person. He never likes to talk much. So be patient with him."

"Okay, this is over." He stood. "Lenny, it's time for you to go."

A small woman came in. Her smile grew as she took in the three of us. She didn't look at all like his mother. Her skin was a natural golden tan I would have killed to have. Still, I guessed it could be his aunt.

"Mrs. Jackie and Mr. Kelley, I see you have a guest. I was just coming to ask about dinner."

His mother spoke next. "Ah, my son has a friend over. Would it be okay to set another place for dinner?"

I still wasn't sure who the woman was. "I have an idea," she said. "Mrs. Joy and her husband are out for the evening. Why don't I serve Mr. Kelley and his friend out by the pool? I don't anticipate Mrs. Joy will be home tonight."

"That sounds wonderful," his mother said.

"Mom, Lenny probably has plans."

"No, I actually don't," I said with a huge grin, opposite of his scowl.

"Wonderful," his mother answered.

The cook or the housekeeper bustled off, leaving the three of us alone.

"Go take her around back." She shooed us with a wave of her hand.

"Fine, but I'll be back later to check on you."

She smiled. "Don't worry. Your father promised to be home in time to watch a movie with me."

His frown deepened. "Let's go, trouble."

I followed him outside. The sun was still fairly high in the sky. We walked around back and entered an iron rod gate. Colorful flower bushes lined the fence, hiding it for the most part. A pool with water the color of one of Kelley's eyes beckoned me to reach in and touch its cool depths.

"It's beautiful out here," I said, spinning around. He sat in a chair that was shaded by a table umbrella. I sat opposite him. "This is amazing."

He said nothing as I spotted the cutest looking cottage in the back corner. It had to be a pool house. The housekeeper came out with a freaking tray of milk and cookies.

"Thanks," he muttered.

She winked at him. "I'll bring dinner out in a little while, and then I'll leave you alone."

What did she think we were going to do? Had he brought other girls out here? I dismissed that because his mom said he didn't bring anyone around.

"Your mom seems nice."

"She is. Now tell me, Len, why are you here? We already had this discussion."

I took a bite of one of the chocolate chip cookies and nearly moaned. It was warm and gooey. "Oh my God."

"Lenny," Kelley warned.

"It's good. You should try it. And your mother says you need friends."

"My mother still believes dreams come true."

"And who says they don't?" I challenged.

"I do." He glared at me. So I drank some milk. "You want to know why I was walking home?"

I shrugged. "If you'll tell me."

"I had to stay after school to use the computer in the library to do my homework and print it out because we don't own one. I don't have a cell phone either. I don't own anything but the bed in my room. But when I leave, and I will get out of this hell hole, it will stay, because I don't have a way to take it."

His words punched me in my chest. But I wasn't going to give him what he wanted.

"You need to stop throwing yourself pity parties. No one I know of has treated you differently in this school. I certainly haven't. And surely no one knows where you live. Why don't you enjoy the moment, enjoy this gorgeous day and accept my friendship?"

"I don't do friends."

"Joel," I announced. "I've seen him around you."

"He's cool. But that's it. And I don't want to be your friend, Len."

"Why not? Do something not in your playbook. Isn't that what you've told me?"

Abruptly, he stood. The chair scooted back a foot when he did. "Fine!" Then he started to strip. "I've wanted to do this since the day I got here."

I would have been impressed by the defined muscles on his body, but the darkish bruise caught my attention.

"Oh no, you're hurt." I was on my feet and gracing my fingers over his bare chest before it registered what I was doing.

"What, you didn't believe me before?" His eyes bore into mine as I continued to let my fingertips travel over the muscles in his chest.

"I did. It's just…"

He caught my wrist, and I felt like a spider trapped in his gaze. His eyes sparkled in the sun. They were beautiful. I almost told him, but he broke the spell by speaking.

"Seeing is believing." He removed my hand.

Then he kicked his pants to the side, which left him mostly naked except for underwear that vaguely resembled the style of my boy shorts. Maybe that's where they'd gotten the name. I stared at what he was packing, but glanced away when I realized I was looking.

He chuckled darkly. "It's okay to look, Lenny, as long as you realize what comes after."

Embarrassed, I glanced away. When I turned back, I got a view of him from behind, and holy hell. Before I could imprint the image on my brain he'd cannonballed into the pool. He shook his head when he reached the surface.

"Is it cold?"

He shook his head. "No. You could join me."

I backed away as he came over and folded his arms on the edge and peered up at me.

"Oh, no, I can't."

"Yeah, right. You wouldn't want to do anything impulsive. I bet Mommy and Daddy told you to date that asshole and you did, because you always do what you're told."

I knew he was baiting me, but he struck a nerve coming way too close to the truth. I didn't want to be the good girl always doing the right thing.

"I don't have a bathing suit."

"Neither did I, and I didn't let it stop me. Besides, isn't a bikini not much more than what you girls wear under your clothes anyway?"

He was right.

"I can't believe I'm doing this," I muttered to myself. I lifted the hem of my sundress over my head and stood there in my undergarments.

"Nice, you match."

I scowled at him. The blush pink cotton set wasn't for show, but comfort. If I'd known what was in store for me, I might have worn the sexy black set Debbie talked me into one day. I'd been saving it for that special day that had yet to come.

Too late for a wardrobe change, I thought as his eyes roamed over me. When the pink garments got wet, he would see all of me. Still, I took the leap and dived into the water.

Warm water cocooned me. When I surfaced, he was way too close. I treaded water as I struggled for something to say. “It is nice in here,” I managed.

“And it just got better. Come.” He beckoned me over to the circle area attached to the pool. It had to be the hot tub. I followed and warmer water settled all around me. I took a seat across from him.

“You surprised me. I didn’t think you’d do it.”

“Why not? I can be fun, adventurous.”

“If that’s what you tell yourself.” He laughed.

“What about you? Why do you play the bad boy and don’t want a relationship?”

I didn’t think he would answer, but I was dying to know.

“Bad boy?” He folded his arms over his chest. “I don’t have a girlfriend because we move too much. Why catch feelings for someone when the next day I could be gone?”

Stunned, I hadn’t expected an answer or anything for that matter.

“So you’ve never had a girlfriend?”

“No. There were a couple of times I got close. We actually lived in one place for a few years. There was this girl next door,” he said wistfully. “She was fun. Only, I liked her more as a friend than anything else.”

“Did you guys…?”

“Have sex? Do you really want me to tell you about the girls I’ve screwed?” I glanced away, and he took advantage. “Has Ox never gotten close?”

“And now we’re talking about my sex life?” I scoffed.

“You brought it up.”

He stood and sank deeper in the water for a second as he crossed the middle to me.

"Do you want to hear about the things I do with my boyfriend?" I asked in challenge.

Half in and half out, he stood over me. I shrank deeper in the water to hide that the tips of my chest had tightened.

"Not especially. But you keep glancing toward my dick, and I wonder if you've ever seen one."

My face must have mirrored a rose bush for all the heat I felt in my cheeks. He yanked me to my feet.

"I know you're a good girl and would never cheat on your boyfriend. So you can blame this on me." He pulled me close with his hand at the small of my back to bring us skin to skin. "Can you feel my dick and what you do to it?"

"I—I," stuttering words formed on my lips.

"You don't have to answer because I very much want to be in you, Len. I bet you're warm, tight and when I do this"—he rubbed against me and my head fell back—"I bet you get wet."

Feeling dazed, I said the first thing that popped in my head. "I have a boyfriend."

Magically, he was gone. He sat back across from me. "I know." Bumps erupted over my skin as I shivered. "Just stay there and let me look at you."

"Why?"

His hands slid down. "Because I haven't fucked in weeks because of you. No other girl will fucking cut it. And my balls will hurt like hell if I don't."

No sex? I couldn't think about that. "Don't what?"

He licked his lips. "I think you know what I'm doing."

The fist he made began to bob up and down. "You have fucking perfect tits, princess. I bet your pussy is pretty and pink too. Has anyone put their tongue on you?" Slowly, I shifted my head side to side. "Then I want to imagine that I'm your first. I want you to hear church bells when I put my tongue inside you. I want you to cum and scream my name before I stick my dick in you. And when you realize that idiot you call boyfriend wouldn't know what a clit is, come see me. I'll show you."

"A clit?" Unconsciously, my hand rubbed over an aching spot that had flared to life as I watched him.

"Fuck," he groaned, and white ribbons floated to the surface. Seconds later, his eyes opened. "A clitoris, Len. The place you were touching. You should really read up on it. It's the female equivalent to a detonator." He waved away. "You should probably get out before my sperm finds its way home."

Quickly, I hopped out of the water and not because I was grossed out. I wasn't. Mortified that I'd touched myself and he'd seen, yes. But more, I was fascinated while I watched him jerk off. For the first time ever, I truly contemplated having sex.

Towels had magically appeared, and I didn't question what the housekeeper might have seen. Instead, I focused on drying myself off. Then I got dressed, deciding I should leave before I did anything stupid.

"Where are you going? We haven't had dinner."

There was humor in his voice. He'd expected me to flee, maybe even wanted me to.

"I should get home. I have homework."

After I got everything back on, I headed for the gate without looking at him.

His voice stroked fire over my skin. "You can run, little butterfly. But we both know I can catch you."

sixteen

KELLEY

IT HAD BEEN A FEW WEEKS, AND I HADN'T SEEN LENNY except a few times in passing. Agitated and wondering if she'd been avoiding me, I couldn't put on a good face for Mom.

"Go ahead. I'll be fine," Mom said.

Her situation frustrated the hell out of me. Every day, she seemed to get a little worse. And although I could fight anything except my father, the damn invisible enemy that coursed through her veins turning her into a virtual baby was beyond my reach.

"Mom, you need to tell me the truth. Everything I've read said with treatment you should be fine."

Her hand, which was more bone than anything else, reached for me and missed. I grabbed it as her eyes held pain from missing the mark.

"I have the severe kind of MS. They call it Marburg. They don't know why it happens. But…"

Her voice started to shake, and she closed her mouth.

"I can stay home tonight."

"No, you should go out. The nurse your aunt hired will be around."

The eyes that had shined into mine over the years and promised a world where I could live whatever dream I wanted, dulled in the dim sterile room Mom was confined in.

The only hand she could move in the crippling episode fluttered, and I moved close to hear what she wanted to say to me.

"Promise me, Kelley..."

I pulled back enough to meet her eyes. "Anything, anything at all." What else could I say to the woman who had given me life and tried her best for me?

Her hand weakly clasped in mine as her eyes widened in horror. I leaned down to hear what she whispered.

"Nurse."

The one word felt incomplete. So I sat back only to see humiliation on Mom's face before tears flooded her eyes. It wasn't long before I realized the problem.

I glanced around, searching for the on call nurse Aunt Joy had hired, but it was just me. I stood and went to the door and looked out. I couldn't say I was too keen on the idea of what I had to do next and not for my sake but for hers.

There had to be a competition of who was more embarrassed, but we got through it. Mom silently cried through it, all while I kept a neutral expression, not wanting her to feel any worse. I balled up the soiled linens and threw them in the corner just about the time my aunt showed up.

"You didn't have to do that." I just glared at her. "The nurse was on a break, but she'll be back."

"It's fine," I said defiantly. I glanced back at Mom, who continued to silently weep.

I walked over, kissed her cheek, and tried for a joke. "It's okay. It's nothing you haven't done for me."

She squeezed my hand slightly before I left, grateful to be away from my unsympathetic aunt, and out of a place I could never call home. I did wonder if I should stay. Though Mom had wanted me to leave, and I could give her that. I didn't want her embarrassment to make things any more awful for her.

Joel waited at the curb, his car idling.

"What took you so long?"

I shrugged. Even though Joel and I had become somewhat close, there was no way I would tell anyone about what I had to do. And not for me, but Mom's dignity.

The drive was short considering we only moved a few houses down. We ended up parking behind a river of cars. "Ox?"

It was a question I already had the answer to considering we were near the guy's house.

"Dude, if I'd told you, would you have come?"

I didn't bother to answer. I'd heard Ox was throwing a party, but he wasn't the only party that night. I just assumed we were going somewhere else. Only, there wasn't anything I could do besides walking back to my empty room and thoughts.

"Fuck it," I muttered.

We traipsed over to the front gate where Trina was leaning.

"What took you boys so long?"

She gave me a passing glance, but her eyes were for my boy. Good for him. Maybe he'd lose his virginity tonight. I left them to eye fuck one another and walked up the stairs to the front door where music pounded away.

I didn't relish the idea of seeing Lenny with Ox. The few times I'd seen her at school, he'd been near, holding her hand or touching her in some way. She'd clearly made her choice, not that I expected any different.

Inside, people were scattered around like ants in mounds cluttered here and there. I found myself herded with the crowd and landed in the kitchen where alcohol was being served. A cup found its way in my hand, and I drank, needing an escape.

The last time should have been a deterrent considering the effects alcohol had on me. Only I watched Lenny go by with Ox's hands around her waist and a smile on her face. Something weird happened in my chest and felt like I couldn't breathe. I ended up choking on a swallow. I cleared my throat, to find a girl I'd seen around school with glazed eyes planted on me.

"Kelley, right?"

"That's me."

It was easier than I thought to turn on the charm. She looped her arm in mine, and I can't say it was a bad thing. She was cute, and I needed a distraction. If only my dick would get on board, it wouldn't be hard to do her as she steered me into the main room.

Time was like a weird loop with no end and no beginning as long as I had a drink in my hand. I never felt more alone than I did in the crowded place. I didn't have friends. Yeah, Joel was there, but he was cool with me keeping him at a distance. I hadn't told him my life's story. No, I'd given those details to a girl who would never be mine.

I had no idea how long I sat with the laughing girl on my lap before she tugged me to my feet.

"Come on." She giggled.

I didn't remember her name. Still I followed her toward the stairs, knowing very well where we were going.

Lenny suddenly appeared, and I couldn't help feeling like I saw an oasis in a desert. She was so fucking pretty it hurt.

Her soft hand landed on me, stopping my forward progress. Certain parts of me stood at attention from her touch.

"Hey, have you seen Debbie?"

I met her gorgeous gaze. "No."

"Maybe she's in a room upstairs," the girl on my arm thoughtfully added.

Lenny's smile turned frosty before she met my gaze again. I turned from her appraising stare and followed the girl upstairs. The long hallway was filled with closed doors. Some were locked and others weren't, but all were occupied. The last door on the right opened easily enough, but the sight thrilled and pissed me off.

"Close the fucking door."

It was none of my business, so I pulled the door toward me. Only a slight figure pushed in front of me, opening the door in the process.

The two people on the bed stopped long enough to glare in the direction of the door.

"Ox?" a small voice questioned.

The guy tossed the girl straddling his lap to the side and stood up, giving us all a good view. The pants he hadn't fully taken off pooled at his feet. I turned away, pulling the girl I'd come with away from what was going to be a fight.

seventeen

LENORA

ANGER SHOULD HAVE BEEN MY MAIN EMOTION. AND while I felt some of it, I was more disgusted.

"Debbie?"

It wasn't so much of a question. What question could there be? Ox was in the room naked with my so called best friend. I turned, noticing Kelley had disappeared.

"Lenny, wait!"

Part of me ached with disappointment. I mean, how could she do that to me? We'd been friends forever. I picked up my pace, taking the stairs down two at a time. I landed on the bottom with a little thud absorbed by all the music. The door was straight ahead, and I took it without knowing where I was going.

The night was a balm to my weary soul. I lived a few miles away and it would give me a chance to cool off. Thankfully, everything I brought to the damned party was with me. I patted the small cross body purse and felt my phone beneath my palm.

Not so far in, I changed course and found a place to sit, surprised by my luck. I covered my eyes with my palm, not surprised no tears came. Betrayal had a way of killing any warm thoughts I ever held for my former boyfriend and best friend.

And that's how he found me. The door opened, and I glanced up seeing his tall frame fill the space as the night surrounded him like a cloak.

"What are you doing here, Len?"

I scrambled to my feet, feeling as though I needed to not be sitting on his bed when we had this conversation.

He stepped forward, closing us in together in the process. Unable to form words, I shrugged. He tipped my chin up, forcing me to meet his steely gaze.

Whispered words fanned across my lips. "Why are you here, Lenora?"

"It's my birthday," I blurted. I couldn't believe the year before Ox had thrown me the sweetest party.

He pulled back. "It's a shitty thing to happen. But you could have gone home. Why did you come here?"

In his eyes was a determination I felt when I marched out of Ox's house. He wasn't going to let this go.

"I want to be with you."

My voice felt small as he towered over me. Whatever I thought he would say, I didn't expect him to put distance between us. In two backward strides he stood flush with the door.

"You can't say things like that, Len."

Stubbornly, I lifted my chin. "Why not? Isn't that what you do? You do every girl in school, but not me."

Because no matter what he said, there were rumors.

"Not you," he breathed, and my lip trembled.

I hadn't wanted to cry when I caught the two people closest to me getting it on. But when he rejected me, I felt on the verge of tears.

Thankfully, my backbone was ramrod stiff. I coerced my feet to move until I was reaching for the doorknob to the side of him.

He caught my wrist. "Tell me why me first."

What did he think? That I was a glutton for punishment? Apparently, my mouth and my brain no longer worked on the same team.

"Admit it, you like me," he said softly.

I bit my bottom lip. "I'll admit you're the first boy to give me butterflies."

His eyes narrowed when he asked, "Butterflies?"

Despite the riot in my heart that thundered in my chest creating a storm of wings in my gut, I was able to answer him.

"You know, flutters in your belly. You get them when you see someone you really like." I blushed, afraid he'd think I was stupid. "You've never had that?"

I wasn't sure I was ready for the answer. If he didn't feel it, I might not be able to go through with my irrational plans.

He huffed. "So that's what it's called."

I nodded. "Have you ever felt it?"

My breath locked inside my lungs as my heart continued its stampede.

"I feel something. And I'm the fool for saying this because one day I'm walking out the door and I'm never coming back. You need a guy who will for sure be here to take you to prom, bring you flowers, whisper poems and shit in your ear."

His eyes never strayed from mine. He was serious.

"Who said I was asking for any of that?"

What was I saying? The steady stream of blood rushing through my body clouded my thoughts, my hearing.

He prowled forward, and I gave myself points for not shrinking back.

"Are you sure about this?"

My words wouldn't be enough to convince him. So with shaky hands, I reached behind my back and tried to unzip my dress. Then he was there. His fingers helped me with the task. When the zipper could go no further, he stepped back.

I shimmied my shoulders a little bit so the dress could fall, exposing me. When he muttered a curse, I had no idea if that was good or bad.

He circled me. "Lenny wants to give me her cupcake."

Nervously, I said, "Don't you think calling my virginity a cupcake is weird?"

He reached around from where he stood behind me. "It's not your virginity I'm talking about." He cupped me in between my legs, and I gasped. "This is what I'm talking about. It's sweet with a creamy center. And I'm going to lick the fuck out of the icing."

I rubbed at my arms, feeling self-conscious as he stood touching me. Gently, he pried my wrist from my arm and placed my hand on the part of his body he talked about once he stood in front of me again. I'd felt Ox before, but Kelley was different. Everything about the experience was different as I didn't cringe. I let him guide my hand up and down his length.

"Are you sure about this?" he asked again, giving me an out.

In answer, I pulled my hand free to work at the button of his well-worn jeans.

When they hung open, he wound his strong arms around me and lifted me off my feet. I had no choice but to wrap my legs around him or I would leave us awkwardly off balance. He turned and took a few steps before gently laying me on his bed. Then he stood up and pulled his shirt over his head. I gaped.

His bruises had healed to more like angry shadows, so I focused on the rest of his body. I had no idea boys could be built like him. Ox was big, but he didn't have defined ridges in his torso like Kelley did.

"What's wrong, cupcake?"

I reached up, but he crawled onto the bed and caged me in on all fours. He leaned down and pressed his lips to mine. Craving him more than I thought possible, I reached up and cupped the back of his head, pulling him closer.

"There's no rush," he whispered against my lips.

He had no idea. My skin felt on fire and only his touch soothed the ache.

"I'll get you there," he said into my ear before kissing down my jaw and lower.

He left a trail of tingles that crackled over me. I felt more alive than I ever had before. Air breezed across my chest as I only then realized he'd freed me of my bra. No boy, not even Ox had seen me completely naked. I'd been felt up, but only through my clothes. I should've been embarrassed, but I wasn't.

His mouth covered my peaks, sending me on a dizzying journey to oblivion. I squeezed my legs together, needing something I couldn't explain. The experience was like no other. When Ox had touched me, I'd only felt dirty like I was doing something wrong.

Kelley's touch felt right, and I wanted more, but he was taking way too long to get to where I needed him.

His kiss met the valley of my breasts as his hand found the junction between my thighs. When probing fingers glided over a place he'd called my clit, my back bowed from pleasure. I had no idea what he planned when he kissed his way to my navel and lower. I opened my eyes to watch him, only to see the top of his head. His hair tickled my belly, and I fought not to squirm. Only his tongue kissed places I never thought would be kissed. My eyes rolled in the back of my head as something built so deep inside, I didn't understand it. His finger joined in the fun, and soon I was over the moon, wondering what planet I landed on as I cried out from the overwhelming amount of feelings that came over me.

Then he was back, saying words that held no meaning for a second.

"This is where you stop me, princess. Otherwise there is no turning back."

When my brain could process what he said, I muttered, "There's more?"

His luscious bow like lips broke into a grin. "A whole lot more."

Whatever I experienced before was a first. And if I had any doubts about Kelley and the rumors about him, in that moment, I wanted him to be my first if it was going to be as mind-blowing as what he'd just done.

"I'm ready."

I reached for him, but he hoped off the bed and removed his pants. I was transfixed by what was about to be revealed. As he pushed the jeans down, I found out he didn't wear anything underneath. What stood out and pointed at me was just as impressive as the rest of him, now that I had a clear view of it. I sat up, eager to touch him. My hand wrapped around its smoothness. And I leaned with a need to taste him as he'd done me.

His fingers wound in my hair, and he stopped me from making contact.

"As much as I want that pretty mouth of yours there, I've dreamed of this moment too long to waste another minute."

Suddenly, I was underneath him. I giggled when in seconds he had me pinned with one leg around his waist and the other in his hand right beneath my knee. His penis poked at the door of my opening. My eyes widened, realizing that this was it.

"Shit, Len. I don't have a condom."

He let go of my leg and fell back on the bed beside me.

"Do you always use a condom?"

His nod was all I needed. I was going against my sex ed class, knowing better. But not caring all the same. "Okay, you can be careful, right? You can pull out?" Because I didn't want to wait for another time. Who knew if I would have the courage to do this again.

I blushed, and he looked pained. He scrubbed his face before he looked at me. "Do you trust me?"

I nodded. He rolled back on top of me. "I'll pull out, even if it fucking kills me."

Then he leaned down after repositioning me and pushed his tongue in my mouth at the same time he pushed a little inside me.

He let out a damn sexy groan. "Damn, Len, you feel so good."

I sucked in a lungful of air just as he stopped. He kissed me hard, stealing my ability to breathe. His fingers threaded through mine when he pulled back.

"On three." His eyes held trust. "One."

An alarm rang in my head. Should I be doing this? He could so destroy my heart.

"Two."

I pushed the thought away, ready to join the masses in my school of those who'd lost their virginity. Who was I saving it for? Ox? No, Kelley was the right choice.

"Three."

My head tipped back, bending my throat toward his mouth as he thrust forward. A piercing pain eclipsed every nerve ending, forcing me to suck in a lungful of air.

"Breathe, Lenny."

I'd heard of the pain. Who hadn't? But it killed all the pleasure I felt before. How could anyone think this was worth doing?

But he started to move, causing me to grip him tight.

"Are you okay?" he asked again, stilling his motion.

Part of me wanted to say no, but the other part of me didn't want my first time to end like this. It couldn't hurt forever. Because I knew people liked doing this.

I nodded yes. He captured my mouth and for a second I forgot what we were doing. His lips, so gentle on mine, eased my burden somewhat. Slowly, his movement sparked to life something other than the dull ache between my legs. He seemed to sense it and moved his lips from my mouth to my breast. And his kiss there super-heated my insides. He let go of my hand and moved it between us. He touched that part of me I hadn't known the name of until he told me, and little by little the pain died away, replaced by a fragment of the pleasure I felt before.

When I moaned, he took my hand again, threading our fingers together. And still he managed the leverage to move inside of me. But each time his body connected with that magic point, pleasure built on contact. I wanted more, so I lifted up to make more of a connection.

"Oh my God," I muttered as the feeling of lighting a spark fused my whole body.

Whatever it was, it was close. And Kelley knew just what to do. He continued to hit that spot until something else sparked inside. Another button was pushed, creating a chasm feeling I wanted to explore until that word he'd mentioned before. *Detonation.*

I think I screamed, not sure. Whatever it was, Kelley sped up, continuing the feeling to course through my body, on a crash collision course. My toes curled when his back bent and all the veins in his neck stood out. His eyes were closed, but he seemed to have found the place I was coming down from as warm wetness covered my belly. A second later, his body lay next to mine.

We both panted and unexpectedly, I felt shy. I closed my eyes, trying to process everything. It seemed like forever and no time at all.

When he got up, I watched as he walked naked over to a bag and searched for something. He pulled out a small towel, then grabbed a bottle of water from the fridge.

"Sorry, butterfly."

My eyes widened, fear moving through me. "What? Did I do something wrong?"

Had I hurt him? Was that why he strained in the end?

His eyes twinkled and his lips twitched. "No…shit…this is going to be cold."

Next thing I knew, he was cleaning the stuff from my stomach and then in between my legs. I should have been horrified. There was blood. But it was so freaking sweet that he thought to take care of me. He flipped the towel over and wiped himself off before tossing it out of sight.

When he lay next to me and pulled me close, I wasn't sure what he meant when he spoke again.

"I don't think I've ever felt like that with anyone else."

"Felt what?" I was still confused and knowing that my lack of skills must somehow be to blame. Instead, I thought optimistically. "Butterflies?"

His fingers pushed hair out of my face. "If that's what they call it. You've got me chasing them."

eighteen

KELLEY

LENNY, BUTTERFLY, LENORA WAS IN MY BED. HER WIDE, innocent eyes were all confused, and I had no explanation for what just happened between us. All I knew was that I wanted to do it again. My dick started to stiffen again, which had never happened before. With her so close, I pushed a little inside her.

"Are you sore?"

It took her a second to catch onto my meaning. She wiggled her hips, which only stirred me to life faster.

"I don't know. It doesn't hurt."

I didn't know what that meant. I pulled back and pushed into heaven, never wanting to leave. "How does that feel?"

"It's not bad." But I saw her wince, and I groaned because I was more than ready.

"What's wrong?" I asked, feeling pressure deep in my balls as my body wanted to move.

"Should it feel sore?"

I nodded and buried my face in her hair. She smelled like berries. I cupped her tit, unable to stop myself. I hadn't been able to touch her the way I imagined in my eagerness to be inside her. I couldn't be sure what I felt as I hadn't fucked in weeks. Could the awesome feeling be because it had been so long?

Something told me shit no. It was all her. And not because she was virgin tight either. I'd had virgins before. Most had complained it'd hurt or some other shit. I'd had to spend a lot of time getting them ready. Something I'd learned over the years, but not my Lenora.

My. When had I started thinking of her as mine?

"Any regrets?"

Why had I asked? If she said yes, would I feel like a shit for taking her virginity?

"No," she said softly but kept her eyes on me.

"Good. And Ox?"

"What about him?"

"Am I going to have to kick his ass when he tries to fight me for being with his girl?"

She pulled back slightly. "I'm not his. Never was. I stayed with him because my father needed his parents as clients. But I'm tired of playing their game. If they use my college fund, I'll just get a loan."

There was more story there, but I felt the grin before I could stop it. "There's my girl."

"Your girl? You don't do relationships." When I glared at her, she reminded me, "Your words."

She was giving me an out. I could say something else. "I changed my mind. You're mine. This isn't a one-time thing for me. That butterfly thing. I'm serious. I'll chase you if you make me."

Wasn't sure why I admitted that. Maybe it was because my dick was still inside her. Clearly making me foolish.

"You don't have to chase me. I'm right here."

She leaned in and kissed me, which led to round two. I took it slow, knowing she wasn't quite feeling up to the task. The shit was I couldn't stop it. And evidently tweaking her breast and clit did the trick. She finally got into it. After round two, I was spent.

"I don't have a bathroom," I said when I finally pulled out of her. Then an idea struck. "But I have something better."

I gave her a T-shirt of mine as I pulled on basketball shorts. Then we snuck down the stairs. My uncle's car was missing, and I was pretty sure they were out for the night. I gave the back door a second glance, feeling bad Mom was alone. Dad's truck wasn't around, but the nurse's car was there.

We made it to the dark backyard where the backdoor light shone on the glassy surface of the pool.

"You aren't serious."

"Why the hell not?" I said, tugging my shirt over her head, leaving her naked and perfect.

I dropped my shorts and counted to three, which felt fitting. Then we jumped in. If my aunt was home, I would know in moments. But the lights remained dark when I broke the surface of the water.

"You're crazy."

"You're beautiful," I said, pulling her in and kissing her.

That in itself was new. I wasn't a kisser but somehow she made me crave her lips.

Her hand lifted the chain from my neck. "Who do these belong to? You're always wearing them. Do you ever take them off?"

So she'd noticed. I didn't want to spoil the moment. But told her anyway. "My brother's, and no, I don't take them off."

"Your brother?" she echoed.

"He died overseas by an IED."

"What's that?"

"I thought you were smart, butterfly."

She tapped my nose. "Don't be mean. Just tell me."

"Improvised explosive device. Meaning some shit planted a bomb in the road that blew up the vehicle my brother was in."

"Fuckers," she said.

Her serious expression along with the curse coming out of her good girl mouth made me laugh, so I kissed the shit out of her. We stayed locked together in the pool for a while.

"Cold?" I asked when she shivered in my arms.

"Yes, I'm pretty sure I'm becoming a prune."

We hustled into the pool house where we found towels, but used the shower first. I went down on her again and because she was new at this, she had no idea I hadn't done it that many times. Never before had I had a desire to do it, but she made these fucking sounds I wanted to hear.

By the time we made it back to my room over the garage, I just held her.

"Please don't break my heart."

Her words were faint, barely a whisper.

"I never wanted to own someone's heart before. I can't promise I won't fuck up. But I won't do it on purpose."

I fell asleep wondering what it meant to own her heart. She hadn't said she loved me. But girls had a funny way when it came to sex. They caught feelings fast, and all I wanted to do was keep her safe.

Morning came with a stream of light that blazed on my skin and had me blinking against its brightness. A noise like a faint buzzing sounded again. So it wasn't the sun that woke me.

"Len, babe."

I shook her slightly. Her eyes popped open, and she smiled when she saw me. Then the phone made a tinkling sound, and Lenny exploded out of bed.

"Oh my God, what time is it?"

When she stared at her phone, her eyes closed, and I knew it was bad.

"Hello," she said tentatively in the phone.

I could hear muffled noises coming from the other end but couldn't make them out.

"I know. I'm sorry. I—"

There was a pause, and I didn't have to make a leap to know her parents were wondering where the fuck she was. *Shit.*

"Yes." She nodded as if they could see. "Okay, I'm coming home now."

She ended the call. Her eyes met mine.

"Your parents?"

She nodded. "I'll call an Uber."

It was my turn to hop out of bed. "Wait, let me see if I can get some money."

I had a stash of cash but didn't want to pull it out in front of her. It wasn't that I couldn't trust her. I didn't want her to know how bad things were for me that I had to hide money. I pulled on my shorts from last night and ventured outside. I would ask Mom if I could borrow some and tell her I'd pay her right back. I would explain about Lenny. I had a feeling she'd be happy for me. I wouldn't tell her what we'd been up to. She could figure all that out on her own.

Only, Dad's truck was outside and a new plan formed in my head. I went into the house through the unlocked side door to their room. Mom was sleeping. Dad was passed out on the foldout bed that Aunt Joy had brought in for him. His keys sat on top of the dresser. I scooped them up and waited a second. He didn't wake up. Just as I was about to leave, my name sounded from Mom's lips.

I darted over, grabbing her hand.

"I'm here. What do you need?"

The nurse was gone. No doubt Dad had sent her packing.

"Where are you going with your father's keys?"

So she hadn't been sleeping after all.

"I'm going to run Lenny home."

"That's the girl, right?" she said with a faint smile and tired eyes. It was like she barely remembered her.

I nodded. "That's the girl."

"I knew she'd see what a catch you are."

"You were right. You're always right. But I need to get her home. Her parents…"

Mom nodded. "Hurry before your father wakes up."

I bent and kissed the top of her head. "I will. I love you, Mom."

She squeezed my hand as if that was all the strength she had left. My chest squeezed and the thought of losing her hurt worse than my brother dying. I scrambled out of the room, forcing back my emotions. She didn't need to see me upset.

By the time I got to Lenny, she was pacing the room.

"Let's go."

"What?"

"I'm going to drive you."

She followed me downstairs without question. She also didn't question my instructions for her to be behind the wheel as I pushed the truck down the drive. I'd told her I didn't want to wake Mom, which was partly true. The real reason was I didn't want to wake Dad.

I followed her directions to her house and leaned over to kiss her goodbye as we parked at the curb. Only her front door opened and angry parents glared at the truck. She smiled at me, and I smiled back.

"I'll probably be grounded. But I'll see you at school Monday."

I nodded, watching her walk away. Something in my gut twisted, and I had an urge to go and toss her over my shoulder and bring her back to my place.

Instead, I drove the short distance home. Worried about how much trouble Lenny was in, I pulled up and parked in the spot I'd vacated earlier. When Dad barreled out the door, I realized my mistake.

He yanked the door open and dragged me out.

"You little shit. I didn't give you permission to drive my truck."

I longed for the day when he would fear me. But as it was, my hits felt like they bounced off steel. His fist to the side of my temple was his go-to punch and had me seeing stars. The kick to the ribs wasn't anything new either. I tried to become a ball as his blows rained down on my back, causing unimaginable pain where I assumed my kidneys were. I heard shouts off in the distance as my vision began to fail.

The screaming words he hurled at me hadn't registered as I wondered if this time I would die. My only regret was that I hadn't told Lenny what I truly felt about her. I was falling for her like I fell down the rabbit hole of darkness.

nineteen

LENORA

THERE WAS NO EXPLANATION FOR MY BEHAVIOR MY parents would accept. But as I sat in my room without a computer or a phone for the weekend, I wondered if I had come home with Ox, would I still be in trouble? Something during my parents' rant suggested not as much.

During my parental weekend incarceration, I had time to think about Debbie's betrayal. I should have seen it coming. There were little things over the last few years that suggested we were growing apart, but it still hurt.

Intermingled with the betrayal was the remembrance of being with Kelley. Sex had been so much more than I expected. In fact, I got the tingles every time my thoughts went there. I honestly couldn't wait to do it again, with him. And what the hell? He'd been the last boy I'd ever thought I would give my virginity to. And the deed was done, and I had no one to tell. That little fact made my thoughts circle back to Debbie.

By Monday, I was so relieved to go to school and out of the house I practically skipped through the halls. Then again, I hadn't seen the outside of my room more than to use the restroom and eat. I was aching for human contact.

Only, Debbie standing by my locker wasn't the human contact I wanted.

I had no choice but to face her if I planned to get my books for my first class. When I went to take a step, a dark shadow crossed my path.

"Babe."

I glared up at Ox and noticed for the first time that he wasn't as cute as I thought he was. He had squinting eyes and thin lips. He paled when compared to Kelley, not that it mattered. I wouldn't have chosen Ox no matter how good he looked.

"Don't *baby* me." I pulled his ring from my pocket and held it out to him. "You can give it to Debbie if you want."

I dropped it in his palm and stepped around him. He stopped me with one beefy hand.

"Lenny, she means nothing to me. She was just willing to give it up."

Years of friendship had me instinctively glancing in Debbie's direction. Her jaw had gone slack and her skin a pasty white. She fled a second later.

"You just pissed off your new girlfriend."

Ox didn't even turn to see Debbie running down the hall in the opposite direction. "I don't want her. It's you, Lenny. I was drunk, and she offered. What the fuck does it matter anyway? It's not like you're ever going to give it up. So why do you care if I screw someone else?"

Clearly he'd been hit one too many times on the field.

"Did you actually just hear yourself? You slept with my best friend."

He laughed as a crowd gathered around us. "That's where you're wrong. She's not your best friend if she's fucked me."

There was no denying that logic. "You're right. But you're wrong about something else. I would give it up to someone, just not you."

I didn't bother to go to my locker. It was too close, and I didn't want any further confrontation with him. As I made my way to my class, I searched long and hard for Kelley, but came up empty.

During lunch, I ate alone quickly before heading to the library. The only reason I went to the cafeteria was to see if I could find Kelley. It sucked he didn't have a phone, not that I had one either. If not for my mother's fear of school shootings, I wouldn't have mine on me. But it did nothing with no one to call. I had no way of contacting him, and I desperately wanted to see his face. If only to confirm that our night together had meant something to him.

I scoured the halls after school, daring to get a tongue lashing when I finally headed outside to Mom's waiting car. Still, I hadn't seen him. He must not have come to school. After I handed over my phone, she gave me a lecture about timeliness. I pushed her voice to the back of my mind as I hoped he was okay and I would see him the next day.

The afternoon and evening sucked eggs with nothing to do outside of homework and my thoughts. The longer I had to think without seeing and talking to Kelley, the longer my thoughts drifted into uncharted territory. Had I been good enough? Did he like being with me? Was he done and going to move on to his next conquest? Had he left like he said he always planned to do?

Tuesday only brought an unwanted conversation.

"You can't ignore me forever."

I didn't bother to look over at Debbie. Part of me wanted to smash my locker door in her face, but that would only get me in trouble.

"I can try," I said sourly.

"I can't believe you'd let a boy get in between us."

I slammed my locker door and gave her a lethal glare. "I can't believe you hooked up with my boyfriend."

"It's not like you were into him anyway."

Her logic was just as faulty as Ox's. They deserved each other.

"That's not what matters. It's trust. Like him or not, everyone in school knew we were together. Of all the boys to choose."

"It's not like that, Lenny."

"Oh, it is. You wanted what you couldn't have." There, I'd said it.

Her eyes narrowed, and I knew I'd pissed her off. "Not all of us want to stay virgins all our lives."

"Was it everything you'd hoped it would be?"

I didn't care who overheard our conversation.

She glanced away. For a moment, I thought shame crossed her face.

"It wasn't," she choked out. "After you left, he got dressed and ran after you. We'd barely started before you showed up."

Did she think I would feel sorry for her?

"Sounds like you got what you deserve. That's what happens when you slut your way to losing your V-card," I snapped back.

"Slut—" she started to say. Then it was like she put something together as her features smoothed out. She cocked her head to the side. "And that's the thing. You were gone from the party, but no one claimed to have driven you home. And you know who else was missing? *Kelley*."

"How do you know that?' I asked in haste, giving myself away.

Her grin was wicked. "His friend Joel came looking for him. Said he saw him run after you. And funny thing is, I got this call from your parents in the morning. They wondered if you were with me. So tell me, how was fucking Kelley?"

Tongue in cheek, I refrained from saying *better than your night*. Instead, I said, "The thing is, my life is no longer your concern. And what I did or didn't do is none of your business."

I started to stalk away as her cold words hit me in my back. I managed not to stumble as she called out, "I bet Ox would be real interested in that info."

School sucked the rest of the day and the rest of the week. Kelley was a no show, which only made me wonder if he'd gotten what he wanted and left town. Since I was under lockdown, I couldn't go to his place and confront him.

After the final bell rang on Friday, I spotted Joel and Trina whispering in a corner. They looked cozy, but I was desperate for answers. So I trotted over to them.

"Hey."

They turned to face me as one and it was cute to find Trina blushing. With that girl's reputation, I didn't think she was capable. But there I went judging. Hadn't I learned that rumors were sometimes far from true?

"I was wondering if either of you have seen Kelley?"

They faced each other and for the briefest moment, I feared what I saw in their faces. Joel spoke first.

"Here's the thing…"

twenty

KELLEY

BLINKING, MY EYES ADJUSTED TO THE BRIGHTNESS OF the room. That was information enough I wasn't back home or in the room above the garage. For a second, I thought I might be on the pullout in Mom's room until a figure came into focus.

"There you are. How do you feel, hun?"

I wanted to ask where I was, even knowing the answer. I wanted to know how I got to the hospital. Instead, my voice came out scratchy and incoherent.

Give it a second. She disappeared and returned with a cup that held a straw. "Why don't you drink something first?"

My throat burned, so I didn't refuse. The cool water coated my throat, giving me the opportunity to voice my questions.

"You're in Mid County Hospital. And I think I should contact the doctor."

"My mom…is she here?"

It was a long shot. Mom barely moved on her own these days.

The older woman patted my hand. "Your mom is here. Let me get the doctor."

Before I could stretch out my hand to stop her, she was gone. I tried to sit up, but a wave of dizziness flattened me. If Mom was there, I figured she'd be in to check on me soon. Maybe she'd finally given my father the boot.

Only Mom didn't show. And maybe an hour had passed when a doctor breezed through my door, all busy like with a clipboard in his hand.

"Ah, Mr. Moore, how are you feeling?"

Before I could answer, he flashed a light across my eyes, blinding me.

"Not very talkative," he said after only a few seconds of silence. "You took quite the fall. Lucky for you, you only bruised a few ribs as we found no fractures. It's the concussion we're worried about. Your dad said you fell down a long line of stairs, which explains why you are here."

So that's how he played it. I said nothing because I couldn't. As much as I hated the bastard, Mom loved him for reasons I would never understand. I needed to talk to her before I went spilling my guts.

"Is my dad here?"

I hoped like hell he wasn't. But I needed to know. Mom wouldn't speak freely if he were in there. I hadn't wished for my brother in a while, but in that moment, I longed for his miraculous return.

"He's with your mother."

"Are they coming in?"

He sighed heavily, and I didn't expect his next words.

"Your father has given me permission to speak with you. Your mother has suffered a complication to her illness."

"She has MS."

"Yes. But she has the rare form of Multiple Sclerosis called Marburg."

"She told me, but what does that mean?"

"It's a rare form of the disease that progresses quite quickly. It's surprising that your mother was able to get out of bed to try to get to you. But stranger things have happened when mothers are confronted with the desire to save their children."

That was all good, but I wanted to understand what was going on. "Is she okay?"

He sighed again, only warning me his news wasn't good.

"My understanding is that your parents were aware of her prognosis and moved here for more assistance."

"You're not answering the question."

"She isn't my patient anymore. After she was admitted, she was assigned a doctor who specializes in that area. What I can tell you is that this form of the disease is usually terminal. And most patients don't live for more than a year or two after onset."

"I need to see her."

I tried to scramble off the bed, but I was stopped by firm hands.

"We want you to see her as well. But let's do this right. I'll get the nurse to get you a wheelchair and take you to her."

"I don't need a stinking wheelchair," I said, managing not to curse.

"You are in no condition to walk that far. Don't worry your mother by walking in looking like a zombie."

He was right. I didn't want to worry her. So I nodded and lay back. "I'm not going to wait another hour to see her," I declared.

"I'll get the nurse in here, stat."

He smiled to himself, but I didn't get the joke. I watched him leave as my mind spun with all the information. She'd explained that her MS was different. Why had I been so self-involved that I didn't find out more? Had I wasted so much time chasing girls than spending time with Mom?

When the nurse arrived, fear lanced me. I wasn't sure what to expect when I was wheeled into the room.

I was rolled up to the bed and given instructions to use the call button if I felt like I would pass out or needed assistance of any kind, including help with my trip back to my room.

My focus was on the still figure in the bed. If not for the beeping of the machines, I might have thought her dead. I clutched at her hand that peeked out from under the covers. She didn't stir. When my head dipped, I said a silent prayer to a God who'd never answered me before.

I glanced up and around the room and noticed my disheveled father passed out in a chair in the corner. Love him or hate him, there was a part of him that cared deeply for Mom. The strange connection they had for each other, I didn't get. But I knew Mom would want him there.

My fist balled and if I'd been on my feet, I might have cold clocked the bastard. It wasn't less than he deserved. My luck, he'd press charges, and I would be locked up like a criminal with no way out.

"Kelley." My name wasn't more than a whisper carried on a breeze.

I met Mom's open eyes. "Mom."

Her lips curled and something in my chest eased.

"You're okay?"

I shook my head yes. "I am. But I'm worried about you."

Her eyes softened.

"Don't worry about me. You finish school and make something of yourself for me."

I nodded vigorously. "I will, but why are you saying this? You'll be fine."

As if she hasn't heard me, she added, "We should have stayed in Galveston so you could play the ball you love. I'm sorry about that. One day, you'll be famous for that."

"Mom, don't talk like you're dying. I need you." A tear rolled down my cheek. "Why didn't you tell me how bad it was sooner? How am I supposed to go on without you?"

But my questions come too late. "I waited to see you and know you were okay. I love you," she breathed out. Her eyes closed, and I thought she'd gone to sleep. Only minutes later the beeping noise went flat like I was in a TV drama.

Everything happened in surreal time. I'm pretty sure I shouted as other voices from nowhere filled the room. Dad jumped to his feet and rushed over to Mom's other side. I was wheeled back, losing my hold on her limp hand as bodies circled her bed. I heard the word *clear* several times, but I could only see a sliver through the wall of people trying to save Mom. Only, they stopped after what felt like seconds in the unreality state I found myself in.

I don't remember the last time I cried. But I felt the wetness on my face as tears streamed down unimpeded. It felt like I had open heart surgery right there as I watched the only person I love leave me.

When they called out the time, I was numb. I had nothing to live for until I remembered my promise to her.

Football was key. The one thing I had left. It was my ticket out of the hell I was living. That would be what sustained me.

Everything that came after was a bad dream.

The sky should have been cloudy. Instead, the sun beat down on us as we stood with my aunt and her husband at a cemetery watching Mom being laid to rest. No one comforted me as I fell to my knees unable to stand under the crushing weight of loss. Mom had left me with my bastard of a father and indifferent aunt. What would happen to me now?

I didn't have to wait long to find out. We'd barely made it back to my aunt's house as she waited for us to exit her car.

"Well, that's done," she said so coldly I wondered how she and Mom were related. My hands trembled at my sides as I tried not to look like a big baby. "I'm afraid I can't have you guys staying here any longer."

My uncle disappeared into the house without ever looking back.

"Your things have been packed." My uncle reappeared with two small duffle bags. "Good luck to you both."

The money I saved most likely hadn't been found. But Aunt Joy didn't look like she was going to allow us back in her house.

"Come, boy," Dad said with pride steeling his words.

My bones ached. My heart completely shut down. School was barely a thought. Aunt Joy didn't meet my eyes when I glanced in her direction. She knew what an asshole Dad was. Yet, she was leaving me with him. What a cold-hearted bitch.

Slowly, I hiked up to get in the cab of Dad's truck on a groan. I felt every stretch of my muscles with stabbing pain. I closed the door and wondered what would become of my life next.

Mom was dead and everyone acted like it was just another day. Just like Sandy. But it wasn't another day for me. I had nowhere to go to wallow in pity. Dad offered no comforting words. *Shocker there.* If I fled, I would dishonor Mom's wishes for me because I would never graduate if I had to get a full-time job to support myself. So I was stuck until I finished school or my father killed me. I wasn't sure which option was better.

We rode in silence as the fancy houses turned into stretches of land and ultimately to a rundown park of trailers. Had Dad already found a place for us? Had that been what he'd been doing all those days he was gone? He parked in front of one that didn't exactly look uninhabited. A woman with dirty blond hair and a pleasant face opened the door with a belly the size of a basketball. Dad's smile ratcheted up to a brightness I hadn't seen before.

"About time you got here," she drawled.

She said something else that was muffled when Dad's door closed. I sat there, unsure what to do until the woman gestured with her hand for me to come inside before she and Dad disappeared.

Slowly, I opened my door, trying like fuck not to assume Dad had been cheating on Mom with that woman and she was pregnant with his child.

I kicked at the truck door, widening it as I got out. My life was something out of a bad dream and surely I would wake from the nightmare.

"Kelley Moore."

I spun around and saw Trina leaning on the back of the trailer next to the one we parked in front of.

"Yeah."

"You haven't been in school all week. And interestingly, Lenny has been looking for you."

Scrubbing a hand down my face, I sighed. "How do you know?"

"Because she asked Joel and me. You should probably talk to her."

There was no confirming or denying. I just nodded.

"Didn't know that was your dad."

I swung my gaze back in her direction. "You've seen him before?"

She nodded. "His truck is here almost every night."

There was my answer, which only made me want to choke the man who helped give me life. I wanted to run, but had nothing to run with. Further, I wanted Lenny more than my next nut. And wasn't that a bitch. When had I ever wanted a girl that much? *Never*.

After an awkward dinner with the woman claiming to be Dad's girlfriend, I slept in sprits between the definite noises of Dad getting it on with that woman. I woke Saturday morning to the smell of bacon.

"I know this is a shock. But you are welcome to stay here."

I scrambled to my feet with an urge to piss so strong, but the need to leave the confines of the trailer. I chose the latter, stumbling out the door with the grace of a drunk. Dad's truck was gone, and I found a spot to water before walking away from the trailer. The bacon had smelled good, but I needed my cash. I needed options.

twenty-one

KELLEY

THE BIG HOUSE LOOKED EMPTY AS I STOOD LIKE A prowler at the corner near a large fence of the neighbors. Finally, I stepped forward and took the stairs two at a time. I prayed to a God that had forsaken me long ago that the door would be unlocked. If it wasn't, I was prepared to break the glass to get inside. My money and my only hope was in there. I turned the knob and it opened.

Once inside, I stood staring at the bed like I'd just gotten my cherry popped. The memory of Lenny and my time there seared on my brain like the steaks Dad used to make on the grill when things were good. I held onto that memory like I did the few others that made me feel human.

Finally, I got to my knees and scooted forward. I bent further to reach under the nightstand and hoped like hell the bag was still there. My fingertips skipped over the wood, searching in vain until I found it. Expelling a breath like it was my last, I pulled the Ziploc free.

I sat and counted the money until I was satisfied it was all there. I was just about to get to my feet when the door opened. All the blood drained from my face as I scrambled to hide the bag in my pocket before the woman came into view.

The sun that blurred my vision was blotted out as the door closed.

"Kelley."

Her soft voice was Band-Aid to my wounded heart.

"Lenny, what are you doing here?"

I found my feet and stood on them. She was so small next to me. I felt oddly protective of her.

"I'm actually grounded. But I had to see you. You weren't in school all week."

Her eyes grew large as I stepped toward her. I stopped fearing that she didn't feel safe with me.

"You're hurt, again."

She moved so fast, the wind she created ruffled my hair, and I sucked in a breath as her finger brushed over my wrapped ribs.

"I fell," I lied because how could I admit that my father was a monster who thought kicking his son in the chest was a suitable punishment for whatever perceived crime he thought I committed.

"Your father did this, didn't he?"

Clearly, I sucked at lying. I nodded. Then the words flew out of my mouth like a caged bird finally set free. "And my mom died."

She gasped and buried deep, wrapping her arms around me as if she could hold me up. My eyes got wet, and I struggled to wrap mine around her. I hurt, but her being there meant more to me than anything else did in the past week. But what use was there in crying. Mom was gone. I remembered what Lenny said about no pity parties.

When her eyes flared large and wide up at me, I leaned down, ignoring the sharp stabs at my chest. I pressed my mouth to hers, wanting to lose myself in her. Virgin as she had been, we didn't speak as our connection became frantic with need and heat. Not soon enough, we were back in the small bed. She on top of me as I guided her down my length. I sighed as heaven found me. There was no other word for it. God had answered my prayers in the form of a girl who showed me the way into the light.

The feeling of her heat wrapped around me dulled the pain in my chest from guiding her hips with my arms to find a rhythm we both enjoyed.

It didn't take long. Never with her. It was a good thing she wasn't experienced. Otherwise, I would be the laughing stock of the boys' locker room if ever word of how quickly I came with her became public knowledge. Good thing she found hers as my dick began to lose its stiffness.

She said the magic words, stunning me. "I missed you, Kelley."

There wasn't a chance to return them before she kissed me again, and I lost myself to her. Forgot about all the missing people in my life, my mom and my brother. I wanted this to be my normal, only a car in the drive changed everything.

I pressed my finger to her lips as I listened to the sounds of my aunt talking to her husband.

"We have to go," I whispered.

Her eyes were wide. "I thought—"

But I cut her off with a hand over her mouth. When I heard a door close, I rolled her off of me and winced.

"I don't live here anymore. I'll explain."

I put the finger to my lips before pointing to our clothes. We got dressed silently. I stuffed the bag of money back in my pocket as her eyes became suspicious. I poked my head out of the door before waving her to follow. We made it to the street and past the neighbor's house before I had a chance to speak.

"What's going on, Kelley? I thought you lived there."

Her narrow-eyed glare would have pissed me off if anyone else. But I put myself in her shoes.

"I did. My aunt kicked us out after the funeral."

Her suspicion died and turned into something like pity. I shook my head. "Oh my God, how could she do that? She's a heartless bitch."

It was true. "But Dad's got a place on the other side of town. I'm not leaving. I just live in a different place."

"I'll drive you back. I parked my parents' car back that way."

I turned around, realizing the ride was a blessing and a curse. No way my aunt didn't notice the car out in the front of her house. We ran, or rather I jogged. Her shorter legs meant my jog was almost as fast as her run. We got in the car and peeled off. She drove me to my new digs.

"This is it," I said in grand fashion, sweeping my hand around. "And it's not even ours. It belongs to some woman my dad's been hooking up with for who knows how long."

She nodded, not looking at all disgusted that it wasn't the burbs.

"It sucks. Not the trailer, just the whole story. But I'm glad you didn't leave. I was afraid…"

Cupping the back of her neck, I seared her lips with a kiss that was more heartfelt than any words I could muster. "I'm not leaving you, Len."

She was the last good thing I had. I would find a way to stay, even if it meant shacking it up with Dad's girlfriend. *Sorry, Mom.*

"Good." She sighed. "I should get back before my parents do and I'm grounded until the end of time, not just the rest of my life."

I actually laughed, a little. Our kiss could have melted ice cream in winter and it was hard to let go.

"See you at school," I said before I watched my girl pull away, not knowing that the shit was only getting deeper.

Once Lenny was gone, staring at the trailer, I felt a betrayal on Mom's behalf. The woman seemed nice, but I buried Mom. Staying there felt all kinds of wrong. It was like being torn in half. Betrayal or leaving Lenny. Those were my options.

Trina obviously lived close. She found me standing outside staring like a stalker.

"Are you hungry?" I asked.

She nodded. With cash in my pocket, I walked back into town with Trina to get a late lunch. I had no desire to ask for something to eat from a woman I didn't know. She was Dad's girlfriend, not my mom.

"She's not all that bad," Trina said, during our semi-conversation.

"She's not my mom and she better not act like it."

"Does she even know your dad was married?"

She had a point. I grunted around my cheeseburger as I let Trina do most of the talking. "I worry about you, my friend. When Ox finds out you're doing his girl, he's going to kick your ass."

The last thing I worried about was Ox. He was pussy sized compared to my dad. I could take a hit and give one too. I worried about how much damage the trailer would sustain when I called my dad out on cheating on Mom.

"Ye of little faith," I said with mirth. "Besides, Lenny's not his anymore, she's mine."

Only my luck was worse than stepping in dog shit on the sidewalk. Ox and his friends sauntered in, having already spotted me.

"Damn, saying his name is like saying Candyman five times."

I stared at Trina.

She shook her head. "It's an old scary movie. If you say Candyman five times, he shows up and kills you."

I said nothing, just watched as Ox moved toward us with purpose. The conversation he and his boys were having died. The guy rolled his head on his shoulders as if that would scare me. Trina placed her hand on mine.

"Don't," she warned. "It's only going to get you in trouble."

But there was no fucking way I'd let him punk me.

"Look who's here." Ox grunted while placing his meaty hands on the end of the table to lean in toward me.

It was an intimidation tactic I had no time for.

"Leave now and I won't break your nose," I warned.

Ox stood, and he traded blustered words with his friends. They taunted me as Trina tried to send me smoke signals by widening and narrowing her eyes in rapid succession.

"What do you say, guys?"

Then the bell over the door jingled and Debbie stepped inside. I gave her points for assessing the situation rather quickly. When she smirked, I knew shit was about to get real. She sauntered over with the determination of someone on a mission.

"What are you doing here?" Ox sneered at her, causing her steps to falter.

Watching her fumble almost made my day. The bitch had done Lenny wrong and seeing her get hers would only be more satisfying if Lenny could be here to witness it too.

Debbie glanced at me as Trina's jaw tightened. Trina hadn't looked back at Debbie, nor had she given up her quest for me to back down.

"There's something you should know," Debbie announced. I was grateful the diner held no other customers but us at that late afternoon hour. But soon, people looking for dinner would arrive. "Lenny spent the night with him after the party. Her parents called me looking for her."

Everyone went quiet as Ox turned his attention back at me.

"You didn't touch her." He pointed his finger at me like somehow he ruled me.

I scooted out of the booth as casually as I could. There was no way I would answer. But he would see that as confirmation.

"I will kill you," Ox claimed.

It took two moves. I dogged Ox's jab while I connected my fist with his nose. He didn't fall to the ground, only stumbled back.

"That's fucking assault. Your ass is going to jail."

Who would have thought the big guy would back down so easily.

"Yeah, you have to call the cops because you're a chicken shit." I took Trina's hand and led her out after tossing some bills by the waitress at the counter.

As we left, Debbie said, "I'm sure the police will want to hear about how you tried to rape me."

Rage almost sent me back into the diner to give her some choice words, but Trina tugged on my hand, pulling me forward. I stewed in the silence that Debbie would be that big of a bitch. She could ruin my life with her lies.

"You didn't?" Trina asked in a soft voice.

I gave her my best are you kidding me glare before I added, "I didn't."

She nodded. "I didn't think so, but I had to ask."

Our walk back to the trailer park was a long one. Neither of us had been in a rush to get back. Our lives were less than stellar. I didn't know Trina's story, but I did notice she was always outside in the short time I'd come to stay at my dad's woman's place.

Flashing lights near Dad's truck had us hanging back. We hadn't walked down the main road to get back home. By silent agreement, we'd walked through a field and behind some buildings so we would avoid any potential ambush by Ox and his friends if they got any ideas.

I peeked my head around the corner of a trailer and watched as Dad shook his head. Officers pointed inside, and Dad continued to wordlessly say no.

"Fucking asshole," I growled.

Less than a minute later, the officers got in the patrol car. Trina and I ducked behind a car as they drove off. Another minute went by before we left our hiding place and walked over to where Dad still stood staring after the police.

"There you are, boy. What kind of trouble did you get yourself into?"

I glanced at Trina, who waved and walked toward her place.

"I—"

"Now we got to fucking leave. If they do a search on me…" He shook his head. "Get your shit and let's get out of here." I pointed to his truck where my bag still remained.

"Fine. Let me talk to her. I ain't going to jail over you, boy."

I had no idea what he was talking about. Why would he go to jail?

"What about the woman you knocked up?" I asked.

He chuckled as if anything was funny. "You see how big she is. She was pregnant long before I showed up. I don't get them pregnant. Made that mistake before and never again. But a piece of advice." As if he'd ever given me any before. "Single pregnant women are a great find. They like to fuck. Something about the hormones and shit. And they are lonely enough to take care of you to keep you around. I had something good here. And because of you we got to leave the state."

I'd pay later as I processed his words. *Out of state*. Immediately, I thought of Lenny. I darted in the direction of where Trina went. She wasn't far. Instead, she stood near a door, hovering like a ghost waiting on the living.

"Hey." Her head snapped in my direction. "You got any paper?" She nodded. "I need to write Lenny a letter."

Understanding crossed her face, and she disappeared inside the trailer door. What were the fucking odds, Dad's shack up girlfriend would live next to someone I knew? There had to be some good fortune I couldn't see.

She returned with a spiral notebook, and I wrote as fast as I could. I heard shouting coming from Dad and the woman inside and wrote faster. When Dad banged the door open, I folded the torn piece of paper out of the notebook into the smallest square I could. I wrote Lenny's name on the outside and handed it to Trina. "Please give it to her."

Her stiff wordless reply was all I had, and I had to trust it. She would most likely read the note, but I had no other option.

She surprised me by giving me a hug. "Be safe."

I nodded and climbed into Dad's truck.

"Where are we going?" I asked, knowing I was tempting fate. I wasn't healed enough to dodge a blow.

"Far from here unless you fancy yourself going to jail. And I got warrants, which means we got to get the fuck out of Dodge and fast."

We didn't drive by Lenny's house on our way to the highway. But it would be almost two hours before we crossed the border into Oklahoma. All I could do was lament that I'd lost the best thing I ever had because of my temper. One day, I would be back. I hoped it would be soon.

twenty-two

LENORA

BY THE SKIN OF MY PANTS, I MADE IT HOME. I'D JUST closed the door behind me when I heard my parents drive up. Hopefully, they weren't smart enough to put a hand on the hood to see Mom's car was warm. I burrowed under my covers, relishing the ache between my legs.

I'd had sex…*again.*

And the second time was even better than the first. And, I was falling in love with Kelley. I didn't think it possible, but the butterflies were still there even when I thought about him. He was everything I thought love should be, smart and beautiful, confident and cocky. He had it all, and I had him, or so I hoped.

My clueless parents had no idea why I smiled the rest of the weekend without my phone. But there was a darker cloud that covered my sky. Kelley's mom died, and he was left with an asshole of a father. I needed to convince him to tell someone at school what was going on. Then the devil on my shoulder pointed out that he could be put in foster care outside of our town. Would I ever see him again? Better yet, wasn't his safety more important? It was, which was why I resolved myself to talking to him about it anyway.

Monday morning came, and I shocked Mom by being ready early to leave for school. I spun the dial on my locker, excited about the rest of the day and seeing Kelley again.

"Lenny."

Spinning around, I found Trina there with her hand extended. When she opened it up, in her palm lay a folded note with my name scrawled across the top. I met her eye, and fear clenched my belly. She wore a concerned smile and it scared me more than any horror movie.

With shaky hands, I picked the note up and took the slow laborious task of unfolding it. Every crease represented a crack in my heart. When I finally held it as flat as it could ever be again, I read.

Len,

I'm sorry that I can't see you one last time. Ox and I had a run-in and Debbie added her two cents, which isn't much if you ask me. But Ox made good on his threat to call the cops and they came looking for me. Dad is convinced if we don't leave town and now, I'll go to jail based on lies. So I'm leaving. I don't want to, but I have nowhere else to go. But I promise you one day I'll be back for you. You mean something to me. You're all I have left that's good. So you just wait. I'll see you again soon.

K.

I glanced up from the paper and saw Trina still stood there. "What happened?" I needed the full story.

When she finished telling me, I moved through the hallways like a raging bull. I didn't care which of the two assholes I found first. Lucky for Debbie, it was Ox I ran into first.

Tears blurred my vision. But with my arms in front of me, I shoved him to get his attention.

"What the—" He turned around to see me.

I didn't wait for him to finish his sentence. "Why would you do this?"

His widened eyes only to narrow as he realized why I was pissed off.

"So it's true."

"What does it matter?" I shouted back, quieting the hall as people stopped and stared.

Debbie came into view, and she would have my full attention in a minute.

"What would you want with him, Len? He's trash. Your parents would never accept him." He may have been right about that. "He's no good for you."

"And you are?" I spat.

He reached out, but I sidestepped his touch. "I can forgive you for cheating on me."

My jaw dropped. "I didn't cheat if you recall. You were the one I caught fucking my best friend. We were done after that."

His mouth closed for a second while he swallowed the truth.

"Baby, we both know she wasn't your friend. And I don't give a shit about her."

I glanced over at Debbie, wondering why she didn't get it. This was the second time Ox said this about her in front of everyone.

"I don't think she knows how you really feel. She's willing to lie to the cops about Kelley just to make you happy."

"Lie?" he asked as if he truly believed her.

"Yes, lie. And if the two of you don't drop whatever silly charges you've filed against Kelley, I'll go to the cops myself and tell them the truth."

I walked away, not knowing if my heartfelt promise would do Kelley any good. All I knew was that my heart hurt in the worst way.

The closer I got to Debbie, I said, "If our friendship ever meant anything to you, you will tell the cops the truth. You and I both know Kelley never did anything to you, you didn't want."

Heartache led me to the nurse's office to get a pass to go home. I claimed to be sick and it wasn't a lie. It just wasn't the kind of sick that could be cured with over the counter medication. Mom picked me up, and I buried myself in my covers for a different reason this time. Kelley was gone, and I wasn't sure if I would see him again despite his promise.

Eventually, I went back to school. My smile was permanently lost in a place I couldn't find. I was ill for weeks as time passed and Kelley never came back. He didn't have my phone number. But I checked my phone every second I could for voicemails or texts, and had none. My grounding ended, but it didn't matter. I had nowhere to go. He didn't show up at school, days, weeks or months later. He'd vanished along with a chance of me ever falling in love again.

part two

twenty-three

KELLEY

ALMOST FOUR FUCKING YEARS IT TOOK ME TO GET TO where I was circled in music and well-wishers. Those first few months had been hell with my dad. Going from town to town, crashing in one place or another. But like Dad said, women love a pretty face and they fell for him every time.

When we'd landed in one spot and I'd finally gotten back in school, I stopped messing around. I had a goal to meet, Mom's memory to honor. I would make her proud. My only regret was the girl I'd left behind. It took a long time for me to let go of hope that I'd ever see her again. But maybe one day, if I made it to the pros, I'd have the money to take care of whatever legal issues I potentially had that kept me out of Texas.

And then I would find her. Face to face, she could tell me why she'd given up on us.

I caught a flying beer from my new teammate while a girl straddled my lap. Her lips bruised mine as we were all celebrating another victory.

"Hey, everyone, our QB is in the house!" my roommate Chance called out.

Clapping ensued with all eyes on me. I shrugged, pulling free from the lip-lock I hadn't asked for. I might fuck her later, but I wasn't down with kissing her. That ended four years ago, when I'd been run out of town and away from the one girl who'd stolen my heart.

Life was great, or so I told myself. I had everything I dreamed of and should have been happy. But getting a transfer this year from a division two to a division one university and being able to play without sitting out a year, wasn't great news when I didn't have the only people I ever loved to share it with. Mom and my brother were dead and buried far out of my reach. And the only girl to make me feel wasn't there either. I buried those thoughts as they did me no good.

"And he can catch," Chance announced.

"Better than you." I pointed at him.

"Never, I was born to catch."

"Is that why you're a Tight End?"

"That's what the girls say. They like my tight end."

He turned to twerk and give me a view of his ass, but I turned away, laughing.

"Dude, go find Sawyer and Ashton and bother them."

"No can do. They've already locked one up." He pointed toward the ceiling and upstairs.

"Why don't you take me to your room?" Shelly said, wiggling on my lap.

And why not? I wasn't in the partying mood. So I stood with Shelly's legs wound around me.

Chance wolf called me along with everyone else in the vicinity as I made my way to the stairs.

Halfway there, I caught sight of a familiar silhouette. I dropped Shelly so fast to her feet, she squeaked and held on to my shoulders to steady herself. I barely noticed as I moved with abandonment toward my target.

It hadn't been coincidence that I'd come to this school. I'd applied at several universities for a transfer, but I jumped on board when coach got me in with Layton. I hadn't forgotten it was the school Lenny had talked about. I'd hoped she had come to school there. But I'd been on campus for a couple of weeks with no sight of her. Granted the school was huge.

When she turned around, it wasn't Lenny. I gave the girl a half smile, trudging off toward the kitchen.

"What was that all about?"

Scrubbing a hand down my face, I stared at Shelly. "Nothing, I just thought I saw someone."

"Why don't we go up to your room?"

She winked, which might have been sexy an hour ago. Right then, my head was plastered with internal posters of Lenny that I'd conjured in my head. Would I ever forget? Four years and a multitude of dreams said no, and didn't that make me completely fucked.

A part of me wished I could just talk to her. Maybe if she told me she moved on, I could too. What should have been a high school fling became my measure for every girl after. And as pretty as Shelly was, she wasn't Lenny.

I drew her back to the circle of our friends and left her to chat with the girls as I went and stood by the guys.

"Dude, I'm telling you, you're drunk. That chick there is an Antarctica ten, but she's a Miami two," Sawyer said.

"Antarctica. Get the fuck out of here. She's gorgeous," Chance said.

"Yeah, that's because you've never been to Miami." Sawyer pointed at Chance.

"Or L.A.," Ashton added.

"Exactly." You would have thought Sawyer solved world hunger the way he said the word. "You can't judge pretty the same in every city."

Sawyer was full of himself, but a good guy. "Who made you the judge?" I joked.

He shrugged. "I've been around. Now see, there's a Miami ten."

We all turned at once and it felt like I'd been sucker punched by my dad. It was her. After all this time. *Lenny*. She stood with her back to me and her face in profile. She wore a skirt that hugged her hips. Her top, if you could call it that, tied down the back. It was one of those…buster things…bustier was the word. My stepmom had worn shit like that to her job and told me what it was called.

Everything faded in the background when she turned and caught sight of me. Bright gray eyes shone for a second. What should have been a moment of happiness for both of us made her smile dim and the light to leave her face. Her jaw slackened before she turned and fled, leaving me no time to close the distance between us.

That wouldn't stop my pursuit. The guys said something as I trailed after her, but their voices were lost to me. I followed her out the door, calling her name. She stopped in her tracks and did a slow turn, makeup ruined from the tears that streaked down her face.

"What?" she sobbed.

Fuck if that didn't gut me.

"Len, I—"

"You didn't come back," she finished for me.

Confused by her words, I halted pursuit, tongue-tied by what to say next. The door opened behind me and my moment was lost. Lenny was soon flanked by two girls who looked ready to castrate me. And a warm arm snaked around my neck.

"Baby, do you know her?" Shell asked.

Lenny's eyes narrowed before she spun around and dashed away. It took everything in me not to chase her. If she went to school there, I would make it my mission to find her again.

LENNY

IT FELT AS THOUGH THE BREATH WAS LITERALLY RIPPED from my lungs. He stood there looking more beautiful, taller and filled out more than my fading memories. His hair had more golden strands in it, suggesting he spent more time outside. That was evidenced by his amazing tan.

My heart hurt because he looked healthy and happy, which meant he hadn't come for me like he promised. Maybe I shouldn't have been so sick over a high school crush, but as the pain lanced through me, I knew I still loved him with all my heart and soul.

The years had been kind to him wherever he'd been. He wasn't the boy who looked troubled from life. And I wasn't the girl who seemingly had it all. My life had turned out so out of focus, my vision blurred to remind me.

More confirmation that my heart was still wrapped up in his was when horns had grown out of my head as I watched the blond beauty wrap her possessive arms around him. I had to turn away as my tears became even uglier.

"What's going on?" Brie asked, while her friend looked on sympathetically.

I shook my head. My words were a jumble of chaotic thoughts and memories. "I have to go," I managed to say, breaking in a jog down the street. I lived on the other side of campus at the very edge. But I waved them off when they offered to drive me. Time was needed to pull myself together. And what better way than in the cool night air.

But time didn't heal wounds. They only dug horrible gouges in my heart as I felt pierced through my very soul.

Steeling my spine, I pushed through the front door and sighed at the silence that greeted me. In the kitchen, I grabbed a glass and chugged down some water while staring out the window above the sink. My grip tightened on the counter as I tried to get a hold of myself.

Surprisingly light fingers wrapped around my wrist before firm pressure was applied. A silent gasp pried my mouth open, but I knew better than to make any noise.

"You're home early. But I don't remember giving you permission to go out." The hot words whispered in my ear were only a precursor to the punishment I would receive.

He was supposed to be out. He shouldn't have been home. Those thoughts meant nothing because I'd hedged my bets and lost. He squeezed, knowing exactly how to create the most pain with little effort. I collapsed to my knees for the onslaught of pain. He stepped back in time so I could fall and not hit my head on the counter on the way down. His kindness extended as he let me catch my breath when he released my wrist. Only, my reprieve didn't last long. In another second, it felt like my hair was being ripped out strand by strand from my scalp. And it only got worse. The sound of his zipper brought tears from my eyes, but any protest on my part would earn me a worse fate.

twenty-four

KELLEY

THE ROCKING OF THE BED WOKE ME FROM A PLEASANT dream or memory. Thoughts of Lenny consumed my subconscious thoughts. So when I opened my eyes, I wasn't able to hold back my disappointment when I saw the wrong girl crawling toward me.

My expression caused her to pause before she brightly said, "Morning, sleepyhead. Since I haven't seen you since the party, I thought I'd give you a wakeup call."

"Shell," I said in vain as she tried to wrap herself around me. I glanced over at my clock. "I have to get to practice."

"I know, silly. I do too." She was talking about her cheerleading practice. "But I thought I could help take care of you first."

She grabbed my junk, and I had to pry her hands loose. My hardness had nothing to do with her and everything to do with a much needed morning piss.

"Shell," I said again, gently rolling her off of me and making my way off the other side of the bed. I sat and took a deep breath before glancing over my shoulder.

What I had to say wasn't easy. As much as I'd fucked, I'd tried not to be a jerk when dealing with women. I didn't want to be my father. So my motto was to always be honest.

She crawled over and shyly sat next to me.

I swallowed. "I think we should cool things down."

Her frown wasn't unexpected; neither was the way her brows pinched in the middle.

"But you just said—"

I cut her off before rehashing everything I thought I wanted, like a steady girlfriend, because it didn't change how things were now.

"Yeah, I'm sorry."

"It's that girl, isn't it?"

"What girl?"

She glared at me. "The one at the party crying. How do you know her?"

Honesty, I thought.

"We went to high school together." It was partially true, seeing that it'd been only a few short months.

The laugh that cracked the silence between us held no humor. "You're making a mistake. If she's an ex, she is for a reason. Besides, I've seen her around. I'm pretty sure she has a boyfriend. You're wasting your time." Standing, she gave me one final glance. "And then you'll be back. Maybe I'll give you another shot, or maybe I won't."

The door closed quietly behind her, leaving me to chew on her bit of information. Then my phone blared to life with an alarm, reminding me I had obligations if I wanted to continue going to school on scholarship. Not only did it require my skills on the field, but I had to maintain my grades too. Neither of which would happen if I stayed lamenting over a girl I was maybe still in love with.

After a quick shower and getting dressed, I headed downstairs to find Chance waiting for me. He was the one of my three roommates I'd felt most comfortable with, probably because his circumstances growing up were similar to mine.

My mom had died, his had taken off. His dad took to the bottle for comfort, mine for the hell of it. His dad was a functional alcoholic, his words. I hadn't seen my dad in a few years. The other guys in the house knew nothing about hard living.

"Dude, what crawled up her ass? She left out of here like her hair was on fire. What did you do to piss her off?"

I shrugged.

"Did you cut her loose?"

I shrugged again, not really wanting to talk about it. I'd never been a big sharer of my thoughts, only with Len.

"Probably for the best," he began. "Although, she was one of the better star chasers."

Stopping my forward progress, I leveled a gaze at him. "Star chaser?" Though I was pretty sure I knew.

"You know, the chicks looking to trap some guy in a relationship before he gets a million-dollar deal."

Exactly what I thought. When I started moving, he added, "At least she was one of the better ones."

He smiled sheepishly at me as I walked by. He didn't have a car, so I expected him on my heels.

"I would have told you, but like I said, she's one of the better ones. And figured you could get a piece before you cut her loose."

Shaking my head, I got in the car to make the short drive to campus. I was fortunate to get a parking pass along with my scholarship.

We were ten minutes late to practice.

"Coach is going to kick our asses," Chance said when we jogged on the field.

And he did.

"Moore and Abbott, two extra laps. And if you don't finish in four, everyone has to do another two laps."

That got us moving, because the last thing we wanted was to have the guys pissed at us. With an additional punishment of the extra reps in the weight room, I ended up missing class.

"Fuck," I said.

"Dude, don't worry. Let me make a call."

"I can't wait. I need to find someone with notes. We have a test next class, and it's based off his lectures, not the book. It's his way to get people in class," I groaned, knowing I was fucked.

Chance held up a finger. "Okay, thanks."

"What?" I said.

"This girl said there is a guy in the library who sells notes."

After getting the description of who I should look for, later that day I made my way into the library after afternoon practice.

I climbed the stairs, glancing at each computer. When I found my target, I had no idea I'd find her. Snagging a seat, I took in her wide eyes glaring at me.

"Why are you here?" she asked.

I pointed to the blue butterfly on the top of her laptop.

"Look, Len, I don't want to fight. I was told a guy with that on their laptop was the person to see about notes."

Though I should have guessed it was a girl when they'd given me that description.

"Just another person who hears a name and assumes someone's gender. You understand that, don't you?"

True enough, although there was nothing welcoming in her casual statement.

"So people call you Lenny around here too."

"Only my customers. My friends call me Lenora."

Strike one, as I'd called her Len. Apparently she didn't consider me a customer or a friend. Though I didn't want to be either. I wanted to be so much more if she'd let me.

"Gotcha. Look, I missed psychology class today. I need the lecture notes. I hear my professor's lectures don't change year to year."

Her frown slipped some. "I may have notes. Whose are you looking for?"

"I don't want a handout either," I said, not sure why I felt the need to say that.

"I didn't offer you one."

Strike two as her eyes were flat. It was as if I meant nothing to her.

I swallowed my pride, needing those notes. "Professor Lange's class. I don't know anyone in there, and I have a test next time. I can't take a chance of failing. I'm prepared to pay whatever."

Her eyes met mine before they went all business. "Twenty for one section notes and a hundred for the full semester."

That class began every other day minutes after practice ended for the morning. And it was the only class that fit my schedule and was mandatory. No doubt I'd miss more classes before the semester was over.

As I decided how I wanted to proceed, I had an urge to find out how she ended up selling notes. The Lenny I knew was all about helping everyone else. Then again, I hadn't seen her in four years. A lot apparently changed. More importantly, her hard expression was something I recognized. She needed the money, but didn't want my pity or anyone else's.

By no means did I have a lot of cash. NCAA rules forbade me to work. But I'd saved up money over the years with odd jobs I did that paid cash. So I dug in my pocket, having already heard the price before I arrived. I placed several bills down and slid them across the round table to her. Her fingers brushed mine when she made a move to retrieve them. Our eyes met before she tugged on the cash, forcing me to let go or make things more awkward. I let go.

She counted the cash, and I realized my mistake. I shouldn't have given her the hundred. Then I would have to make up some other excuse to see her again. It was too late. She pulled out an accordion folder out of a bag in the chair next to her. She riffled through it before coming up with a binder clip wad of papers.

"Here."

I arched a brow in surprise. "You don't have a thumb drive or something?"

"If I gave them electronically, my business would end. My hard work would be posted on the web for anyone to use."

She had a point. "But someone could scan these."

"And they could copy them too. Luckily for me, my customers aren't that smart. They don't think out of the box."

There was nothing to argue. Besides, there were other things I wanted to talk about.

"Len—"

Her scattered movements stopped my words. She was shoving things in her bag, including her laptop.

"Look, I'm late. I have to go," she announced.

There was no stopping her as she was already walking away. I wanted to call out, but we were in a library. And I didn't think she would appreciate me drawing unwanted attention. Besides, I knew where she'd be after class. I could try again tomorrow.

twenty-five

LENORA

MY FEET BURNED A PATH THAT LED STRAIGHT OUT OF there. Being close to Kelley after all these years shouldn't have affected me so. Those bi-colored eyes of his, one blue, one green were just as captivating as the first time I saw them, which was why I had to run and fast.

I didn't dare look back. Not a first. I had to steel my spine and resolve. But too soon, my steps slowed, and I glanced over my shoulder to find he wasn't following me. My heart sank even though it was for the best.

When I turned back, Brie was in my path.

"Lenora, where are you off to in such a hurry?"

I came to an abrupt halt. "Jesus, what's your superpower, speed? How did you just materialize out of thin air?"

She laughed. "I was headed in your direction. I waved, but you didn't see me. It was like I wasn't even there." My head had been elsewhere. "So where are you going like there are hot coals under your feet?"

"Just headed home." I tried my best to sound cheery.

Her eyes softened, and I braced myself. Brie was a psych major and a good one. She'd been the first girl I'd met on campus. She'd volunteered for welcoming committee. She became somewhat of a friend, although I hadn't let anyone in since Debbie's betrayal. Trina had been the closest thing since, though I'd rarely talked to her since graduating high school. But Brie never gave up. She'd stuck through all my excuses for not hanging out and never being available. She didn't push for answers, but I felt like that was quickly going to change.

She reached out and placed her hand lightly on my wrist. I tried not to flinch, but the grimace of pain must have registered on my face because she pulled back. "You know you can tell me anything. I won't judge."

"What's there to tell?" I said, though I didn't expect an answer.

Her pitying smile said it all. "Len—"

Embarrassment colored my words an angry shade of red. "Don't psychoanalyze me, Brie."

Pursing her lips, she nodded. "Sorry, force of habit. I just want you to know you have a friend. You don't have to go through this alone."

She had no idea and wouldn't even learn the truth if I had my way about it. She ended the ensuing silence with, "You should come out with us this weekend to the bonfire."

Little did she know how impossible it would be for me to go.

"I doubt I'll be able to make it."

When I went to pass her, she added, "Is that you or him talking?"

There was no way I was responding to her, so I kept going. For as much as I thought I'd hidden from the people who knew me, they'd seen more than I was comfortable with. How many of my bad decision were they aware of?

My hollow steps were as empty as my heart. Brie and everyone else could judge me all they wanted. I'd made choices I had to at the time, and I'd lived with them. And quietly, I'd been making alternative plans. But that took time. I would endure in order to do what was best for the immediate future.

During the long walk across campus I replayed my every decision since Kelley drove out of my life. I thought about the girl I used to be, strong and fearless, to the woman I'd become, weak and helpless, and I hated it. When had I morphed into a spineless woman with no options? After one stop that brought a smile to my face, I plastered a fake one when I opened the door to my personal hell.

Maybe I wasn't brave anymore.

"Hey," a finger snapped in my face. "I have a rugby game this weekend. So I won't be home."

Of course he wouldn't. "I'm not surprised. You would have been at your fraternity otherwise, so why bother to tell me."

He raised a hand, but balled it closed and lowered it.

"You know if I didn't like that smart mouth of yours to open, I would permanently close it."

Whether it was fear or practicality, I said nothing else. Instead, I quietly made plans to hang out with Brie again, at the bonfire. My bold defiance was working its way out of my pores, little by little. The previous weekend turned out to be a bust in many ways. But when Friday arrived, I wouldn't be taken by surprise by Kelley's existence. Though I hoped he would be there.

"Oh my God, Lenora's here."

I waved and bit back a biting retort. Shelly or Shell as everyone called her hadn't been my biggest fan. She and Brie had been friends in high school, though I didn't see it. Shell had a bit of mean girl in her, though she wasn't as bad as some. Or maybe it was because she'd wrapped herself around Kelley the other night. It also could have been that she reminded me too much of Debbie. And thoughts of my former BFF still stung. How could an age old friendship turn so wrong?

Shaking it off, I just smiled.

"Don't mind her. I think she and her boyfriend broke up."

Good thing the clearing was packed with bodies everywhere because both girls had glanced away and missed the shock I tamped down. I also managed to hold in a smile as we found the keg and got a drink. I had the red plastic cup up to my lip when a seriously good-looking guy strode over to where we stood.

"Brie," he said.

"Chance," she said frostily.

"Still the ice princess."

"Still a case study in douchebagness."

He shook his head. "I don't know why I bother."

"I don't either. It borders on desperation. But we both know you need appointments for the revolving door of your bedroom."

His jaw tightened and it looked as though he might say something more. Instead, he marched away.

"What was that all about?" I asked.

The question popped out before I could stop it. I didn't normally ask questions because I didn't want to reciprocate in answering things about myself. But Brie looked ready to talk. Only Shelly sauntered over first.

"I see Chance is still panting after you," Shell said.

Shell acted as though that was a surprise. But Brie was gorgeous. Long dark hair with giant honey eyes had guys tripping over their feet whenever I was around her.

"He wants what he can't have. And no way am I giving my virginity to him. I've waited this long. I might as well wait until I'm married."

Shell shook her head and said, "You are like the last Junior virgin on campus," before walking away.

"You're a virgin?"

Again, I hadn't finished my first beer. Who was I to question anyone else's choices?

"Don't be surprised. Anyway, it isn't for lack of trying. I've just had bad luck," she said while glaring at the back of Chance's head.

The guy hadn't exactly gone far and when he shifted, I caught sight of Kelley walking over to him.

Glancing away quickly, I moved out of his line of sight. But that wasn't enough.

"I'll be right back," I said to Brie.

She nodded as I made my retreat. *Keep calm. You can't keep running from him,* I thought.

That turned out to be true. I stepped behind a tree that lined the clearing to take a breath. Then I thought about all the horror movies that started off this way. Girl walking away from her friends. No one knowing where she was headed. I moved to walk back and ran into a solid wall of muscle.

"Len."

I glanced up and shadowed eyes hypnotized me in their depths.

"Damn, Lenny, don't look at me that way or I'll—"

Whatever he was saying got lost somewhere as my brain shorted. My libido kicked into high gear, and all I heard was white noise. Caught like a deer with the mouth slightly parted in awe, I was helpless as his lips descended to press against mine.

Sparks exploded behind my eyelids, wings fluttered in my belly, and for a second I rejoiced that this connection really did exist and wasn't in my imagination.

When his tongue tried to dart past my lips, I jerked back.

"Lenny—"

He called out. But I was several steps ahead. Tears burned in the back of my eyes because I wanted that feeling. I'd been living a lie so long, I didn't think that feeling was more than a dream. And seeing him again changed all that. Only it was far too late.

Before I made it back into the throngs, Shelly appeared.

"Well, well, well. Your lipstick is smudged. You should fix that before someone sees and tells your boyfriend."

twenty-six

KELLEY

SHELL'S WORDS TO LENNY HAD BEEN SAID LOUD ENOUGH to hear. As Lenny ignored her, I didn't.

"Back off, Shell. Leave her alone. She didn't do anything. It was me."

Lenny turned around and gave me a look filled with so much relief, I wanted to recoil. The guy she was dating must have meant a lot to her. And fuck, as much as I wanted to, I wouldn't be the cause of them breaking up. So I had to distract Shell.

After Lenny disappeared into the crowd, I closed the distance between Shell and me where she stood with accusatory eyes.

"I kissed her. You were right. She's not into me anymore."

"I warned you," she said smugly.

I pulled her close to me, enough she felt the hardness in my pants that had nothing to do with her and everything to do with Lenny. But if Shell thought otherwise, maybe she'd keep her jealous mouth shut.

"You did, and you look good tonight," I whispered in her ear.

And she did. Shell was a stunner, which was why I'd asked her out in the first place. But she wasn't Len. Still, I would take one for the girl who had stolen my heart. I would play a game for a short time at least to secure that Shelly wouldn't ruin Len's relationship.

Shelly wasn't a pushover, which had also attracted me to her. "You think I'm just going to go home with you tonight?" She shook her head. "I'm not that girl. Your dick can find comfort in your hand tonight. And maybe I'll consider giving you a second chance."

She sauntered away with an extra bounce in her step that should have had me drooling. Instead, I found it a blessing she was so easily appeased and left without me asking her to. I wasn't sure how far I could take the ruse. But her smirk meant that she believed I was hard for her, and she hadn't mentioned Lenny again. So hopefully, that'd worked.

I melted into the crowd and found my roommates where I left them. Instead, now Sawyer was wrapped around a girl, whispering something in her ear that made her giggle. Ashton stood watching as he always did in the short time I'd known him. He didn't say much unless he thought he was alone with Sawyer. They'd grown up together and had been best friends forever. There was more of a story there. I just hadn't figured it out yet. I did know they hardly did anything without the other, including girls.

When I turned back to Chance, he stood brooding, glaring off into the crowd. I followed his line of sight to where Lenny stood with a cup to her lips and a smile on her face. My jaw clenched, and I was about to say something until I realized he was staring at the girl next to Lenny.

"Who is she?" I asked quietly.

His eyes left the girl in question and found me. "An ex."

So he and I had more in common. His wistful crossed with annoyed expression reminded me of me.

"Is that a good or a bad thing?"

He shrugged. "She's better off."

I understood that statement all too well.

"Then it's better not to watch."

I turned away myself, having spent the entire conversation with my eyes glued on a girl I could never have. Lenny seemed happier without me near, yet I felt like dog shit without her.

The bonfire raged, and I found a spot near it. Long ago, huge logs had been heaved around it like planks to perch on. So I found an empty spot and sat, trying my best to not search for Lenny in the crowd. Eventually Chance came around and sat next to me. His eyes looked a little glazed, and I realized he'd reached his happy limit.

"Why is it I never see you drinking?" he asked.

Oh, I'd taken a sip or two of beer here and there, especially at parties. But I'd always ended up nursing what amounted to one drink the entire night. It seemed Chance was more astute than I'd taken him for.

"Not much of a drinker. Besides, coach said anyone caught with a hangover tomorrow wouldn't play. No exceptions."

"Yeah, well, I guess we should get ghost then. It's not like anything's going on here."

Several girls had approached him, and he'd quietly sent each one away. If I hadn't been in my own private hell, I might have tried to puzzle out what was going on with him and the blonde.

In silent agreement, we got up and strode over to our last vacated spot. I planned to give Ashton and Sawyer a heads-up about our plans.

Sawyer was grinning like a loon, handy with the girl wrapped around him. She didn't seem to mind, while Ashton frowned at Sawyer.

"Don't mind him," he said to the girl. "He's the silent type. He likes to watch, but he'll get in on the action if you let him." Just as I was about to cut in with a peace out, he added, "Have you ever had two guys at the same time? You'll love it."

"Ah, we're out," I said quickly and strode away as Sawyer grinned at Ashton, who appeared to sigh in resignation.

I wanted to get home before they did. I was grateful my room was across from Chance's and next to Ashton's. The noises that emanated from Sawyer's room when I found myself in the hall would keep me up at night.

On autopilot, I'd navigated toward Lenny. Maybe subconsciously I wanted to check on her before I left. Whatever it was, she swayed on her feet with wide eyes and a wide smile.

"Come on, just one more," she said to Chance's ex, who held a cup out of reach.

"Lenora, you've had enough."

Lenny made a go for the cup and stumbled. Automatically, I reached out and snagged her before she face planted.

"Kelley, Kelley, Kelley," she said.

Her friend glanced between us. "You're Kelley?" she asked, like she'd heard all about me. I nodded. Her lips formed an O.

"Look, I'll take her home. My truck is just over there."

"You can't take me home," Lenny protested, but her eyes went unfocused, and she slumped in my arms.

Repositioning my hold on her, I lifted her up, cradling her like a baby.

"I would take her," the girl said. "But I'm too drunk to drive my car."

Chance cut in. "I'll drive you home, Brie."

Brie's eyes narrowed, but she wasn't stupid. She nodded. I quietly asked, "You sure you're up to driving?"

He nodded. "I only had one drink."

"She lives in the Montague apartments just past the park," Brie said.

The campus was located in the middle of nowhere, boarding a small town. There wasn't much of anything, including apartments. I knew which ones she was talking about.

With a head nod, I carried Lenny to where I was parked. Brie and Chance were headed in the same direction and helped me get Lenny into the cab of my truck.

"How are you going to get home when you leave her car?" I asked Chance. Just because we were near a small town didn't mean the campus wasn't as big as one on its own.

He shrugged. "I'll find a way."

"Why don't I pick you up after I drop her off?"

Brie said, "I'm in the Sadie Hawkins dorms," which were the same ones Shell lived in.

I nodded. "I'll text you when I'm close."

Chance nodded, and I got in as Lenny quietly breathed in her sleep. The rumble of my engine didn't stir her. I wondered if she lived with someone. Her boyfriend? But I didn't let that stop me. If she did, it was his fault for not being there to keep her safe.

I drove the speed limit the entire way. I wanted more than the couple of minutes it would take to get her home. I wanted the impossible—*her*.

Parking in front of the small complex, I had no idea what apartment number was hers. I touched her arm, and her skin was soft and warm under my hand. Sliding my hand down her arm, I slowed at her wrist, which was covered in rubber band bracelets. Her eyes jolted awake, and she pulled her hand way, protecting it like I'd hurt her.

"Sorry."

Large eyes filled with fear took a few moments before they cleared and blinked until anger replaced the expression.

She turned and saw where she was. "You shouldn't be here."

Scrambling, she fumbled with the door handle before I could help her and nearly tumbled out of the car, trying to get away from me.

"Lenny, please—"

She shook her head. "Thanks for the ride. But you need to leave."

The door shut on anything I could have said before she disappeared across the street and down the path. She pulled a key from her pocket and darted inside. I sat like a creeper and waited until a light turned on in the second floor. A few seconds later, it went out before another popped on for a short second before it too went dark. And then nothing. With no reason to stay, I fired the engine back to life and made my way back to the other side of campus to pick up Chance.

twenty-seven

LENORA

THE WARM SUNNY DAY SHOULD HAVE BEEN A BRIGHT spot to my morning. But the meaty hand on my hip wasn't Kelley's, and it created a wave of revulsion in my gut. Slowly, I rolled away from his hold, wondering why he was home. Had he lied about being out of town to test me? If so, I'd failed.

My day began with chores that couldn't be avoided as much as I wanted to flee the confines of a prison of my own making. Eventually, I made it to the park across the street. Feeding the ducks, I sat in the sun, trying to remember what happiness felt like.

But I wasn't off the hook. By Monday I scurried into class with the evidence of my attempt at independence shinning on my face. No amount of makeup would cover it, so I did what I could and entered class at the very last minute, sitting in the back with my head down.

For each of my other classes, I did the same with good results. Nobody noticed. By lunch, I wished I could go home, but that wasn't in the cards. I headed to the café to use my lower than basic meal plan, which allowed for me to eat one meal a day on campus.

I was halfway down the hall when he stopped me.

"Lenny."

The cadence of his voice was filled with a plea. I stopped and did a slow turn. Somehow he'd caught up to me by the time I did.

His eyes widened and his hand reached out to brush light fingertips over the yellow, greenish bruise on the right side of my face as he peeled my sunglasses off.

"What happened?" he growled, as if he planned to defend my honor. Little did he know how far I'd fallen, and no amount of rope could pull me out of the hole I'd dug for myself.

I didn't know how much of a liar I'd become until one popped out of my mouth without thought.

"Nothing but drunk face planted. My fault, I knew better."

Wasn't that the lesson I'd been taught yesterday?

"You shouldn't drink so much."

I understood his words. Hadn't I seen the evidence of his father's drinking? But I'd been chastised enough. And I didn't have to take it from him too.

"Why do you care? You never came back."

"Lenny," he called out as I turned, fleeing my past and into my present nightmare.

Brie found me in the lunch line. When she touched my arm, I'd flinched and whipped my head around, thinking Kelley had followed me. But he hadn't. And I shouldn't have been disappointed. It was better that way for both of us.

"What's up, chica?"

I shook my head, glad for the dim lighting in the buffet area. It hid the uglier side of certain mystery meats and worked in my favor since I'd left Kelley holding my sunglasses. She hadn't noticed my face yet. I moved to the checkout line and breezed through. We stood searching for a place to sit in the crowded seating area when arms circled around me.

Brie glanced up and her lips barely curled. She had no love for my boyfriend, and I understood why. She'd figured out what a control freak he was.

"Prescott," she muttered.

"Brie," he said, matching her tone.

"Looks like we're late today. I see two seats. Why don't you let Lenora sit with me, so we can have girl talk?"

His reply made him sound suspicious. "Why? Has she told you she doesn't want to sit with me?"

I felt him go rigid behind me. Pleading without words, I stared at Brie, willing her not to say anything that could make this worse.

"Of course not," Brie said. Her smile warmed, while not reaching her eyes. "It's not that. It's just I hardly see her. I wanted to hang out a little bit, unless I can convince her to go to dinner with me tonight."

I said nothing. Some lessons had taken time for me to learn, but they were now ingrained in my brain.

A cool hand snagged my left hand and held it out in front of Brie. Shock registered on her face and it was too late. His other arm snaked over my right one before he gripped my wrist in what appeared to be a loving gesture. Pain brought tears to my eyes, but I couldn't let them fall.

"Lenora has obligations as my future wife. If she goes to dinner with you, what am I to eat? We're building something. And maybe you don't understand that. The future of our family depends on each of us fulfilling our role."

For anyone listening who didn't know our dynamics, it might sound reasonable, even romantic especially the way he held me and the plastic smile on my face. But Brie was no dummy. I continued to silently beg her with wide eyes to let it go.

"Well," she began after letting out a deep breath. "Putting it that way, I guess I understand."

I closed my eyes in relief as she said her goodbye, and I was grateful that I remembered to put the ring back on before coming into the lunchroom. I didn't wear it unless absolutely necessary.

But Brie didn't give up that easily. A week or so later she sent me a text shortly after my last class, perfect timing on her part. I met her on the quad where she was setting up tables with some other people.

"What's up?" I asked when I reached her.

"We're shorthanded. I'm hoping you'll help us out." She waved a hand like it was a magic wand over all the boxes stacked. "The guys need to get more supplies and my other cohort hasn't showed up."

She launched into what she needed to do. When she was finished, I was already prepared with my excuse.

"I really have to get to the library," I said. If he came to check on me and I wasn't there, I'd have hell to pay.

"Is he hurting you?"

"Who?" I asked, even though she was talking about the same he I'd been thinking of.

"Prescott."

Her eyes were soft, and I wanted to tell her the truth. But she wouldn't understand. I would have to confess it all for her to know. And I'd kept my secrets for more than two years by staying on the fringes. I'd gone to class and home with little to no social activity. I'd kept people at a distance so they wouldn't ask questions about things I didn't want to answer. Despite all that, Brie had never given up on me. She kept trying to break down my walls and be a friend to me. What would she think of me if she knew the truth? And could I trust her?

"No, of course not." The lie came out as smooth as satin.

She rolled her eyes. "Anyway, if you're not busy, then help me, please."

When she started to bend on one knee, I laughed and hauled her back to her feet.

"Okay, okay, I'll help. But I don't have a lot of time."

twenty-eight

KELLEY

WITH MY BOOK OPEN ON MY LAP, I TAPPED MY PEN ON the empty page in my notebook. Although I had a laptop, a used one my high school coach had given me, my typing skills sucked. I blamed that on not having a computer in the house growing up. I hardly ever got to use it unless I went to the library. So I still used pen and paper for notes.

I couldn't focus. All I could think about was the last time I saw Lenny in the café. I'd been heading to a class I couldn't be late for. Her smile was missing in action like it always was these days with the brief exception of her drunkenness at that party. She was so different from the Lenny I remembered. I'd been rushing not to be late, so I couldn't chase after her. Which was why her sunglasses sat like a trophy on my dresser.

Sawyer's voice broke through my thoughts. He and Ashton were coming downstairs but hadn't noticed me yet.

"I don't know what your problem is. You had your share," he said.

"Maybe I'm tired of sharing," Ashton said.

Sawyer huffed. “Then get your own, bro. No one’s stopping you.”

Ashton reached out, eyes dark as night. He snagged Sawyer’s arm to stop him. Ashton mumbled something I couldn’t hear. But so far, he’d said more than usual.

Sawyer’s eyes narrowed. “That shit happened a long time ago, and I’m not going there.” He snatched his arm out of Ashton’s hold when he spotted me.

He changed his path, and a smile curled on his mouth.

“Kelley, what are you doing here? It’s Friday. Coach gave us off for practice. I thought for sure you’d be with Chance chasing pussy tonight.”

I shook my head. “Nah, studying for midterms.”

“Dude, don’t be like Ashton.” He hooked a thumb in the guy’s direction. “Life is short and pussy is never going to be better than it is now. We have no fucking responsibilities. No wife or kids and shit. We are like gods at this school. Pussy is never in short supply.”

I shrugged.

“Don’t tell me you have a thing for that brunette.”

Tightening my jaw, I ground my teeth together. Apparently, my silence was answer enough.

He shook his head as if he were disappointed with me. “She’s dating one of my fraternity brothers.” Over his shoulder, he glanced at Ashton. “If you can call him that. He wouldn’t have been voted in if his father wasn’t legacy.”

“Prescott is a douche,” Ashton said.

“Yeah,” Sawyer concurred. “He’s pussy whipped. He treats her like those porcelain dolls my mom collects. There is no in. Trust me, I tried.”

“And I ended up saving your face,” Ashton muttered.

Sawyer waved him off. “I had no idea. She’s hot as shit, but believe me when I say she has an unavailable neon sign strapped around her. Don’t waste your time.”

Thankfully, Chance came through the door and tossed me my keys. “Many thanks, man.”

He held up a six pack of beer. “Want one?”

Ashton nodded first, and Chance tossed him a can. Sawyer held up a hand and didn’t even really look but caught the flying can with no problem. When they stared at me, I shook my head. Chance shrugged and popped the top.

I hadn’t realized I’d wrapped my hands around the tags until Sawyer asked, “I’ve been meaning to ask you. Who do those dog tags belong to? Your dad?”

The metal bit into my skin as I shook my head. “My brother.” Before they could ask, I told them. “He died in Afghanistan.”

It was a story I didn’t tell often, but these guys were different. In the weeks I’d lived there, they’d accepted me on and off the field. I hadn’t had that in so long. And I’d slept better in years since moving away from her. So I told them the ugly truth about the roadside bomb that killed my brother.

“Damn, man, that sucks,” Sawyer said.

Even though he and Ashton had grown up far different than me, with parents who were still living, I believed Sawyer felt bad for me.

“So it’s just you and your mom.”

He and Ashton had been there when I moved in. They believed that the woman who’d come with me had been my mom. “My stepmom. My mom died from complications of MS.”

“Fuck. You’ve had some shit to deal with.”

I nodded, grateful when Sawyer got up and didn't ask about my dad.

"Wanna go get free ice cream?" Chance offered, ending the awkward silence.

Ashton grunted. It was unusual for him to opt in before hearing what Sawyer was going to do.

"We've got ice cream here," I said when Chance glanced at me.

"Yeah, but here we eat alone. There we find pussy for the night."

Sawyer's eyes brightened. "Hell, I'm in."

I sighed. "Fine."

"Good, because you're the designated driver."

As odd as that sounded, I figured we'd be out until late and there would ultimately be a party with alcohol and whatever else. They all piled in my truck. Sawyer and Ashton opted to sit in the flatbed. After we were underway, I asked Chance a question.

"Who's giving away free ice cream?"

A little too quickly, he said, "The science club. According to the flyer, they've mixed alcohol and ice cream in several experiments. They need human testers to prove out theories or some shit. Whatever it is, it's free ice cream and beer, what else matters?"

"Un huh," I said, knowing there was more to the story. Chance had been relatively girl free since the bonfire.

"The psych club might also be involved. They are studying human behaviors. Something like that."

He'd tossed that in. Chance was a math major of all things. I wasn't sure why he was interested in the psychology or science clubs.

We parked and made the short walk between buildings onto the quad. The afternoon was scorching, so it wasn't surprising to see the line near some tables set up near the center.

Sawyer sped up when he spotted all the available women dressed in very little due to the heat.

I spotted Lenny's friend Brie first. A glance over at Chance said he caught wind of her too. Then she took a step to the side, and I saw her. The breath escaped my lungs like I'd taken a hit in the solar plexus.

"Jesus," I said out loud.

"I know," Chance said next to me.

Ashton glanced between us, then shook his head before rushing off to catch up to Sawyer.

"We're fucked," Chance said.

"Yes…yes, we are."

Lenny's legs from her toes led straight up to unnaturally tiny shorts. I wanted to cover her in a sheet so no one could see. Her long hair was pulled up, exposing her neck, and I had to lick my lips.

My stomach flipped over several times as I made a beeline for her, which probably wasn't the brightest move. But logic had fled the building long before I stepped behind her and fought the urge not to press my lips to the nape of her neck. Instead, I touched her shoulder.

She spun around, eyes the size of quarters that shone like they were newly minted.

"Can we talk?"

"Kelley," she said breathlessly.

"That's my name, but I prefer you saying it like that when you're underneath me."

Her fucking perfect cheeks flamed, and damn if my dick didn't swell all proud like.

"Please," I added.

"You aren't going to give up, are you?"

I shook my head. "I think you want me to chase you."

Her mouth parted but snapped back closed. She glanced around before facing me.

"Fine, but make it quick." Then she whispered to her friend, who was already caged in by Chance. I couldn't hear what she said at first, but she added, "I'll be right back."

Brie nodded, trying not very hard to remove Chance's hands from her waist. Lenny stomped off and stopped under one of the trees that had been planted on the quad to provide some shade.

"What do you want to say? And no, I don't want you to chase me."

"Too late for that. Ever since I met you I've been chasing you."

She rolled her eyes, and it was almost cute. "That's not true. You didn't even like me."

"The problem was I liked you too much when you had someone else, and that problem hasn't changed."

Her eyes sparkled for a second like maybe I was breaking through her walls. But then they dulled and narrowed. "I don't have time for this. What you and I had was a crush."

"Was it?"

"Whatever it was, it's over. I am with someone else."

I licked my lips before I bit my tongue. Her annoyance with me was further evidence she was happy with someone else. And she seemed perfectly fine without me. It wasn't a repeat of the past when she didn't want to be with that asshole and I'd been there when she realized it. Still, we had to get something straight.

"Fine, you keep saying I didn't come back," I began. "And you're right. I didn't. But I called you, Len. I called your house several times once I found your house number and had a phone I could borrow."

"What?"

I nodded. "Your parents shut me down every time. Their excuse was you weren't home, you weren't available, until they flat out told me you didn't want to speak with me."

Her jaw dropped, and I continued.

"I even mailed you a letter after we got settled. I thought if you read it, you'd understand why I couldn't come back."

twenty-nine

LENORA

BETRAYED. I FELT IT DEAD CENTER AND WITH SO MUCH pain.

"They never told me you called, and I never got a letter other than the one Trina gave me."

His eyes closed and something like relief was in them when he opened them again.

"When I finally got my truck, I toyed with the idea of coming to see you. So much time had passed. I wasn't sure. Plus, I didn't want to get caught with a warrant on my head."

"Warrant?" I asked, confused.

"Remember the cops came for me? Ox and Debbie, they lied to the police."

Frantically, I shook my head. "I stopped that. Debbie retracted her statement to the cops, and Ox dropped the charges."

"What?"

It was his turn to look dumbfounded. "I went to the police myself and made a statement. You were clear to come back anytime."

He stared at me for the longest second. But we'd stood alone together too long. No doubt my actions would be reported and my punishment for daring to talk to another guy would be swift and painful.

"I didn't know," he stuttered.

"Now you do. But it doesn't matter. It's too late. You've said what you had to say. And I'm going to ask you to leave it alone. Leave me alone, Kelley. I'm not the same girl you remember."

I walked away and prayed he wouldn't say anything more. On the verge of tears, I wanted more than anything that things could be different. But I was trapped like a mouse in a maze. And I couldn't puzzle my way out.

He didn't leave, which made me uncomfortable in ways I didn't want to think about. No longer was he the boy from high school. He'd grown more beautiful in the years we were apart. His frame had filled out with lean and powerful looking muscles.

When I couldn't take watching girls fawn all over him, I made my escape. Brie was lost in her own world as Chance was another target for scantily clad females flocking like ants over a group of very hot guys.

Kelley didn't follow, which was a good thing. There was so much I wanted to share about what happened after he left town. What was the point when I was stuck in my circumstances with no way out? Not yet at least.

With my ear buds in, I sat in the library, transcribing notes for one of my customers. He'd taped the lecture while he slept through it. It was my job to type up the notes for him.

Movement had me glancing up to see Kelley slinking into the chair opposite me. I pulled one of the buds out and gave him my best bored expression.

"You are starting to look desperate."

Where I hoped to strike at his ego, he said, "Maybe I am desperate."

"Desperation doesn't look good on you. Why don't you go sit with those girls over there? They might appreciate your company."

He glanced over at the giggling girls who made no attempt at hiding they were vying for his attention. I rolled my eyes and started to put my earphones back in.

"You left these with me." He slid my sunglasses back over to me. I snagged and tucked them in my bag. "Look, I know you have a boyfriend. But do you think we can at least be friends?"

Was he serious? "Why?"

He sat back and stared at me. I started to squirm under his scrutiny. "I don't know, Len. Maybe because you're the last person alive I ever gave two shits about."

His chair scrapped back, causing more than a few heads to turn in our direction.

"Kelley, wait." I felt like gum under someone's shoe.

"Oh, of course you're here."

We both turned to find Shelly standing at our table. But then something happened I didn't expect. The room suddenly got brighter. Only I saw that Kelley had dialed up the wattage on his smile.

"Shell, I'm glad I ran into you."

He stood up and whispered something in her ear. She smiled like she'd won a Miss America pageant. His hand landed on her back as he guided her from the table without even a goodbye.

Green was so not my color, because envy didn't change that I could never be as free as Shelly. And I couldn't have Kelley even though I wanted him.

thirty

KELLEY

THANK GOD FOR SMALL FAVORS. SHELLY HAD CLASS, SO all I had to do was walk her there and pay her a few compliments before she forgot all about Lenny. A small price to pay so Lenny could have the happiness she had every right to. It made me sick in my gut, but I'd do it because I was pretty sure I was still a goner for her.

When Chance and I walked in the house, we found Sawyer and Ashton sandwiching a redhead.

"My eyes," Chance called out.

"You blind too?" I said in all seriousness while trying to hold back a laugh.

Sawyer's reply should have pissed out his guest. "Caring is sharing. You guys can join in."

"Um…" I pretended to think about it while holding my chin. "No, I'll pass."

Chance brushed by me and headed to the kitchen on the left. "No thanks for me either. I, uh, don't like my sexual experiences buffet style."

Sawyer sighed, while Ashton remained silent. "Let's take this upstairs."

He took the girl's hand, and they were at the foot of the stairs before I caught Ashton roll his eyes before getting to his feet. I glanced away when he started to look in my direction.

"Mark my words," Chance began. "Sawyer will own a sex club before he's twenty-five. That guy…" He shook his head.

"And what about Ashton?"

"Don't underestimate him. He's more Batman, and Sawyer is Robin. I'm telling you."

"And what does that make us?" I asked, more amused by his analogy.

He shrugged. "Mere mortals."

The next day found me in class staring at my grade back for the psychology exam. I needed help. Out of all the classes I had, that one was kicking my ass. So I found myself back in the library.

"He's back," she announced when I sat down. "Though I'm not sure why. Shouldn't you find your girlfriend?"

It was the way she said it that had me smiling on the inside. She was jealous. Calling her out on it wouldn't do me any good. So I used another tactic.

"I need a favor." Her eyes narrowed, so I rushed on to explain. "Your notes didn't exactly help. I failed the test." I pulled out the evidence and slid it across to her. "I can't see how I answered the questions wrong. You did take this class, right?"

She nodded and lifted the paper to look it over.

"Here is your problem. You answered the questions verbatim like you memorized his lecture word for word. You should incorporate the text to show you did read."

She slid her chair over and started to explain. For several seconds her words diminished against the faint scent of wild berries. However, I caught myself and focused on the task. She used my text book to illustrate what I should have done.

After the first example, I'd gotten it. Yet, I let her go through each question just to spend more time with her.

Her phone chimed much later, and the lines etched in her face looked as though she'd gotten seriously bad news.

"I've got to go. I'm late."

As organized as she was, it didn't take even a minute before she was packed and on her feet.

"Can you help me tomorrow?"

She paused. "We both know you've gotten it. You let me go on because you know my weakness for helping people. You're smart enough that you don't need me. But if you really need help, you should ask Brie. Psychology is her thing."

I wasn't calling Brie, and she knew it. The other part of her statement about not needing her was wrong as well, which made me dumb. She had someone and yet, I wanted to chase her until she saw reason.

That night our place was far too quiet except for the noises coming from down the hall. I swore that Sawyer would win gold in the sex Olympics if it were considered a sport. The guy had a girl every night. The only thing I had was a couple of pictures I'd snapped on my phone of Lenny at the ice cream thing on campus. She hadn't known, and I stared at her imagine like some lovesick fool.

Channeling my aggression, I worked out my Lenny issues with the weights that next morning. Thankfully, I didn't have psychology that day, so I didn't have to rush to class.

"Moore," Coach said as I walked by his office. "Come in."

I did and sat where he indicated.

"You're doing really well, son. I appreciate your dedication."

That was new. Coach was easy about showing his displeasure and harder on doling out the compliments.

"Thanks, Coach."

"But don't kill yourself in there on the weights. You got girl problems, find another girl, or do whatever. But don't risk hurting yourself or this team because of chicks."

Shit, was it that obvious.

"Yes, Coach."

There was so not anything else to say. So I headed out when he waved me in the direction of the door, feeling like I was in the middle of the final play of the game with Lenny. I had to either throw a Hail Mary or admit defeat. The next time I saw her I could easily put my heart on the line, or walk away. It was time I made that decision.

thirty-one

LENORA

After leaving Kelley in the library, I practically ran. By the time I got home, I was tired and hungry. As much as I wanted to crawl in my bed and get some early sleep for once, I had responsibilities. I made dinner, which was the least that was expected of me.

A hand clamped around my throat. "What is it with you these days? I feel like you're testing me."

I could barely get air in my lungs, let alone speak. He pulled me back into his chest and worked a hand around my waist to my jeans. Bile rose in my throat. I hadn't realized I was doing it until he said, "Stop shaking your head. It's always no with you. I feel like I need a crowbar to spread your legs."

On instinct, I locked my thighs together. Violently, he shoved me, and I stumbled forward. Too late to stop my momentum, I connected with the wall and went down. As I lay there panting, I thought, and not for the first time, to make a run for the kitchen and a knife. I could kill him. Then again, life in prison didn't seem worth it. So I stayed down, playing possum. Air left my lungs when I heard the front door open and close.

The next day, I wore an infinity scarf around my neck, the first layer tightly against my throat. I needed to rework my schedule so I could get a job. I wasn't sure how much I could take.

When I reached class only to find out it had been cancelled for the day, I thought for sure luck was in my favor. That was until I turned to find Kelley leaning on the wall, staring at me.

I felt like a fish being lured to the bait despite knowing it was a trap. What choice did I have? I asked myself as I strode in his direction. The closer I got, I heard passersby say things like, *Great game, dude, you were awesome. Call me*.

His eyes never strayed from mine as I watched him say things in response.

"This is boarding on creepy," I stated.

"What? Me getting out of class and seeing you?"

I scowled, having no response.

"Fine."

I didn't get two steps away before he said, "Do you want to grab lunch?"

"What, so we can reminisce about the past?"

"Kind of. I have some questions, like do you know what happened to Joel?"

Defiance had already formed roots in my gut. And I'd paid dearly for it. Still, I couldn't help taking back my freedom in small ways. So I found myself following him to the café.

"He and Trina took off after graduation. I've seen a few pictures of them posted online. But other than that, I haven't talked to him."

“I saw that coming.”

“Yeah, they were a thing all the way until graduation and still are if the pictures are to be believed.”

I thought he’d ask about Debbie and Ox. Instead, I was surprised.

“Did you get your prom? The limo, the whole deal?”

I could have told him the truth. I could have outed myself right then.

“Did you?” He shrugged, which only made me realize my mistake. “You know what? I have a free hour. I should probably go to the library and get some work done.”

My escape opportunity came when a gorgeous blonde walked up to Kelley as if I didn’t exist.

“I heard about tonight. I’m so going to be there,” she said to him, totally ignoring me.

The way she touched his arm felt like a brand, and I wanted to slap her hand away. Clearly, as I stayed put like quick set concrete had been poured over my feet, I’d lost my mind.

“Lenny.” I glanced up. I had no idea what he’d said to the blonde. She gave me the once-over and dismissed me as she walked away. He spoke again, and I trained my focus on him. “I get it. I lost my chance with you. You have someone else to make you happy. You’re happy, right?” I nodded because I couldn’t choke out the lie. “We’re having this thing tonight at the house. It’s just a small group of us. You should come. Bring your boyfriend and Brie.”

“Brie?” I asked, like the idea of bringing my boyfriend was even possible. If I even explained whose get-together it was, he would go Mike Tyson on me.

“Yeah, you know. If we could get her and Chance in a room, maybe they can work things out.”

“I never saw you as a matchmaker.”

His broad shoulders rose and fell as he pushed back his hair from his face. "It's easy to see when two people want to be together."

Mismatched eyes so vivid in color stared at me with so much intensity, I swallowed.

"I don't know. Maybe. Anyway, it's the middle of the week. What's the occasion?"

The smile that graced his beautiful mouth was the saddest I'd ever seen. A phone rang in his pocket. He pulled it out and glanced at the screen.

"I finally got one of these." He held up the phone. I caught a flash of a woman's picture. "Sorry, I have to take this. But to answer your question, it's my birthday."

thirty-two

KELLEY

I TOOK THE CALL WHILE HEADING INTO THE CAFÉ. LENNY could have come, but she didn't.

"Hey," I said into the phone.

"Kelley. Happy birthday."

"Thanks, Mom."

I could hear the smile on her face. She got a kick out of me calling her that.

"Do you have plans?"

The plans I wanted with Lenny weren't happening. She was happy, and who was I to break that up? I shouldn't be selfish wanting her for myself if someone else was there for her. Wasn't that what a good guy would do? But was I good?

"Aww, you know, this and that."

"Un huh, like you don't have all the girls in that school in some sort of mating frenzy." She laughed.

I groaned. "Don't say mating. It's weird."

As her laughter subsided, she said, “I taped your game and watched it. You were every bit as good as I knew you were.”

“Thanks.”

“I’m going to get off and come to one. It’s hard, though.”

“I know,” I said. “Don’t worry about it.”

“I feel bad. I used to make all your games.”

“Really, it’s cool.”

“I should probably get back to work, but I wanted to call you. There’s just one thing.” Her pause was a little too long.

“What is it?”

“Your dad.”

He wasn’t a topic of our conversations. Once we’d rid ourselves of him, he wasn’t brought up unless the school reminded me that a parent needed to sign certain forms.”

“What about him?” I asked through clenched teeth.

“I ran into him. He’s in town and has been asking about you.”

Asking implied she’d talked to him more than once.

“Is he bothering you?”

“No.” Another lingering pause suggested that the asshole had gotten to her. He had that charm about him. Had she been duped? I wouldn’t be.

“If you see him again, tell him I’m not interested in anything he has to say. Okay?”

“Kelley?”

“Pam, no.” I regretted saying her name. I didn’t have to see her to know she cringed. “Look, Mom, I’m sorry.”

“It’s okay. Like I said, I should get back to work.”

“I’ll call you later.”

"You better. I have to sing you happy birthday."

"Are you sure about that?"

She laughed, and I knew we were good. "I feel like maybe I should Skype you and sing it for all your friends to hear."

"Now I know you hate me."

"Never that. You have the best day, and I'll talk to you tonight."

Later, after our small get-together turned into a full-blown party, I stopped watching the door when Lenny didn't walk through it.

Standing by the kitchen island pouring drinks, Shelly appeared with a large cake in her hands. People started singing and all that faded away when the door opened and Lenny finally walked in.

My eyes had been trained on her. I hadn't even noticed that the song had ended. I didn't notice Shelly until it was too late.

"Happy birthday, Kelley."

Warm lips met mine as everyone cheered. I pulled back and searched for Lenny. I caught sight of her back as she made a hasty exit.

"Lenny," I said, moving around the counter and to the door.

I caught up to her outside. She spun around, her dress catching the breeze, giving me more view of her gorgeous legs. Her mouth opened as if she started to say something, but closed before she could.

Jumping on the opportunity to explain, I said, "Len—" before she cut me off.

She shook her head and her dark hair spilled around her shoulders. "It was a mistake to come here."

"Why, because you wonder what there could be between us?"

Fuck it. I was tired of being the better guy. I wanted who I wanted.

"Exactly. I do wonder what would have happened if you stayed. But you didn't."

"It wasn't my fault." Fucking Ox had ruined my one chance.

"Does it really matter?"

Our conversation was eclipsed by piercing words not too far from us.

"You're never going to change, given what I saw in there. I'm not like those girls, Chance. All we can ever be is friends. So just stop, okay? I don't want to hate you anymore."

We faced each other, and I saw resignation in her eyes. "She's right. The best we can hope for is friendship."

She must have thought I was fucking around again, and I had to set her straight.

"Len, I can explain about the phone call earlier."

Her hair danced around her face as she shook her head. "You don't have to."

"I do. It was my stepmom. Well, sort of." Pinched brows added to her confused expression. "My dad didn't exactly marry her, but she did become my mom."

As I told Lenny the story, I slipped into the memory.

We'd been staying with Pam for a few months. Dad had steady work, and Pam was easy-going. I'd started school for my senior year, and with football practice, I wasn't home a lot. Things were semi-normal. Only, I knew it wouldn't last.

Summer storms that included some lightning had canceled practice that day. So I'd gone home on the bus.

The small house wasn't much, but it reminded me a lot of our old house in Galveston because Pam had decorated it to feel like a home.

I walked in on an argument. A part of me wanted to turn around and go to the library, but the slur in Dad's voice was all too familiar, and I couldn't leave Pam to face that alone.

"You can take your sorry ass out of here if you think you can talk to me like that."

His fist balled as he growled, "Woman, don't you—"

My bags thumped to the floor as I quickly moved to stand between them.

"Don't," I warned.

I wasn't small anymore. My growth had come quickly and so fast, I didn't have clothes that fit.

Dad huffed. "So what's it going to be, boy? You think you can take me?"

I'd avoided Dad's fist for the most part since we left Texas. So I had no idea if I could. But I held my ground.

"Try me."

He laughed and turned his head to the side. I'd been taken by surprise too many times to know his game. So when the swing happened, it missed me by a mile. I, however, landed a solid punch his chest, sending him backward to fall on his ass.

"You don't know what you've done. You've gotten us both kicked out. And I ain't taking you with me."

"He can stay," Pam said in a rush. I turned to look at her over my shoulder, and she nodded. "You can stay with me, honey."

I faced my father again as he got to his feet and teetered to stay upright.

"He's my son. You can't have him if I call the authorities."

"But you won't," Pam said smoothly.

"And I'll be eighteen soon."

"So get out, James. And don't come back."

Blinking back into focus, Lenny gave me a hesitant smile and something I didn't name swimming in her eyes.

"I'm happy for you. She sounds great."

"She is."

"You deserve that and more." She lifted on her toes and kissed my cheek. "Happy birthday, Kelley."

The kiss ended far too quickly, my face all tingly and shit. I watched her fall back to her feet and cast her eyes away. She began to turn away, but stopped.

"I forgot. I got you this. It's nothing big, especially seeing that fantastic cake. You can throw it in the trash. They didn't have much of as selection. It was this or one with Barney on it. I hope your birthday wish comes true."

"If it were your birthday, what would you wish for?"

Her response was curious and made me wonder if I had hope.

"Freedom." The word bounced in my head. "What about you?" she asked, walking backward as Brie linked her arm through hers.

It was my Hail Mary. "A second chance."

My attention wasn't on the small box she gave me. I watched as her smile disappeared as they hopped in Brie's car and drove off.

Chance stepped over, grief wafting off him. "What did she give you?"

I opened the box to find a perfect cupcake inside. It reminded me of the ones she'd made me for my birthday years ago. The only difference was the candied butterfly stuck in the icing.

thirty-three

LENORA

BRIE APPEARED ON THE VERGE OF TEARS.

"What happened?"

She glanced over at me. "You know, the same old shit, just another day."

"And?"

"Oh, now you're playing therapist?"

"Whatever it takes."

"Fine," she began. "He wants us to get back together. But the past is the past. And I could never be with him knowing I'll always resent what he did."

After she dropped me off, I thought about what she said. Even if I left him, would Kelley and I honestly have a chance? I finished all my chores for the night and thought everything was cool until he caught me in the jaw unawares.

"You are making a habit of coming home late and that's unacceptable. Do you want to tell me where you were, or should I?"

His question was rhetorical as he didn't really want an answer. I stumbled back as hits two and three sent me succumbing to the darkness.

In the middle of the night, I woke up with vomit nearby. My mouth tasted foul, so it had to be my own. I rolled to the side and pushed myself up, hardly able to see. I didn't search for a mirror. I cleaned my mess first, not wanting more pain for being so fucking untidy. Once done, I found the couch and a bag of ice I laid across my eyes, before sleep claimed me again. Morning came with no fanfare or apologizes. I made breakfast with a new pair of sunglass covering my eyes. I slunk to class, wondering who I'd become.

And for that reason, I plunked myself in the library chair with determination. Complicated could describe my situation, but I had no intentions of staying in it forever. I had a plan, but I needed money to leave.

Nodding off from lack of a full night's sleep, I didn't notice his approach.

"Long night."

His voice was unmistakable as I jolted upright in my seat.

"How did you find me here?" I asked.

"It didn't take a genius to figure out you would switch to a different library." We had two on campus.

"What do you want?" I asked wearily.

"I wanted to see you." Before I could stop him, he reached over. "You aren't a diva. You don't need to wear sunglasses inside."

My hand clasped air too late as his shock was evident. The glasses clattered to the table as he dropped them.

His tone was sharp but tempered due to our surroundings. "Who fucking did that to you, Lenny? And don't give me a bullshit excuse about falling down."

I snagged the dark glasses and repositioned them back on my face before others would pay attention to the growling guy in front of me.

"What does it matter to you? I'm no longer your concern."

His hand balled into a fist. "You don't understand, Len. You are my butterfly effect."

My eye hurt when I tried to narrow my other one to slits, wondering what he was talking about.

"You aren't making sense."

"You're wrong about that. The theory behind the butterfly effect is that the flapping wings on the continent of, say, Africa can be the catalyst of a hurricane in Mexico. The bruises on your face are like that. They are the death blow stabbing through my heart. I watched my dad hurt my mom year after year. I tried to be her buffer, but it didn't always work. And now she's dead. There is no way you can expect me to say nothing or do nothing."

"That's exactly what I expect you to do. You have no idea what my life is like. Maybe I wanted this." That was a lie, but I had to do my best to discourage his interference. "Or maybe using your theory, your leaving way back when is my butterfly effect."

His jaw slackened as though I'd slapped him. And I took the opportunity to pack my things quickly. "Don't follow me, Kelley. Just leave it be. I'm not your mother. And God rest her soul, but she died because of a disease, not your father. So don't interfere."

I practically ran out the door, looking over my shoulder. But he didn't follow. With every step, I pretended I wasn't that girl trapped in a bad relationship. Or that he hadn't looked at me like I was smarter than that. Maybe I once was. The cage I'd built was woven in actions too late to change.

Once I knew he wasn't coming after me, I slowed my pace. I had no reason to rush. There were only a few hours in the day that I could call my own. The rest was spent at school or home with responsibilities I'd never asked for, but couldn't take back. I hadn't wanted to be a wife. But I played house every day.

When I made it home early as it was, Dina came out the door. For a second, I wanted to be angry. The girl shouldn't have expected me this early. But maybe she was picking him up.

But then Prescott came out the door and everything changed in a matter of moments.

thirty-four

KELLEY

WHAT HAD LENNY BEEN TRYING TO TELL ME? HOW had my leaving her changed her life? I pulled myself together and followed her. But she'd disappeared like a scared rabbit. Only, I knew where she'd end up. So I drove to her street and parked behind another SUV and waited. The asshole who hit her needed to be taught a lesson.

Almost an hour later, when I was ready to give up my stalker routine, she appeared. Her face was radiant, with a smile worthy of a toothpaste commercial. How could she be so happy? Then I saw her lips move. The closer she got, I saw the tiny hand she held and my heart stopped.

What the fuck?

She was nearly to the front door of her building when a woman around the same age came out. The boy let go of Lenny and ran toward the woman as she knelt down. Lenny stayed back and watched.

I sighed after almost coming to the wrong conclusion. Was Lenny a nanny? I had so many questions until a familiar figure exited the apartment doors.

My reality was blinded by the conclusions I'd drawn. I'd exited my truck long before I realized I was beating a path in their direction.

The boy was still wrapped around his mother several feet away. So I didn't mince my words.

"What the fuck, Lenny?"

Her startled eyes darted between the two of us like she'd seen a ghost.

"Kelley fucking Moore, what are the chances?"

I barely glanced at the guy. Instead, I said to Lenny, "Ox, really, you're with Ox, Odin Prescott?"

"I can explain," she pleaded.

My head spun in disbelief.

"Oh, she can explain." Ox snagged her wrist, and she winced.

I might have sympathized with her if he didn't rub it in my face that she wore a familiar engagement ring as he held her hand for me to see. Disgusted, I stumbled back a few steps, when the boy ran to Ox and called him "Daddy."

Pressing one side of his face to his father's chest, he eyed me wearily with one blue-eyed stare.

I turned, stomping my way back to my truck. Lenny called after me, but my head was full of confusion. Ox had cheated on her. She'd left him and come to my bed. How could she end up with him again? Was the kid hers or the blonde's?

Something was so messed up with that situation, I couldn't see through it. I didn't sleep that night, so when practice came in the morning, I was not on my game. We didn't wear full pads in the morning. It was more of a conditioning practice. Still, I got knocked on my ass by the defensive linemen more than once.

"Moore, what the hell is up with you today?"

I shook my head, more to clear it than in answer to the coach's question. My teammates stared at me as well. But I wasn't about to bare my soul about a girl who had the power to shred my heart.

"Go sit this out. And you have stadium stairs after practice this afternoon to further clear your head."

"Yes, Coach," I said before jogging over to the bench.

I let the shower rain down on me after practice, knowing I would be late for class. Most of the guys were gone when I got out of the tepid water.

"What's going on, Kel?"

Chance had slung his bag over his shoulder, heading for the door.

"Nothing," I said, shaking my head, unsure I could make sense of it.

"You know I got your back and I won't say shit to anyone else."

I nodded. He'd proven himself in the time I'd been at the school. I'd told him things I hadn't told Ashton or Sawyer. Things he could relate to. And he'd never ragged me about it or said anything to the others.

"I know."

"Did you hear from your dad or something?"

"No," I said sadly.

"Is it that girl, Lenora?"

I exhaled heavily. "What do you know about a guy named Odin Prescott? He might also go by Ox."

He shook his head. "Never heard of the guy. Why?"

"He's the shithead Lenny went out with in high school who called the cops on me when I kicked his ass. He's the asshole who forced my father to make us move."

"Oh, shit. He's here."

I nodded. “And she’s with him even though he treated her like crap then. I don’t get it.”

“Women. I’ll never understand them. Maybe you should let her go. She sounds like one of those who like guys who treat them like shit.”

I would have argued, but why? “Yeah, maybe.”

“Well, get your head out of your ass. The big game is this weekend. I hear NFL scouts will be there and they are looking at you.”

Shrugging, I said, “I don’t know why. I haven’t declared anything.”

“Yeah, well, you’ve already made a name for yourself. You could enter the draft and be picked in the first round. Think about it. It could change your life.”

I had thought about it. But Mom wanted me to go to college and get an education. If I gave it up for money and fame, would I dishonor her wishes?

Late in the afternoon, my legs felt like jello after fifty reps of stairs. And I walked as though I were threading cement. Not listening to Chance’s advice, I was determined as fuck to get answers. So I’d headed toward the library at a snail’s pace. Only, I came up short.

Her hair swung side to side from her long ponytail as she hurriedly walked toward home. I was in good shape, but two hours in the hot sun with weight training and running the stairs had left me useless. I watched as she continued to put more distance between us.

Resolute, I found energy enough to finally keep pace. I knew where she was going, so I didn’t run after her to catch up. Only she stopped at a small building just on the other side of the street from the far side of the campus.

While she was inside, I closed the distance and heard noise coming from the back side of the building. Children’s happy chatter filled the air with remembrance of a time long past. As I crept around the side, I saw a walking trail that probably led to the park not too far away. That was a good thing because I didn't want the staff of the daycare center to think I was a potential kidnapper.

That's when I saw her talking to some kids. Did she work there? I'd come too far not to ask her. So I walked toward the chain link fence that separated the kids from the outside world. Several children darted away, but the familiar kid from yesterday spotted me.

"Mommy, who's that man?"

My heart thundered to a stop and not because of the little boy's words. Lenny stood and turned slowly as if she already knew it was me behind her.

"Kelley?"

There were no words to describe my feelings. I clenched my jaw, forcing back what I wanted to say. It was Lenny's kid.

"You need to explain yourself," I said as calmly as possible.

I curled my hand around the metal bar that formed the top of the fence. The bits of metal that twisted the ends of the crisscross design bit into my palm. I didn't care.

"Mason, go play with your friends. I'll be there in a minute."

The kid nodded and ran off. Then she stood straight and looked at me.

"I can explain."

"Good," I barked. "You have two minutes to tell me why that kid has my eyes."

Because there was no doubt in my mind the kid was mine. I hadn't gotten a good view of him with his face buried in Ox's chest the previous day. Then, he hadn't looked like a miniature version of me. Up close he did. But what clenched it was the fact that we shared the same bi-colored eyes.

thirty-five

LENORA

TIME COULD HAVE BEEN MARKED IN TWOS, TENS, FIFteens or hundreds. It didn't matter as time didn't slow enough for me to think. Why hadn't I prepared for this moment?

"You left," I said as my only defense. "I had no way of contacting you."

"Yeah, but you've seen me for weeks and said nothing."

"What did you want me to say? *Hi, Kelley, it's been four years and you look great. By the way, you're a father.*"

"I don't know, Lenny, but pushing me away wasn't the answer. Don't you think I have a right to know? And fuck all to hell, my son calls that asshole Daddy."

His eyes skipped over me in search of Mason.

"I didn't know what to do. He found me on the day I took the test in the bathroom at school so my parents wouldn't find out. It was weeks after you left with no word from you. Once it showed that plus sign, I knew my parents would have kicked me out and there was no way I was getting rid of it."

"Him of all people?"

His condemnation hurt. "I didn't see another choice. He offered to take care of me, of us. And I didn't take him up on it at first. I waited and waited to hear from you." She waved it away, placing a hand at her temple. "But you know how that went. So when I had no choice but to tell my parents because they were going to find out, he claimed he was the father to my parents and his. And things were good. Until after Mason's first birthday and his left eye changed colors. It happened gradually, but became apparent by the time we were here for school. There wasn't any denying that he had one blue and one green eye. Ox changed after that. I hadn't told him who the father was. As much as Debbie told him about us, he chose to believe I'd been date raped, and I let him. So with the truth out, he became mean and then violent over time. And I had nowhere to go. I had to stay for my son."

"Has he ever hurt *my* son?"

I closed my eyes as his frosty words hit me. His worry was over Mason and not over me. And that was a good thing, though it still stung.

"No, not really."

"Not really?" he roared. "He either did or didn't."

"He hasn't, not like what he does to me."

When he focused on me, I almost shrank back due to the venom that stretched his lips into a thin line.

"I want to know my son, Lenny. And I want him to know me."

He had every right, but…

"Kelley, he's just a child."

"And I've lost three years or more with my son. You won't deny me this."

I licked my dry lips. “He’ll kick me out. I have nowhere to go. My parents have washed their hands of me.”

“So, you’ll move in with me.”

The laugh was more of a snort. “And what, live in a dorm? We have an apartment because of that very reason. Children aren’t allowed to live in dorm rooms.”

“I don’t live in a dorm.”

That shocked me, but I hadn’t made any inquiries about him for fear it would get back to Ox.

“And what? Are we supposed to be a happy family all of a sudden?”

“No.” He shook his head. “I’m so angry right now I want to break something. But I’d never lay a hand on you. Still, you are the mother of my son. And it’s my job to take care of you.”

Was that all? I’d seen tenderness in his eyes over the last weeks, but that spark had faded.

“How, Kelley? What job do you have? Last I heard you were the starting quarterback, which means you’re probably on scholarship.”

Determination wasn’t the only thing that had him standing tall. He was a proud man, and I shouldn’t have expected less than what he offered next.

“I have money saved. And I’ll quit the team if I have to.”

“No,” I snapped with a shake of my head. “My life is already ruined. I won’t take you down with me.”

I thought he might balk at my stubbornness, but his next words hurt.

“Fine, you can stay with that asshole. But I will get to know my son. And he will know who his real father is. And if I ever find out he’s hurt my son, I will end him.”

Kelley turned and stalked off. I covered with my hand the choking sob that threatened to wail out like a tornado siren. A few minutes later, Mason came over.

"Mommy, did that man make you cry?"

I bit back the hurt, anger, and frustration and tried to find the smile I used at home.

"No, baby. He didn't. Mommy's just sad."

"Are you sure?"

I nodded.

"Well, let me give you a kiss. You always say it will make me feel better."

Falling to my knees, my son gave me the biggest hug and kiss on the cheek. I had to smile, because he was the reason why I endured. That was the one thing I learned since becoming a mother. I would sacrifice everything of myself to protect my son.

The next few days were calm. I'd hoped that Ox wouldn't be home as he'd left the night before and didn't return for a few days. Instead, I walked in from my time with Mason at the park to find my sometime babysitter on his lap.

"Mason, why don't you go to your room and play while I fix dinner?"

He nodded, but stopped to wave at Dina before he darted off to his room.

Ox might have been my jailer, but he didn't have to throw it in my face. "So for how long?"

The girl tried to answer, but Ox stopped her. "What's the problem? It's not like you put out. You act like I need the Jaws of Life to open those legs of yours."

With my spine stiff, I said, "I don't care where you stick your dick as long as it's not in me."

He pushed the blond girl, who was barely legal, off his lap where her butt hit the floor. He stood to intimidate me like he always did. But I'd been hit enough and was used to the blows.

"Leave," he said to the girl sprawled on our floor.

He barely glanced at her as she said his name. His reply was a thunderous, "Go." She hightailed it out the door as I glanced down the hall, hoping Mason wouldn't come out of his room.

Ox's M.O. had always been to keep the bruises hidden and his punishments quiet. I knew that was for the neighbors. No one would ever say they heard a word. But his violence had slowly increased, and he seemed to care less and less about who saw and heard what.

"I take care of you and the kid. I buy your clothes, feed you, and keep a roof over your head. You owe me respect."

"Respect maybe, but not submission. Not anymore."

"What, you think Kelley's going to save you? He can have you for all I care, but the kid stays with me."

No way in hell. "He's not your son."

We both understood that fact, but I hadn't ever said it out loud.

"I've taken care of that kid since the day he was born. That's a father." He had me there. "Besides, my name is on the birth certificate."

"No, it isn't."

And that was when the first blow knocked me to the floor. Still, I smiled as I told him how I hadn't put his name there out of respect for Kelley. And smiled more when I let him know how I planned to tell my son who his real father was. Where I found the strength to stand up to him after two years of hell, I don't know. Maybe it was because Kelley would take care of Mason if I couldn't.

thirty-six

KELLEY

THE MOOD ON THE BUS WAS SOMBER. EVERYONE HAD earbuds in their ears, or they were asleep. The cheerleaders shared the buses with us, and Shell had her head on my shoulder. I hadn't asked her to sit with me, neither had I asked her to leave.

It was a bad move on my part. She would think somehow we were good. The thing was, as mad as I was with Lenny, I was pretty sure I was still in love with her. Which didn't make sense, but there you had it.

I'd been cold with her after finding out about my son, but it fucking hurt she was with Ox of all people and that asshole was raising my son.

My son.

It was surreal. And my anger had fueled my words toward her. Still mad, I hadn't tried to get in touch with her, but I would. I just needed to wrap my head around everything and figure out my next move.

A tap on my shoulder had me glancing across the aisle.

Chance sat across from me with a different cheerleader next to him.

"It's one game. We have two more left. I'm sure other scouts will show up."

I didn't know what to say to that. My performance was abysmal at best. The scores we got on the board weren't because of me. The balls I'd thrown had been too long, too short, or too high. The ones that were caught were all because of the players stretching themselves to make the play.

Before finding out I was a father, I hadn't cared so much about scouts. I had one more year of eligibility. I could use it and graduate before entering the draft. It was a risk, because if I got hurt that could be the end. But I'd been leaning in that direction. Something about having a family to support changed everything. I couldn't afford to play like shit for the last couple of games and not make a bowl game either.

Chance frowned and pulled out his phone. I lifted my shoulders in the universal sign for what's up. He shrugged back and answered.

"Brie."

He said it as shocked as I felt. There was more than something between them, but based on the other night neither would act on it.

Chance's frown only deepened. "Hold on," he said into the phone before holding it to his chest. "Brie says that something's happened and she thinks Lenora is in trouble."

Unconsciously, I gripped the seat like I planned to destroy it.

"What kind of trouble?"

He relayed that.

"She says she's not sure. She's just worried. She wants you to meet her at Lenora's place."

I didn't want to care, but I'd seen the bruise. As much as I wanted to hate her for being with that asshole, I wouldn't let him hurt her. There was no way I could stand back and watch another female I loved be hurt that way.

Fuck, I was going to kill that asshole if he'd laid a hand on Lenny.

As soon as the bus pulled in front of the school, I made it my mission to be the first one off.

"Kelley, wait up."

I turned to see Chance running after me.

"I have to go. You should ride with Sawyer and Ashton."

"No way, man, something's up and you might need backup."

There was no need to argue. He was right. We got in my truck, and I peeled off like the cops were chasing me. And maybe they would if Ox had hurt my son or Lenny in any way.

Brie hopped out of a tiny car when we parked on the street near Lenny's complex. She hustled over. "I don't know what apartment she lives in. She's so secretive. And she's not answering her phone. I'm worried. I think that asshole is hurting her."

I marched over to the entrance only to find it locked. Just as I was about to beat on it, a person stepped into the hall, heading in our direction. The woman eyed us suspiciously as she pushed through the door, but didn't stop us from going inside.

A crash sounded above, and I hit the stairs at a dead run. From the sounds of pounding feet, Chance and Brie were behind me.

On the second floor, a few bystanders stood in open doorways, staring at one spot down the hall. It didn't take a genius to guess which apartment Lenny lived in.

Purposeful strides in that direction helped keep my anger at bay. I beat the side of my fist on the door at the same time another clatter sounded inside. Imagine my surprise when Mason opened the door.

Brie sucked in air and Chance muttered a curse. They didn't know about our son. Still, I ignored them both and bent down to talk to Mason.

"Hey, little man. Where's your mom?"

Our perfectly matched eyes connected as his finger lifted and pointed toward the back of the apartment.

"My daddy is hurting my mommy."

Tears welled in his eyes and my vision clouded. I ground my teeth together as my own frustrations in the past with my inability to save my mom rushed to the surface. I wouldn't allow Mason to feel so helpless. Lenny would be leaving Ox whether she liked it or not.

"I'm going to save your mommy. Okay?" Mason nodded. "I need you to stay here with Brie and Chance."

I glanced behind me as I pointed to them.

"No way, man. Backup, remember?" Chance stubbornly said.

Focusing on Mason when every muscle in my body was ready to charge ahead, I said as calmly as I could, "Wait with Brie."

My son was smart, and he made a good point. "Mommy said I shouldn't talk to strangers."

The words locked in my throat as I held back the revelation that I wasn't a total stranger, just his absent father, which stung in the worst way.

"Brie is your mommy's friend. And your mom knows me, right?"

His next statement kept me from charging to where the muffled words came from inside the apartment.

"You made Mommy cry."

Our brief talk at the daycare played in my mind. I'd seen the beginning of tears in her eyes, but had been preoccupied with the knowledge that I was a father and no idea what to do with that information. I'd stormed off to process without thinking of anything else.

"I didn't mean to. And I won't ever again."

It was a promise I probably wouldn't be able to keep, but I had to say it. And for Mason's sake, I would do my best to make good on it.

When he nodded, I stood. I glanced at Brie, and she silently gave me the go ahead.

"I'll be back."

The layout of the apartment was simple, with furniture on par with what Sawyer had in our place. Simple, though it didn't feel like a home. Pam's place had worn furniture, but it felt lived in. I sped toward the one hallway and followed it to the place where the voices were heard the loudest. Turning the knob yielded nothing. Lenny's choked sob broke all reason in my head. I wouldn't let this happen again. I would be what my brother had been all those years ago. Unknowingly, I clutched at his dog tags, not knowing for how long I'd done it.

Letting go, I became the man I should have always been. I kicked the door, not caring about the damages. It swung open, but remained on its hinges.

Immediately, I saw clothes spilled out on the floor from an open suitcase. Had Lenny been about to leave?

Ox stood with his fist balled a few feet away from Lenny, whose battered face was a contrast to the straightness of her spine as she faced off her abuser.

I moved like the Man of Steel, faster than a quickly thrown punch.

"If you fucking dare hit her again, you'll go through me." I stared in his eyes, challenging him to say something different.

The asshole had balls. His lips curled in a snarl, and I imagined smoke blew through his nostrils.

"Fucking Kelley, figures. Did the bitch call you? Did she think she could leave with my son after all I've done for her? I fucking own her."

Even though my father hadn't said those words, I could see his face overlaying Ox's.

"You don't own shit. And I think it's pretty clear who Mason's father is."

Ox was about to leap at me, when Chance appeared. I had no idea where he'd been in the room, but he was suddenly by my side.

"I wouldn't," Chance said to me before giving his attention to Ox. "As much as I know my boy can handle you on his own, I'm here to make sure you get that backing off is the better option. Let Lenora go and he won't clean the floor with your head."

Not totally stupid, Ox knew he was outnumbered. "Fuck you. She can go, but this isn't over. I'll sue you for custody, Lenny. I'm the only father Mason has ever known."

I hadn't moved because the fight in me hadn't gone. Chance tried to force me out of the room as Lenny strode by, looking worried about what Ox said. "I'll never let you have him," she said before fleeing to check on Mason.

But I wasn't yet ready for it to be over. "You think you're some kind of man hitting women. How about you try and hit me? I'll guarantee you'll lose."

My balled up hand ached to connect with his jaw and loosen a few of his teeth.

"He's not worth it, man," Chance whispered, still by my side.

"You're right," I said to Chance. Then I turned stony eyes back on the douche. "If you ever hit Lenny or my son from this day forward, I will ensure your parents have to have a closed casket funeral for you."

Giving Ox my back, I made for the door. Chance was in front of me, so when Ox charged and took a swing, it was only my excellent reflexes that saved me. His fist connected with the doorframe. Bone crunched in a satisfying way, but not enough. I launched a throw in response that was guaranteed to ring his bell, only Chance pulled me back. My arching arm missed by a mile as Ox was bent over, staring at his ruined knuckles.

"Let's go," Chance said.

Lenny stood by the open front door with my son's face buried in her neck. She patted his back and managed holding him with the other arm while carrying a bag. Brie stepped in and took the bag from her.

"Don't you come back here," Ox called, feeling the need to have the last word. "Everything in this place, I bought. None of it is yours."

"Have you heard of Target, asshole? She doesn't need your shit," Chance declared. My feet had unwittingly turned back in the direction of the hallway. "Let it go, man. Do it for Mason, Kel."

That was enough to cool the fury that burned beneath the surface of my skin. I ushered Lenny through the door and closed it behind us.

On the way out the building, Brie was rambling on, but I didn't understand a thing. It wasn't over between Ox and me. Not by a long shot. We would settle it like men, just not in front of my son. He'd seen too much violence apparently. I wouldn't have him afraid of me like I'd been afraid of my father. I would be patient. Ox would pay, and unfortunately for him, he would pay additionally for sins not even his own.

When we made it back to the house, I finally got a really good look at Lenny's beautiful face. It was destroyed by puffy purple bruises as if she'd entered a heavy weight boxing match and lost.

I dug my keys back out of my pocket and said to no one in particular, "I'm going to end him." Because I shouldn't have left until he couldn't breathe any longer.

"Wait," came a chorus from in front and behind me.

"Wait for what? Him to kill her?"

Then Brie helped my son out of the car. He curled himself around his mother with twin red-rimmed eyes.

"Kelley, please," Lenny called.

I strode to her, stopping only to brush light fingertips over the few spots on her forehead that were untouched. "Don't worry. I'll take care of it."

"No," she begged. "He'll only call the police, and you'll get in trouble. I need you to watch Mason for me. I have no one else."

My eyes bugged out. "You're not going back, are you?"

"She needs to go to the hospital, you idiot," Brie declared.

"Mommy, why are we here? He's making you cry again."

Lenny kneeled down, which took considerable effort based on the pain frown lines on her face. "He didn't make me cry."

Mason wiped as his mother's tears.

"Did Daddy make you cry?"

I fisted my hand around my keys and struggled not to tear out of there and rip Ox a new asshole.

"There is something I need to tell you."

My breath hitched. The moment had come. I did my best to smooth out my features.

"I've told you before that some daddies aren't the daddies who brought you in the world, but take care of you."

My son nodded. It sounded as though Lenny had been prepping her son for this eventual knowledge.

"Odin is that kind of dad. He wasn't the dad who helped Mommy give you life."

"Who is?"

Her small finger pointed at me. The boy's neck craned back to look at me.

"Is that why he has the same eyes as me?"

She choked out an unintelligible word but nodded.

"You're my dad."

I knelt down to meet him man to man. "Yes, I'm your dad." And I didn't need a blood test to confirm that. He looked like my brother and me as kids.

"What's going on here?" I glanced up to see Shell. "Oh my God, your face," she said, pointing out the obvious with her finger in Lenny's direction. Then Shell turned glacial eyes at me. "You didn't, did you? I will so have your ass. You know I'm from around here. What you didn't know was that my brother is a cop and my dad is a lawyer."

"It wasn't him," Lenny choked out. Her voice sounded like walking over gravel.

"What are you doing, Shell? Why are you here?"

She held up a finger before she punched in some numbers on her phone. "Greg, get your ass over here, now!"

"Language," Brie admonished.

Chance had made it over to Brie's side, wrapping an arm around her shoulder.

"First, I'm here because you left your hoodie on the bus." Shell tossed it at me as Lenny's eyes found mine, and I shouldn't have felt guilty. "Second, my brother's coming over so he can arrest whatever asshole did this."

In less than fifteen minutes, the cops and the rest of my roommates stood with us as Lenny gave a statement to Shell's brother.

"I wanted first crack at him, Shell," I whispered a few feet away.

"I know you did. I saw your eyes. You would have done something stupid to mess up the case. If you fought, he could claim his bruised knuckles happened in the fight with you. That asshole needs to go down. So calm yourself."

Everything she said made sense, and I respected Shelly more in that moment than I ever had.

"So," she began. "That's your son."

I nodded.

"Well, at least I didn't lose you to just any girl. A baby momma is a respectable person to lose to."

"Shell—"

"You don't have to explain. I see how you look at her. I want that one day. Now go be there with her."

The cops were walking away. Shell's brother, Greg, was just saying something final to Lenny. Shell left me in favor of Ashton and Sawyer, who were tossing a ball to Mason. I moved toward Lenny.

"Take her to the hospital, Brie," Greg said as I walked up.

Brie nodded.

Chance said, "I'll go with you."

"Me too," I declared.

Lenny's eyes shot over at me. "Please stay with Mason." I glanced over at my friends. "I know they are having fun, but I don't know them. And I trust you."

The fact that she trusted me was a win. But somehow I nodded, still feeling helpless. I couldn't kick Ox's ass, and I couldn't be there for Lenny. I would be there for my son. The resilient little boy didn't seem fazed that his whole world had changed. He was more interested in playing ball. What did that say about Ox as a father?

"I could bring him with me," I offered.

She shook her head. "He's seen enough. He needs to get ready for bed soon." The sun that had been low in the sky when we arrived was long gone. "I managed to pack him a bag while Ox was in the bathroom before I headed out. Everything he needs is here."

The bag she held seemed so small. What did kids need? Was he potty-trained? Did he need a special diet? But she trusted me, and I needed her not to worry. So I didn't ask. I figured Mason might be able to answer some of my questions. If not, I would call my stepmom. Maybe she could help.

"Don't worry, he'll be fine," Shell said, coming up behind me.

thirty-seven

LENORA

THE JEALOUSY I EXPECTED DIDN'T COME. I WAS TOO sore and tired to worry about Shelly playing house with Kelley. Mason would be safe, I chanted in my head as Brie drove to the hospital.

"That asshole better hope he stays in jail overnight. Otherwise, I'm going with Kelley to show him what it feels like to be helpless," Chance said.

"You're not helping," Brie complained.

"I am. He's not going to stop until he gets his ears, nose, and throat test."

Even I was baffled by his statement, but Brie asked the question before I did. "I'm almost afraid to ask, but what test are you talking about?"

"You know, the test they'll run on him after Kelley uses his fist to give the guy a nose job that will most likely send his front teeth into the back of his throat and cause his ears to ring. They'll need to test to make sure everything is still functional after that."

I almost laughed, but my face hurt too much. Lucky for me, my time at the hospital was limited to only a couple of hours. They had to run tests to see if I had a concussion, along with X-rays. The humiliation came when Greg showed up with a forensic photographer from the county to catalog my injuries. Another round of questions and after I'd given my official statement, I was sent home with the knowledge that Ox was in custody.

I didn't go back to the apartment. Brie dropped me off at Kelley's. They'd called ahead, and I learned Mason was asleep. But I needed to see him more than going back to the hell hole and getting a change of clothes for myself.

One of Kelley's roommates let me in.

"Lenny, your son is funny as hell."

"Thanks, Ashton." I thought that was his name.

"I hope you're staying the night. I promised the little man we would finish our game in the morning."

"Yeah, okay."

I didn't want to brush him off, but I needed to go see my son was safe.

"He's in Kelley's room," Ashton called out. "It's the first door on the right down that way."

He pointed upstairs. I let out a sigh of relief when I entered Kelley's room and saw Mason curled on the bed fast asleep. I leaned down and listened to his soft breath before kissing his forehead. Then I left the room in search of Kelley.

"Are you looking for him?"

I turned and saw Chance hadn't gone with Brie. I'd left them in the car when we arrived. I nodded.

"He's in the shower," he added with a smirk on his face.

There was a challenge in his eye, and I took it. I followed the sound of running water to a closed door. I held the knob a second before I talked myself into turning it. And lucky me, it opened.

Steam filled the room as I watched Kelley's shadow behind the opaque curtain. He didn't move from his position under the spray and hadn't seemed to notice I'd come in. I shouldn't have peeked, but I did only to be disappointed when I found him standing fully dressed under the water.

"Kelley," I gasped.

He turned eyes cloaked in shadows on me. Then his arm snaked out, and I was yanked into the shower. Before I could process what was happening, he turned us so that water rained down on me.

"What are you doing?" I asked.

Kelley didn't speak. He fisted his hand in my soggy clothing and pulled me closer. He leaned in and nuzzled at my neck.

"I need you, Len," he growled.

I needed him too. So I nodded. Then we were helping each other out of our wet clothes. They plopped down on the tiles in a dripping mess. But none of that mattered. He pressed gentle kisses on my eyes and nose and brushed his lips over mine. He whispered, "Were you safe with him?"

He wasn't talking about safety, but rather protection of the small square foil kind. But the last thing I wanted to do was think about what sex was like with Ox. Still, I answered, "Always."

"Good, because I don't have a condom, and I can't wait."

Gingerly he lifted me up and his mouth was on my bare breast, sucking as my body hummed with lust and burned with fire.

"What about you?" I managed before he tested my wetness with his finger.

"Always, except with you."

My back pressed into the cool tiles, which didn't bother me in the least. He slid me further up until I felt the tip of him at my entrance. "Now," I begged.

Too slowly, I rode the happy trail down his length. It seemed to take forever as he stretched me in ways I hadn't been stretched since we were last together.

"God, Lenny, you're so fucking tight."

The better to grip you with my dear, the inappropriate change of the nursery rhyme made me giggle out loud when there was nothing funny. I was drunk on joy because the moment was everything I'd hoped it to be with Kelley.

His eyes laser focused on mine made me feel special in a way I'd never felt before. My stomach dropped and flipped over a few times in excitement. I'd never thought I'd be with him again. It felt like coming home.

"If you're laughing, I'm not doing something right."

I bit his ear, making him laugh. "See, some things are funny. But believe me, I'm so fucking glad to be here with you."

Then he moved and all talk disappeared. Each movement hit every magic button inside me. He rolled his hips, keeping my happy clit even happier.

"I'm close," I called out automatically and bit my lip, not wanting to think of Ox and his requirements.

Kelley didn't know or didn't care. He sped up and his thrusts became more frantic until we were both moaning and groaning out our pleasure.

After catching our breaths, he pulled back. "I hope you're on the pill, otherwise I'm sure I got you pregnant."

Somehow we made it back to Kelley's room. I fell asleep with Mason curled in the middle of the bed and us on either side of him, our fingers twinned together. When I woke, the clock read it was too early to be up, and I was alone.

Making my way downstairs, voices grew clearer the closer I got.

"You know how to make breakfast?" Mason asked.

"Yes, we men need to know how to cook for ourselves," Kelley answered.

"My…"

"It's okay for you to call him Dad," Kelley said.

"He hurt Mommy a lot. I'm glad he's not my dad. What's his name?"

"Odin."

"That's a funny name."

I didn't yet see Kelley as I paused on the stairs, but I could imagine him shrugging.

"He never cooked. Mommy always did."

"Your mom is sleeping. So if you want breakfast, I guess I'll have to do."

"Okay, Dad."

And just like that, my tough three-year-old accepted his new father as easily as changing a channel on the TV. And I guessed some kids were like that. I was sure he would pepper Kelley with a million questions. And part of me wanted to sit on the stairs and listen to it all. Instead, I turned back, not wanting to interfere with their bonding moment. On the way back up, I lamented on the fact that Mason had seen Ox hurt me. Unfortunately, I couldn't take that back. I could only hope in the years to come, Mason's young mind would forget those awful moments. However, the best thing about this whole ordeal was how easily Kelley had taken on the role of father.

Midmorning, Kelley entered the room. "Hey."

"Where's Mason?" I asked automatically.

He held up a hand. "Slow down, Mom. I just left him outside with Sawyer and Ashton. They're tossing a ball around, trying to teach him to catch. I thought it might be a good time for us to talk."

The talk. His seriousness freaked me out.

"You're not going back to live in that apartment."

It wasn't a question. Still, I balked. "We can't stay here."

"Why not?"

"We can't. What, are we all going to sleep here on your bed every night? Do you know how long it took me to get Mason to sleep on his own?" I shook my head. "Besides, we're not together."

I'd said it, hoping he would contradict me. It was a passive move on my part, but my nerves were frayed.

"We aren't together, yet. But he's my son. You're both my responsibility."

I bit my lip to stop it from trembling. I'd wanted last night to mean something. And apparently it only had for me. But I took a deep breath and tried a different tact.

"I'm not your responsibility."

"Fine, you go and Mason can stay with me."

My jaw dropped. "No way!"

He wasn't taking my son away from me, which was part of the reason I hadn't told him right away. It might have been selfish, but I wanted to know my rights and Kelley's as well.

"Then stop playing games. You have to know by now how I feel about you. But I'm still so fucking mad. I need time. But I also need you both safe. I have some money saved up. I can probably pay a couple of months' rent somewhere for the both of you until I can get a job."

"Job, you can't get a job if you're on a sports scholarship." That much I knew.

"I know. I also know I'm a dad now. I won't be like my father and let you support our kid. I will do my part."

We were at an impasse, because there was no way I would let Kelley give up his future for us.

thirty-eight

KELLEY

BEING INSIDE HER AGAIN HAD BEEN A MISTAKE. SHE HAD my head so twisted up in knots, I didn't know north from south. As much as I wanted to claim her, I had to do right by my son first. I wouldn't repeat the mistake of our parents.

Mom had loved Dad fiercely. And I think he may have loved her once too. But my brother and I had come along and tied them together forever in a binding he eventually resented. I couldn't jump into something with Lenny too fast until I got my shit right.

The townhouse we lived in had been built in recent years with students in mind. The upstairs held four bedrooms and one bath. There was also a full bathroom downstairs. It was rarely used. Still, Lenny was right. There wasn't enough room for Mason to have his own space.

I'd left Lenny in my room to put Mason down for a nap. Sawyer came into the main living area, and I signaled for him to give me a minute.

"What's up?"

His dad had gotten the place and worked out the details for all of us to pay rent. It wasn't a problem for Ashton because his family had money too. But for Chance and I, who were on scholarship, our rent came through the school. Living off campus had to be approved by the powers that be at the university.

"Do you know what's required to get an apartment?"

Sawyer narrowed his eyes at me. "Are you leaving so soon?"

I shrugged. "I need to find a place for Lenny and Mason."

His head tipped up in understanding. "She and the kid can stay here."

He'd said it so casually, like it wasn't a problem in the slightest. As much as I appreciated the offer, I explained about Lenny's stubbornness. "Fine, we'll empty the office, putting everything in the garage, and they can stay there."

There was a room off the back that currently held two desks and chairs. I wasn't sure how often it was used. So it could work. But he really needed to think about this first.

"That would mean no more late night parties." He shrugged. Again, I could have hugged him for how cool he was being. For all his no care attitude, he had more of a heart than he let on. "You would do that?"

"I won't be able to use the garage, but it's cool. The kid is fun, and we know that asshole will get out of jail eventually. She's safer here."

When Lenny came downstairs, Sawyer proudly announced, "You're moving in."

"I can't," she argued.

"Ah, but you can. And here's why."

He laid it out for her about safety in numbers. In the end, she said, "Thank you. And it will only be temporary. I'll find a job and a place of my own."

"Sure," he said and winked at me. "Now, go get your shit before that asshole makes bail. Ashton and I will clean out the room before you get back."

Brie came over to watch Mason while I drove Lenny back to her place. When we pulled up, she put her hand on mine.

"Your friends are—"

"Great."

She nodded. "If we stay that means you don't have to give up your scholarship."

We were back on that subject.

"For now." I had plans, though, a lot of them.

"Kelley, promise me. Otherwise, I'll go back home to my parents before I let you give up your dreams for us."

"They're my dreams. And maybe I never thought I'd be a father. But I am. And I've never felt more inspired to do the right thing until now."

I got out of the truck and helped her out as she sat looking at the door to the apartment house.

"What if he's here?"

"Then I'll have an excuse to kick his ass if he touches you."

She nodded, and I put my hand at the small of her back. She was so tiny in that moment as she slowly made her way to the door. I wanted to kiss her, but it was too soon. I'd let things go too far last night because our emotions were raw. And it had been as good as it was the first time. It hadn't been my imagination. She'd been the only girl I'd wanted more from after the deed. And that still held true.

Inside, the place was nicer than it looked from the outside. I hadn't paid attention the first time. And I was treated to the knowledge that Ox could take care of my family better than me. A while later, she turned in my direction.

"Do you ever talk to your dad?" she asked, making conversation.

I paused from stuffing Mason's clothes in a suitcase.

"Nope. I haven't seen him since he left Pam years ago."

"What is she like?"

I let the air out of my lungs and felt a smile form.

"She's great. Almost as great as my mom. She was there for all my games. She worked nights, but made me breakfast every morning. She encouraged me when I wanted to give up. I stopped wondering when the next hit would come or when we would move. I was *safe*."

The word nearly choked me up. I hadn't thought about how much she changed my life.

Once I started, I couldn't seem to stop. "She was like my mother, hardworking and strong. Her only rule for me was to stay out of trouble. She forged Dad's signature on things so I could stay in school and graduate. She was my lifesaver, and I owe her everything."

"She sounds amazing."

"She is. And I should call her and tell her about Mason. She'll probably drive here so she can meet him."

"She should. I can't wait to meet her myself."

I had questions too, but I didn't exactly want to know how Ox had been a father to my son the last couple of years. He'd probably been there when he was born. They probably had pictures. I felt the anger stirring inside me. I wasn't mad at Lenny or even Ox. I was mad at myself. If I hadn't lost my temper that day, Dad might not have moved us out of the state. Though even I knew better than that. Dad would have gotten kicked out of that woman's house. But maybe not before I found out I was going to be a father. Then I could have found a way to stay.

"What's wrong?" Lenny asked.

I met her eyes. "I just wish I had known."

Silently, she came over and took my hands in hers. "It wasn't your fault. It was my parents and Ox and Debbie. If any of them had done something different, you might have known sooner."

She rolled to her tiptoes and brushed her lips against mine. I wanted to kiss her back, but I wanted out of that place sooner.

"We should hurry," I said, pulling back.

I watched disappointment cover her face. She didn't know it, but she wasn't ready for a relationship. How could she be?

"And, Lenny?"

"Yes," she said, her lashes fluttering in anticipation.

"We can't start anything. I won't be your…" I snapped my fingers as if that would conjure the word I was thinking of. "Rebound. Yeah, that's what you girls call it. I won't be your rebound guy. I'm here for you. But we can't be together. Not yet."

She nodded before turning and giving me her back. As we worked to pack up all her things, I thought I heard her crying. But every time I saw her face, her eyes were dry. She claimed they didn't have much, but we made over a dozen trips between the apartment and the truck to bring everything out.

It took the rest of the afternoon and evening to get them settled in. We ended up driving into one of the bigger small towns to a Walmart to get a futon and a toddler's bed for them to sleep on. Thank goodness for my truck.

When they were settled, I was more at peace for the first time in what felt like years.

It wouldn't be until the middle of the following week before the guys came to get me from my room to tell me it was time.

The gleam in their eyes said they were just as pleased as I was for what we were about to do. I knocked on the downstairs room that had become Lenny's.

She opened the door dressed for bed. Her legs looked appetizing in her sleep shorts. Even though her breasts were hidden beneath her shirt, they were firmly in my memory. I swallowed.

"We're going out for a while. You'll have the house to yourself," I said, trying to get my thoughts back on track.

"Where are you going?"

"We're not together, Len. I don't answer to you about my comings and goings. Neither do you. This is just courtesy so you're not alarmed if you went looking for one of us and found that no one was here."

She bit her lip, and I swear my dick jumped in my pants. I wanted so badly to kiss her, but we needed more time apart. I had to focus on getting to know my son and making sure he was safe before I would start anything with his mother. I didn't want him to see us together and then apart if it didn't work out.

"Keep the doors locked."

She nodded, and it took a herculean effort not to toss her over my shoulder and fuck the shit out of her. My dick wasn't happy, but my conscious was clear. I had something to do tonight. And it would take God himself to stop me from what I was about to do.

thirty-nine

LENORA

MASON WAS ASLEEP ON THE TINY BED THAT WAS STILL too big for him. I cradled my phone to my ear, wondering when it would be cut off considering it was in Ox's name.

"So what are you going to do?" Brie asked.

Brie had wanted in for so long and when she proved herself by coming to me in my time of need, I finally gave in. Not every girl out there was Debbie. And Brie was trustworthy. She hadn't told anyone about my son. It wasn't a total secret as it wasn't anyone's business.

"He hasn't touched me since..." I blathered the whole story to her in tears. It was a good thing Mason slept like the dead. He hadn't stirred through all my sobbing.

"Do you want him back?"

"Of course I do. But he made it clear there was nothing between us."

Brie huffed into the phone. "Do I need to come over there? That guy has it bad for you. Maybe he just wants to take things slow."

"I've waited four years. I don't want slow."

"Then you know what you need to do," she said.

We ended the call, and I got dressed, or rather undressed. I had to leave some clothes on in case I ran into the guys, but I would make it easy for Kelley to get to my important parts effortlessly.

After finding and setting up the baby monitor, I was halfway to the stairs when my phone rang. It was late, so I figured the only person calling me would be Brie.

"Don't worry, I'm on my way to his room right now."

"Whose room?"

The deep voice shocked me stupid for a second. It took a few seconds to register who was on the phone.

"Mr. Prescott?"

"Yes, Lenora."

I veered from the stairs and sank deep into the couch. Humiliation flamed in my cheeks.

"I'm calling on behalf of my son."

"Figures," I said out loud and covered my mouth when I realized I'd done that.

"I'm sure you can imagine how heartsick my wife and I are. We are very sorry about what our son did."

"So you believe he did it."

"The detectives showed us your picture. We are hoping you would drop the charges since part of this is your fault."

"My fault?" I practically yelled and then glanced down at the baby monitor. Mason's gentle breathing didn't change tempo. "You've got to be kidding me."

"He was upset about finding out Mason isn't his."

I sat there slack-jawed for a second. "He's always known that."

"Then why did he allow you to put his name on the birth certificate?"

"His name isn't on it if any of you had bothered to ask. And besides, he knows damn well he wasn't the father considering we hadn't had sex when I got pregnant."

Okay, so I made myself out to sound like a whore, but I didn't care.

"So my son helped you out. That's got to count for something. Do you even know who the father is?"

Of course he would go there. He should have put his wife on the phone. She wouldn't have said something so blatantly stupid to someone who was holding most of the cards.

"You know what? Your son is a liar, but that doesn't make me a slut. You want to know the truth? The truth is I caught your son having sex with my best friend on my birthday. If not for that, I might not have taken that next step with someone else. And Kelley was my first and only until your son offered to help me out with my problem."

"Is that the guy you're staying with?"

"That's none of your business," I spat. "If you're here that means your son is out. And I have to worry about my safety because even if you don't want to believe, this isn't the first time he's hit me. But I'm damn sure it's just the last. I'm tired of paying for his help by enduring his wrath."

"I can assure you he won't harm you."

"How can you? He's done it for two years."

"Lenora, I'm begging you to drop the charges. We are willing to compensate you. And my wife is bereft at the thought of never seeing Mason again. Even if he's not our blood, we love him as if he were our grandchild."

I closed my eyes. They hadn't ever been horrible to me. In fact, they worshiped the ground Mason walked on. "I have to think about it."

"That's all we can ask. And for what it's worth, we're sorry this happened."

He hung up, and I sat on the sofa curled into myself. The tank top and shorts I wore didn't help the sudden chill I felt.

When my phone rang again, I jumped. "Hello."

"Lenora Wells?"

"Yes, this is her."

"Hi, this is Greg, Shelly's brother."

"Oh, yes."

"I wanted to let you know that Odin Prescott has been released." That wasn't news thanks to the call from his father. "You should know that a condition of his release was that he shouldn't get within fifty feet of you, on purpose that is. He does attend the same school. But if he sees you, he should go the other direction. If you feel threaten by him, give the station a call, and he will be picked up."

Not having anyone else who may know how to advise me, I said, "His father called me actually a few minutes ago."

"He did? I imagine they want to settle this out of court."

"Yes, they want me to drop the charges."

"I can't tell you what to do, but I can say that my experience with domestic violence is that the person doesn't change, not without consequences."

"They offered me a settlement."

"I'm not a lawyer like my father. But I can tell you that you don't have to drop the charges in order to sue them in civil court. It won't be easy, but you have options. I'll get Shell to talk to you. She's the future lawyer in the family. And who knows, my dad has a soft spot. He might be willing to take you on as a client pro bono. But you have to talk to him."

"Thanks," I said before we hung up.

It was strange that a girl I thought was my rival might turn out to be the helping hand I needed.

When my phone rang for a third time, I muttered, "You've got to be kidding me," to the air.

I read the display and put the phone to my ear. "Mom."

"Lenora, we heard."

Ox's parents must have called them because I hadn't. I didn't hate my parents, I just didn't respect them. Everything they'd done indirectly had screwed my life.

When I didn't respond she said, "You have to know your father and I are sick over this. But maybe you should consider the Prescotts' offer. Think of your son."

"Or maybe you and Dad are thinking of yourselves. If not for you guys pressuring me to date him, none of this would have ever happened. Even though I would do it all over again to have Mason."

"You have to know both your father and I love you."

"I know, but your love has ruined my life."

"Lenora."

"I need you to tell me the truth."

"Okay."

"Did a guy other than Ox call the house for me over the past years?" She said nothing and the silence was my answer. "Did he send me a letter you never gave me?"

"You have to understand. Your father was understandably upset when he found out you were pregnant."

"I haven't forgotten. I had to live with the Prescotts until Dad let me come home. That's something I won't ever forget."

She sighed. "Your father was only mollified that your trouble came from a respectable boy in the community."

I rolled my eyes, wishing she could see I wasn't buying the bullshit.

"The way the boy begged to talk to you, I guessed he was most likely the father. He was the boy you'd been tutoring, the one who drove you home after you spent the night away." She paused, waiting for an answer, but I gave her none. "It was easy to put it together that he'd been the father. Your dad not understanding how a woman's body worked didn't put it together. But I did. The math worked. Plus, even if Odin had taken responsibility, I knew you barely tolerated him. But he had money and could give you a good life. That other boy, hell, he even called collect a few times. He couldn't offer you anything. I couldn't let him destroy your life."

"And boy what a good life I had, Mother. I want you to send me the letter."

"I don't know—"

"Find it. I have to go."

"Lenor—"

But I hung up. She may have meant well, but that didn't mean it was right. I tried not to be angry, but I certainly didn't feel the least bit sexy anymore. Instead, I felt drained of every drop of good will and humor. I felt like an M&M with no chocolate, naked and hollow and alone.

forty

KELLEY

Chance eyed me as we stood in a dimly lit room. He and I were the only ones not dressed in dark cloaks. The hooded figures stood in a semi-circle around a chair. It felt like the start to a good movie, but fuck if it wasn't real.

Cloaked in shadow, one of the hooded figures spoke like he was Dark Vader come to life.

"Odin Prescott, you have failed us. You have broken one of our sacred vows."

When the guy didn't elaborate, I gave Chance a what the hell is this all about look. He shrugged.

"And for this reason, you shall be punished."

Someone stepped forward to where Ox was bound to a chair with a sack over his face. As I hadn't pledged any fraternities, I didn't quite understand why he would willingly submit to being almost hog tied. A hand snaked out of the robe and quickly yanked the covering from Ox's face, leaving him to blink and let his eyes adjust from darkness to the little light we had.

"What the fuck? Why is he here?" Ox ranted.

"I'm your punishment," I said darkly, getting into the spirit of the atmosphere. "Untie him."

There would be no satisfaction in beating his ass if he couldn't try and defend himself. When no one moved, I glared at the hooded guy who had taken the sack from Ox's head. Someone else nodded dramatically, and the guy got to work with his bindings.

Free, Ox rubbed his wrists and got to his feet. With a humorless laugh, he asked, "What? Are you pissed I've been fucking your little slut for the past four years?"

I uncurled my arms from across my chest and took two steps away from Chance. It was time. And as much as I liked to keep my business personal, I needed to bait him.

"Funny, she felt practically virginal when I was with her the other night."

That did it. Ox lunged at me. I didn't move, needing him to strike me first. If the asshole tried to claim I assaulted him, I would have witnesses who said I only defended myself. I dodged some, not wanting to take a direct hit to my face. His fists connected with my shoulder and the blow rattled through my bones. I knew it wouldn't be easy to take him down. He wasn't a small guy.

Big and clumsy, he left himself open to a gut shot that knocked the air from his lungs. He stumbled back but didn't go down.

"Is that all you've got, pretty boy? I'll mess up your face and then your shoulder. And we'll see who Lenny comes to cry when you're no longer the starting quarterback."

"She won't have time for crying. Her mouth would be otherwise occupied."

Again, I hated to say that out loud, but I got the desired results. Ox barreled forward like the unskilled fighter he was. He used his brute strength and overall size to bully people. But he was only a little wider than I was. And I knew how to fight.

I went for another body shot and lifted my elbow in the same motion to clock him under the chin. Blood flew as he no doubt bit his tongue. There was no time to step back and enjoy. I had to finish it. Ox didn't give up. He got in a few blows to my side that would hurt like hell in the morning.

"I'm going to kill you," he said, sending bloody spittle everywhere. "And then I'm going to have her begging to swallow my dick to take her back."

Speaking of dick, he was busy missing his blows to my face, so I got a knee to his balls.

"Don't think about her. Don't talk to her. Don't fucking dream about her. Or I'll make you a fucking eunuch. Then all you have to do is shave your head and you can be cast as Varys' stunt double on *Game of Thrones*."

He made a loud indiscernible sound. It didn't matter. I was done. It was time to stop toying with him and end it. With my left hand, I throat punched him, which caused him to stumble back and try to catch his breath. Then with my right, I caught him squarely in the nose with an arm rattling blow. He went down, lights out for him.

We all waited a second in silence as we watched for the rise and fall of his chest. When he did, one of the hooded guys nodded at me. I turned on my heels and left with Chance in tow. We ascended stairs we weren't supposed to know about. Sawyer and Ashton had got us in with their fraternity. A group based on how many zeros your family had in their bank account. And it showed because sublevel rooms just didn't exist very much in these parts. But apparently, some wealthy alumni had it built long before our time. Our lips were sealed, never to speak of what we knew. I'd eagerly agreed for the opportunity to make my mission clear to the asshole.

Chance prattled on about the fight on the short drive home. I was ready to see that Lenny was safe. Ox wasn't a threat, but my protective instincts were on high alert. And growing up the way I did, I understood that Ox wasn't the only threat in the world.

What I didn't expect was to find Lenny curled in a ball on the corner of the sofa. She had her arms wrapped around her legs with her phone next to her and what I learned later was a baby monitor curled in her hand.

"Damn, man, I'm not creeping on your girl or anything. But she looks cute as shit like that," Chance whispered. "And she snores."

She did, so I nodded. "Don't laugh. I like her snoring. It's soft and at least I know she's breathing. And you don't have to be so quiet. She sleeps like the dead."

And she didn't stir, but I bet money if Mason cried out for her, she'd be on her feet in a nanosecond.

"You should get that straight between you and her." I glanced over at the guy who was fast becoming my closest friend. "Hey, I'm just saying. You don't always get a second chance."

Either he didn't realize he'd said his name or he was in his own head.

"What happened between you and Brie?"

He sighed heavily. "There isn't enough time to explain it all now. Let's just say, when you leave your house for the first time in your life and have freedom—I mean the real kind—and pussy is everywhere in all shapes and sizes, I wanted to have a taste of it all before settling on the one. And when I realized who the one was, it was too late. Now get your girl. You don't want Sawyer to see her like that." He laughed and left me alone.

Sawyer was a huge flirt and spent too much time trying to help Lenny settle in. Sawyer wouldn't cross the line, but

Chance was right. What if Lenny saw she had way better options than me? Should I let her find out?

She was so light in my arms when I scooped her up. I couldn't believe Ox thought he was a man hitting her. It boiled in my gut and reminded me of my dad. A part of me had wanted that fight to go on forever as I rained down my fury from pent-up aggression from all the years my father had beaten Mom and me. Somehow, I managed to keep my head, but little did he know how close I'd been to snapping his neck.

"Kelley?" Lenny stirred in my arms.

"Yeah."

"Where are you taking me?"

"To your room. You need your rest."

She wiggled in my hold. "No, take me to your room."

"Lenny," I began.

"I have the baby monitor."

I made the mistake of looking into her eyes, and they were red and puffy. Damn if seeing her like that didn't make me feel like I'd been run over by a freight train.

"Please," she begged again.

There was no denying her looking so lost. I changed course and headed upstairs. Gently, I stretched her across my bed and freed the baby monitor from her clutches. I listened to the breathing through the monitor before I rested it on the nightstand and stared down at her.

"Now what?" I asked at a loss. "Who made you cry?"

Frantically, she shook her head, and she closed her eyes tight as if she were holding back more tears. I fisted my hand at my side, daring not to touch her.

"You have to tell me what happened if you want me to fix it."

Tear-streaked eyes met mine. “You can’t fix it unless you’re ready to fix us.”

“Len, you need time. You just got out of a bad relationship. Don’t you want to have some time on your own?”

Her head moved slowly side to side. “But if you don’t want me, just give me one more night. I don’t want to think, Kelley. There’s too much to think about. I just want to feel.”

She rose to her knees and crossed her arms over her belly as she tucked her small hands under the hem and lifted her tank top before I could protest. Her gorgeous tits bounced slightly as her hands fell to her sides. She stared expectantly at me.

“I’m not a saint, Len.” My dick wanted out from behind my fly. It pulsed as every thought I had headed south for the foreseeable future. “If this is what you want...” She nodded. “Lean back and take your panties off.” She did as I commanded. “Spread your legs, baby, because I’m going to eat you alive.”

forty-one

LENORA

As I complied, he tugged off his own shirt and thumbed open the button on his jeans. Anticipation made me squirm as thoughts of him inside me made me wet.

He said nothing as his eyes skimmed over me. I closed mine, afraid he might see something lacking, and I didn't want to know if he did.

"Open your eyes and watch me."

I opened them in haste as the bed dipped under his weight. He lifted my legs as he positioned himself between them.

I nearly came as soon as his tongue made contact. Reaching over my head, I closed my hands around the sides of the mattress. His little flicks and quick sucks weren't everything I needed. I must have made a sound of protest because he chuckled darkly.

"You want more."

"Yes," I complained and arched my back, wanting his mouth on me again.

Done with tormenting me, he slipped a finger inside along with his tongue. His thrusts drove me wild, and I bucked underneath him. When he moved to suck my clit, I was pushed over the edge with the addition of another finger for perfected friction. Or it could have been when he stroked that spot inside me.

I'm not a screamer, but I let out an ear-piercing one. Kelley moved to cover my mouth as I continued to ride out my pleasure. When I came down from the high, I bit my scream back and listened for my son. Kelley rose up and only turned back to me when he was satisfied Mason hadn't woken up.

"You're going to have to keep quiet if you don't want Chance to know what we're up to."

Too late for that, I thought a second before he slammed into me. He stilled as my eyes found the back of my lids. I'd never felt so full except when he was inside me.

"Fuck," he growled. "You never answered me before about the pill. Are you on it?"

"No, not really," I said, slightly annoyed he hadn't moved.

"Okay, we'll talk about that answer later. But I'm okay if Mason gets a little sister or brother."

My mouth opened, but he covered it with his own. He kissed me like there was no tomorrow and we would be joined forever. I gave as good as he did, meeting his thrusts with my own.

"Fuck, baby, you're so goddamn wet, I'm not going to last."

There was nothing soft in the way he fucked me. I knew I'd have bruises the next day and didn't care. I couldn't get enough. My insides felt raw but in a good way.

He'd had to cover my mouth a second time when I found my next orgasm. When I could think, I bit his hand.

"So you want to bite me, huh?"

Wickedly, I grinned. He pulled out and flipped me over. Lifting my hips, he rammed into me again, and damn if that angle didn't send me flying over the edge.

Too soon, his rhythm lost its precision as he squeezed my breast and spilled into me just as my pussy clamped down for a third time.

He groaned and tumbled us onto our sides after a few more jerks inside me. With his dick still sheathed, he pulled me close and cupped my breast.

"So we're going to do this?"

I should have been shocked how easily he switched gears or maybe even a little surprised. But I'd been thinking about the very thing.

"Yes, if you want to."

"I've wanted to the moment I saw you. I wanted to give you time and space."

"We've talked about this. And frankly I feel cheated. What we had was just building when you left."

"We were just kids."

"And now we're not. And I know what I want."

Of that I was one hundred percent sure.

"Okay, but we're taking it slow. I'm going to take you out on a proper date."

Flashing a teasing smile, I said, "Does that mean no sex?"

He rolled me and ended up on top of me. His cock was hard and ready. "Fuck no. I'm going to burry myself in your pussy every chance I can. You're going to think I live here," he said, testing my wetness with a finger.

"But one thing is for sure, living here, you're going to learn all my bad habits." He thrust into me.

Catching my breath, I said, "And you're going to learn mine."

He paused and caught my lip between his teeth before letting it go. "Like your snoring."

I slapped at his ass, a damn fine one. "Not funny."

"I am, but not right now."

And he was right. There was nothing funny about what came next. Pleasantly sore and on my way to drifting off to sleep, he spoke in the darkness of the room.

"On a serious note, I wondered if you'd come to my last game here."

He sounded as though he thought I might say no. "Of course. I'm sure Mason wants to see his dad play."

His arm tightened around me and it felt so surreal. I never thought I'd see Kelley again, let alone be in his bed. I fell asleep, feeling safe and warm. That meant he and I scrambled to find our clothes when Mason started knocking on the door first thing in the morning.

Later that week on Friday, he didn't have practice and was waiting outside my classroom door.

"What are you doing here?"

He'd insisted I give him a copy of my class schedule, and he'd given me his as well. I'd learned from Ox's parents that he'd withdrawn from school. It wasn't clear if he'd been asked to leave or if he'd left on his own because the school had received information about the assault. Still, Kelley wanted me to be cautious, though he assured me Ox wouldn't be that stupid.

I hadn't been stupid either. That night he'd found me curled on the sofa, I'd seen his bruised knuckles and other bruises on his body. But I'd said nothing. I'd wanted him, knowing what he'd probably done to protect me.

"I'm here to take you out on our first date."

Smiling like a loon, I took his hand as we walked down the campus. We got curious looks and some glares from girls probably pissed off I'd claimed one of the good ones. I didn't care. I felt like I was walking on the moon.

"Where are you taking me?"

He eyed me with a wide grin. "It's not like there's a whole lot to do in this town. I thought maybe mini golf, but if I did something like trip because I'm too busy looking at you instead of where I'm walking, Coach would kick my ass."

I giggled. "I'm going to give you points even though you don't need them. I'm a sure thing."

"I don't know about that. I have a feeling if I don't keep my A game, you'll have twenty guys waiting in the wings for you." He was crazy stupid, because the only guy I wanted was him. "So anyway, with the hazards of mini golf, I figured it's a movie and dinner if that's fine with you. We'll do something else when the season's over."

"Sounds good."

He let me pick the movie. I hadn't been to see one not kid related in, well, forever. I chose a romantic movie about a bull rider because I'd read the book.

When it was over, Kelley squeezed my hand. "You know, if that'd been you and me, I would have given up riding way before that guy did."

"How do you know?"

"Because I was ready to give it all up that day you showed up needing me."

Damn, he made me weak in the knees.

"Are you ready for dinner?" he asked.

"Would it bother you if we went home? I haven't seen Mason all day, and I miss him."

He chuckled. "I have to admit I miss him too. Chance will be disappointed."

"Why?"

"Because Brie's there."

"What do you know?"

He shook his head. "Are you going to tell me what Brie's thinking about my boy?" I moved my head to signal no. "I guess we are keeping secrets from each other now."

"That's the only secrets. I would tell you if it impacted us or our son," I said. "Now let's get home before all the pizza's gone and then we can take Mason for ice cream."

I glanced up, and he nodded in agreement.

We didn't get to go to his game that Saturday because it was far away. I didn't want to put Mason through a three-hour road trip each way since we wouldn't be staying the night. But I half watched it on TV and played with Mason, missing Kelley the entire time. They won, but barely. And that was important based on how he'd explained it. If certain things happened, they might get to play in a bowl game after next week's game. Whatever that meant. I needed to study up on football, just so I wouldn't feel so clueless.

We went out a few more times alone and once with Mason. We took him to mini golf despite the unseen tragedies waiting to happen. Kelley made it unscathed, so I didn't have to explain to his coach that we'd taken a careless risk. We laughed about it the entire time. Poor Mason wanted to know what was so funny. Kelley would just whisk him on his shoulders, giving our son the time of his life and freaking me out in the process.

By Saturday, I sat in the stands with Brie, Shell, and Mason on my lap.

"He's so hot," a girl in front of us said. "I'd like to be his ball right now."

"Get over it, ladies," Shell admonished. "He's taken, and his son is listening, so keep it PG."

The girls turned back with sneers until they saw Mason. The day was bright and clear and his bi-colored eyes could be easily seen. Their mouths parted as their twin expressions grew to epic proportions. Then they huddled to no doubt talk about us. I didn't care, I watched Kelley snap the ball. And then I watched him go down as a guy twice his size, who wasn't blocked, took him down, making Kelley resemble a chalk outline.

"Is Daddy okay?"

I didn't know how to answer my son. I was surprised he even grasped who his Dad was on the field.

"I hope so."

forty-two

KELLEY

In a daze, I lay wondering how my life might have just gone to shit in three seconds. In that time, I might have failed my son and his mother. I didn't want to be my father. If I believed in such things, I would wonder why a curse had been put on my family. And better yet, I prayed that it ended with me and not got passed down to my son.

Muffled sound came from everywhere as a bright light passed over my eyes. I hurt like a motherfucker, but that was to be expected when a three hundred plus defensive linebacker drilled you into the ground so hard they would need a spatula to get me off the turf.

Questions were hurled at me in rapid succession.

"Three," I said, counting the fingers placed in front of my face. "No, my head doesn't hurt." Just every other bone in my body. "No, I don't feel like vomiting." I answered to unseen faces.

Finally, I had enough. I pushed up to a sitting position and noise erupted like a lion's roar from the stadium. Helping hands were there to get me up, but I did it on my own. I prayed I hadn't scared Mason, so I waved at the crowd in the general area he and Lenny should be sitting.

More noise and I was ushered off the field. It was protocol with the fear of concussions. I had to sit out at least one play to be further evaluated.

"I'm fine."

Back slaps from my teammates didn't help the ache. But I endured. The doctor ran a few more tests, and evidently I passed because I was pushed back toward the field. There wasn't much time left. And if I had any chance in hell in playing in a bowl game, we had to win here. And my future career meant not letting my team down. More importantly not letting my family down.

I glanced at the sideline where the coach looked like he was doing a rain dance with his signals for the next play.

The guys were in the huddle. "Okay, Minnie Mouse swept right." It was a bootleg play to the weak side of the defense. It had a crazy name, but the guys wouldn't forget it. It was four down and less than twenty seconds of play left. Despite getting mowed down by the human lawnmower, I trusted our guys to protect me. So when the ball was snapped in my hands, I stayed in the pocket for a second or two. We had two wide receivers, including Ashton, and my right hand tight end, Chance, in the play, getting in position. But since our starting running back got benched, it was Sawyer who was there to help me sell the fake handoff. He ran left, and I ran right after, pretending to give him the ball while I surveyed the field. He sold the play as I had time to find an opening before a defense end came barreling toward me. I let the ball fly.

The clock ran out and the field was soon flooded with parents but mostly students. We won in spectacular fashion, and I was lifted up on shoulders as the hoots and yelling came to a crescendo.

More than anything I wanted down. That moment wasn't for the crowd. It was for me, my girl, and our son. But when I was finally let on my feet, a microphone was shoved in my face.

"So what's next for you, Kelley? Will you be entering the draft?"

I gave non-committal answers to every question. I hadn't had time to think. Pam, my stepmom, should have been at the game and was meeting me at the house. More importantly, I needed to see Lenny and Mason.

So after some polite brush-offs, I jogged off the field, searching every face along the way for them both. When I saw them, I stopped. Mason scrambled out of Lenny's arms and ran for me. My heart swelled with gratitude that he'd accepted me. And I'd spent every second I could with him, making up for lost time.

"Daddy, you're okay."

"I am."

Then Lenny was there, and I drew her close. When I kissed her, Mason laughed. I didn't want to leave them, but I wanted out of there after spotting a familiar face in the crowd. I took the fastest shower ever, knowing I'd take another more thorough one later with Lenny.

TV cameras had followed me out of the locker room as I found Lenny safely near the entrance.

"Kelley, can you tell us who this is?"

With my son in one arm and Lenny tucked to my side, I said, "This is my son and my future wife."

Lenny's cheeks reddened and it was so damn cute, I kissed her again, giving the reporter a show.

I hadn't seen Pam at the game. There hadn't been any messages on my phone.

"What's your hurry?" Lenny said.

But I'd been spooked. I wasn't yet ready to talk about it and just got us home. When the doorbell rang, I opened the door. "Hey, Mom."

Pam would never take the place of my real mom, God rest her soul. But she'd earned that title by being there when my own blooded aunt had kicked me to the curb and my father never looked back when he left me with Pam.

"Now you know," she said, squeezing me back. "I missed you, boy. Saw your game."

But then I saw the person standing on the sidewalk behind her and stiffened.

"Kelley, I wanted to tell you—"

Her words drifted over my head when I saw red. I moved outside, shutting the door as if somehow my family would be protected. I vaguely heard Pam say Chance's name, but didn't pay attention.

"What are you doing here?" I bellowed, uncaring of what our neighbors heard.

"I wanted to see you play, Son."

"Son," I barked. "When was I ever your son?"

"I deserve that." Dad glanced at the ground as if he understood what eating humble pie tasted like.

"And more," I yelled. "Like maybe jail time." He winced, but I didn't care. "How dare you show up here?"

His words had been calm while mine felt more like a nuclear countdown. He extended his hands palm out, and I almost flinched. He caught that and dropped them.

"You're right. I shouldn't have come. It was selfish of me to want to see you play. I'm clean. I'm sober, and I have been for the better part of a year. Part of the program is to apologize to everyone I've wronged."

"Too bad Mom is in a grave. Even dead she'd be more likely to accept your apology than me."

He closed his eyes, and I got satisfaction my jab had hit its mark.

"If I could go back—"

"But you can't. I'm not the son you wanted to survive. You wish I'd been the one to die not Sandy. I'm sorry for that."

"Kelley—"

"Don't bother. Don't waste your second chances on me. I don't want any part of it. I'm that ugly reminder that you had to stay with Mom when Sandy died. If you hadn't had any other kids, you could have left Mom and started fresh."

"That's not true."

"Isn't it?" I barked.

He stood there silent until he glanced over my shoulder. I turned around and saw Lenny there with our son in her arms. She walked over to us.

When she reached us, Mason held out his arms to me. I took him, feeling calm come over me.

"Who is he, Daddy?"

I had a moment to make a choice.

"He's my father, your grandfather."

Mason waved. "Hi, Grandpa."

The smile that graced my father's face was nothing I recognized. It seemed sincere, which only made me angrier.

"Hey, Mase, why don't you go inside and ask Uncle Chance to get you a cookie?" I cajoled.

He practically jumped to the ground and ran on his tiny legs back to the house. He was just tall enough to get a hold of the knob and that scared me. I added baby proofing to my list of things to do. Then I turned back to my father.

"He looks just like you when you were little."

I wasn't moved by his words. "And it's time for you to go. Don't think I did that for you. I did that for my son. As much as you are a bad person, he still deserves to know his family tree. But if you ever lay so much as a finger on him, I will consider it an act of violence and kill you."

He nodded to me, then to Lenny. "I'm sorry for disturbing you all."

Lenny, the picture of sweetness, said, "That's okay."

"I assume you're my grandson's mother." She bobbed her head. "Well, take care of my son. I didn't do a good job. And I know you'll take excellent care of my grandson. Just remember that time is precious and there isn't a whole lot of it. When it's gone it's gone and there is no turning back." He glanced back my way. "I'm sorry again, Kelley. Maybe one day you'll forgive me."

Then my father turned and headed toward a beat-up car that didn't look like it would make it down the street. I wondered what happened to his truck. But I didn't care enough to ask.

When his taillights somehow made it to the end of the street, I relaxed.

Lenny had her arm around me and her face pressed to my chest. I wrapped her into a full hug.

"Why'd you come out here?"

"I heard the yelling. So did everyone inside."

"And you thought you'd come out and protect me with our son on your hip?"

She shrugged. "Pam clued me in to who was out there. But I would have come anyway, to protect you."

I kissed the top of her head. "The only person I need protecting from is you."

Her head popped off my chest and craned back to glare at me. "What do you mean by that?"

"You stole my heart four years ago. And now you've taken my soul. If you leave me, I'll be left a shell of a man. Because unlike my father, I would never take for granted the gifts you bring into my life."

The wattage on her smile couldn't have gotten any brighter, because months after then when we'd settled into a grove, her smile remained just as bright. Even when I'd piss her off. But I would always remember her smile in that moment. Her next words would solidify the memory.

"Do I still give you butterflies?"

I laughed. "When I first saw you that day at school, I thought I had indigestion. I didn't know then what I know now."

"What's that?"

"I'd never had that weird feeling in my gut like I was unsure of myself. When I saw you, I knew you were too good for me. But I couldn't give up. Even when I didn't have a name for it, I knew it was unique to you. And no matter what women came into my vision, no matter how attractive they were, none gave me that feeling."

"Do you like that feeling?"

"I wouldn't have chased you if I didn't."

epilogue

LENORA

NERVOUS, HE KEPT TUGGING AT THE COLLAR OF HIS shirt.

"Stop," I whispered, hoping no one heard me. "You look great."

"It's a suit and every guy here has one on."

"But you look the best."

His smile stole my breath. "You trying to say I look good, baby?"

"You know you look good. Now rein in your ego. More people want to come in the room."

His deep chuckle vibrated through his chest.

"You look even better in that dress. I can't wait to get you out of it." I slapped at his hand on my thigh. He grinned at me before planting a quick kiss on my lips.

"I saw Daddy kissing Mommy," Mason said, pointing at us.

I put a finger to my lips, quieting him as the man came to the podium.

"This is it," I said softly.

My son put a finger to his lips, admonishing me.

"And for the second pick of this year's draft..."

I squeezed Kelley's hand. "It won't be me, Len. But I'm hoping to be selected in the first round."

The announcer had gone on and on with words that weren't that important, until he said, "Kelley Moore."

We froze together until it sank in. Kelley uprooted himself to standing. I looked so far up from my seat to his six plus feet height as I whispered, "Congratulations."

Sexy as hell, he made his way down the aisle with my eyes glued on him until his agent whispered to me once my son sat in his father's vacated spot.

"You know everything will change for him. You should prepare yourself."

Something about how she said it made me turn to look at the woman with her gorgeous Asian features. I'd hated her on the spot for how poised and beautiful she was. She pushed back her long, glossy hair, making mine feel dull and lifeless.

"Prepare for what?"

"For the enviable. Good-looking and smart women will toss themselves at him in every city he plays in. And he'll eventually give in. The loneliness and need for release will make him crack. You'll find out and then you guys will fight. It might even mess up his game. I'm just saying protect yourself. Leave him before he can truly break your heart."

I gaped at her. Only she'd voiced some of my own insecurities I'd kept at bay. But never let them see you sweat. Wasn't that what that commercial said?

"You're wrong. He's committed to me and our son."

She huffed out a laugh. "You aren't the first baby momma. And some other woman will find herself pregnant.

These women are scandalous. They'll do whatever it takes to snag your man. You're better off leaving now and finding an accountant to settle down with."

I wanted to claw her eyes out, but Kelley's voice broke in.

"And most of all, I want to thank my future wife. She was the first woman outside of my mother who believed in me. She made me feel that I was capable of more, and I hung onto that. She gave me the most precious gift, our son."

But I read between the lines. Although he meant our son with every fiber of his being, I also knew that he was talking about the gift that led to our child, my virginity. He went on to thank his new team for the opportunity. And when he was done and ushered to the back, I did the only thing I could.

In the most undignified way, I stuck my tongue out at his agent and resisted the urge to say nah, nah, nah, nah, nah. Clearly spending half the night in the hotel room making love with Kelley had left me sleep deprived, and I was acting like a three-year-old.

She rolled her eyes, but her point clawed at me. I didn't like to have doubts, but how could I deny all the stories of men who gained fame and left their wives and girlfriends for better, shinier models?

I pulled the letter from my purse to remind me why I didn't have to be insecure. Mom had finally found it and sent it to me. She claimed she'd lost it. I opened it and read it for the tenth time.

Lenny,

I'm not a poet or anything. I'm not sure I even have the right words. Other than to say, I haven't been with anyone else or had the need to be. You're my butterfly, with wings that give me that feeling whenever I think of you.

Shit, I sound stupid, especially since your parents have made it clear you're done with me. But I thought maybe if you knew I'd be willing to wait forever, you'd wait for me too.

I picture you in my head when I remember how alone I am in this world. With Mom and my brother gone, and my dad is gone too, not dead unfortunately, I have no one but you.

Right now, I live with a woman named Pam. She's good people. She wants nothing from me, which seems strange. I think she's making up for the son she lost custody of. But you probably don't want to know about that. All I know is I can't imagine anyone not wanting her for a mom.

I'm getting my shit together so one day I can come for you. I'm playing football again. ~~Girls are everywhere.~~ Scratch that. Just know they don't hold a candle to you. I'm focusing on school, keeping my grades up and staying out of trouble.

I feel like I'm bugging you, or begging you. But call me. I've left my number below. If I don't hear from you, I'll guess this is goodbye. And I hope you have the world. You deserve it.

Kelley

Folding it again, my trust shouldn't waver. Kelley could have any girl he wanted. He'd never given me any reason not to trust him. Would so much money be our game changer?

After waiting forever, we made it back to the hotel. It had been a long day for Mason, so I let Kelley take him and tuck him into bed like he did every night.

"Man, he fell asleep as soon as he hit the pillow."

"Is the monitor on?"

He nodded. "Now I have you all to myself."

"I think I'm tired."

I got up to leave, but he tugged me to fall in his lap.

"What's going on? You haven't been yourself since they announced me being picked."

"It's nothing," I said.

"Remember, we promised no lies."

I exhaled, knowing he was right. "Everything's going to change. You'll be gone. I'll be at school."

His eyes narrowed. "Are you letting what my former agent said get to you?"

"Former?"

His head moved slowly up and down. "Yes, I gave her credit for being honest with me about what she told you. I still fired her. She doesn't know me or what I've been through. She hasn't walked in my shoes. I've seen the good, bad, and ugly that life has to offer. I've lived in a home, in a room, in a car and wherever my father could get for us for the night. I've had a full belly and an empty one. I've been beaten and I've kicked a number of asses. And I've had plenty of women. So I know what I want. I may be young, but I've lived two lifetimes."

He shifted his hip up and reached in his pocket before he continued on.

"I know how you feel about your father. So I couldn't ask him. I wanted to do this in the morning, so Mason could be a part of it because I asked him instead."

"Asked him what?" I was mystified by his mini speech.

"I asked him if I could marry his mom because I'm so in love with her."

Tears clogged my throat. I cleared it and said, "God, I love you too. But what did he say?"

"He said as long as I was good to you and didn't make you cry, he was okay with it. So all I need to know is if you'll be my wife."

He pulled out a ring that made my eyes dazzle.

"If you don't like it, the guy assured me we could exchange it for something else. It's not huge. I didn't think you would want a ring that would require you to have a bodyguard with you when you left the house."

"No, it's perfect. But, how could you afford it?"

He brushed my hair over my shoulder, making me unable to hide under a curtain of it.

"I told you I'm a saver. And apparently I have good credit."

"What about my school?"

"They're bound to have a university nearby where I'm going. I'll pay for your school or whatever you want."

"You can't waste your money. Football contracts aren't guaranteed."

He kissed my lips. "You're cute when you're trying to argue with me. I know better than you that contracts aren't guaranteed. But my new agent—"

"You have one already?"

"Yes, and if you'd let me finish..."

"Sorry," I said.

"Some of the money is guaranteed. I don't have a deal yet, but my agent let me know what he'll fight for. And it's more guaranteed money up-front. If we're not crazy and buy a decent house in a nice neighborhood."

"But you'll be famous."

"And if the house is sitting on a couple of acres of land, our neighbors can't be nosy. I don't need more than my truck, but I'll get you a car. We'll put most of the money away so we can live off of it for years."

"Or until you get tired of me."

"Tired. I'll never tire of you and my two sons."

His hand landed on my belly. "How do you know it's a boy?" Because Kelley was apparently potent. It hadn't taken long for me to get pregnant. And with summer looming, I would pop soon.

"Because if God gives a shit about me, he'll give me a son so I don't murder any boys for looking at my daughter if she looks anything like you."

He was everything to me. I loved him more than life itself with the exception of Mason and my growing peanut.

"I bet you say that to all the girls," and that time I was truly teasing.

He cupped my cheek. "There's only ever been one girl I've chased. And if she'll say yes, I would have caught the most beautiful butterfly of them all. What do you say?"

"I say…yes."

His kiss was long and lingering. When he pulled back, he said, "It's a good thing you said yes."

"Why?"

He smiled and my stomach did backflips. "Because it's only ever been you. And I wouldn't have given up. Because you got me chasing butterflies."

a thank you

I'd like to thank you for taking the time out of your busy life to read our novel. Above all I hope you loved it. If you did, I would love it if you could spare just a few more minutes to leave a review on your favorite e-tailer. If you do, could you be so kind and **not leave any spoilers** about the story? Thanks so much!

about Terri E. Laine

Terri E. Laine, USA Today bestselling author, left a lucrative career as a CPA to pursue her love for writing. Outside of her roles as a wife and mother of three, she's always been a dreamer and as such became an avid reader at a young age.

Many years later, she got a crazy idea to write a novel and set out to try to publish it. With over a dozen titles published under various pen names, the rest is history. Her journey has been a blessing, and a dream realized. She looks forward to many more memories to come.

You can find more about her books at: www.terrielaine.com.

stalk
Terri E. Laine

If you would like more information about me, sign up for my newsletter on my website or use one of the links below. I love to hear from my readers.

Website: www.terrielaine.com

Facebook Page: terrielaineauthor

Facebook: terrielainebooks

Instagram @terrielaineauthor

Twitter @TerriLaineBooks

Goodreads: terri e laine

other books co-authored by Terri E. Laine

Cruel and Beautiful

A Mess of A Man

A Beautiful Sin

Made in the USA
Middletown, DE
15 July 2017